HST 10/13

HST 2/14

This book is to be returned on or before the date above.
It may be borrowed for a further period if not in demand.

Essex County Council

DISTRACTIONS

STANLEY MIDDLETON

Distractions

HUTCHINSON OF LONDON

Hutchinson & Co (Publishers) Ltd
3 Fitzroy Square, London W1

London Melbourne Sydney Auckland
Wellington Johannesburg and agencies
throughout the world

First published 1975
© Stanley Middleton 1975

Set in Intertype Plantin

Printed in Great Britain by The Anchor Press Ltd
and bound by Wm Brendon & Son Ltd
both of Tiptree, Essex

ISBN 0 09 124840 X

I only took the regular course . . . the different branches of Arithmetic – Ambition, Distraction, Uglification and Division.

LEWIS CARROLL, *Alice in Wonderland*

I

The five limousines glided along the street, chrome bright under a spring sky, halted without fuss. Five mutes in black opened doors, heads bowed, as the mourners unstiffened limbs, tumbled out to the pavement where conversation sobered itself. The smaller cars, drawing up behind the quintet of Rolls, banged cargoes loose, and in some semblance of order men and women made their way up the short drive, past bare limes and the already sprouting mountain ash, towards the house.

Edward Fielding, straight-backed, stepped ahead. He wore a charcoal grey suit, a dark tie, but no hat, though the smoothed hair matched his status as widower. His mistress, Hilda Gascoigne, all in black, walked at his elbow, at ease, as if aware that every man in the party would look first at her.

Staid relatives followed, and behind them the younger people, saddened not by the death but by the callous talk of their elders, breathing the cool air, enjoying the sudden bursts of sunshine on orange brick, all relieved that the ceremony was over.

In the hall Mrs Makepeace the housekeeper cheerfully indicated clothes-pegs, easy chairs, lavatories, sandwiches.

'Do make a start, now,' she called. 'The girls will bring tea and coffee. It's ready.'

Her voice was plummy, autocratic, not quite suitable to

her untidy grey hair and her stout legs. Rings flashed as she pointed.

'There's food laid out in both the dining and sitting rooms.'

The elders chose the front with its sunshine, and sighed as they reached for proffered cups, but immediately they were catered for began conversation. As was proper, they commented on the service, the arrangements, the weather.

'Went off well, to say.'

'Spoke nicely, didn't he?'

'Yes. Not much he could have said, in the circumstances.'

'We dodged the rain. Up on that hill. Looked black as my hat.'

'That's the trouble with burials. They're outside. Whatever else there is against the crematorium, it's dry.'

'Good job.'

They laughed; they leaned forward, biting into their sandwiches. Some wore mourning, but even amongst these respectable people were those who had not bothered, or who had failed on principle. Not that it mattered. The effect of the group was sombre, and substantial; well-cut suits over paunches, shrunken legs and heavy wallets.

In the dining room the younger set had already opened the french doors so that one or two couples ventured on to the patio, sandwiches in hand.

All were relieved that the interment had been no worse.

Anna Fielding had committed suicide on weekend leave from a mental hospital while her husband had been at the coast with his . . . They all knew. While the balance of her mind . . .

Upstairs, in the large bedroom which overlooked the garden, Edward Fielding said he'd better go down, say a word or two. Hilda Gascoigne at the dressing-table mirror vigorously dashed at her hair with a silver-backed brush, one of Anna's, whose bedroom this had been, and hummed, pursing her lips humorously, a tuneless recitative.

'I'll be with you in a second,' she said.

Her voice reassured him, so that he raised a hand and made for the broad staircase. She finished with her brush-work, straightened tights and walked to the window, where, hiding behind, holding on to, a curtain, she watched a young couple hand in hand on the path.

Fielding had completed an unobtrusive entrance into the front room.

One of the hired maids handed him tea while Mrs Make-peace took her place at his shoulder.

'I think everything's in order,' she said.

'I'm sure it is. Thanks, Ivy.'

Mahogany furniture bloomed dark in here, rich and polished, huge along the white walls, substantial as the gold-framed Victorian land- and sea-scapes, while in the middle of the room stood the round table from his grandfather's house, heavy as lead on the carpet, beautiful as an unruffled puddle.

'Edward.'

His aunt Olive, wedged in an armchair, Father's last surviving sister, chubby and afraid; the Mount of Olives, he'd called her.

'Yes?'

Barely interrogative, his monosyllable troubled, so that she dropped her eyes, folded ringed hands.

'It went well,' she said.

The rest waited for his answer, as if it mattered.

'Yes,' he said. 'We can't complain.'

He stood by her chair, smiling down on her, tall, very handsome, not looking his age.

'I wonder what poor Anna would have made of it,' she said.

'She liked parties.'

9

'Not funerals. She looked dreadful at your father's, and at Harold's. As if her face were frozen and cracked.'

'You know these people?' he asked, bending.

'Pretty well.'

A delighted smile gleamed, mischievous pleasure, and the hovering Mrs Makepeace raised a warning finger to her lips. 'Now, Lady Rosen.'

'I know, Ivy. I know. I've been as smooth as butter. Get yourself a sandwich, Edward, and then do your round.' She loved curtness; it protected her. He obeyed, leaving her in the care of the housekeeper, who now knelt at the chair's side, solemnly scandalizing.

Fielding shook hands. Two cousins and their wives, three business associates, Anna's brother, her sisters, their husbands, people from the parish church, committees and societies, the family doctor forgoing his golf and staring glazed at the vicar, women from Anna's clubs, who'd talked money or good works out of her before she dropped from life, all cheerful because there had been no awkwardness, no reminders of embarrassment. They seemed glad to have Fielding acknowledge them; men patted the back of his hand, while three of the women stretched tiptoe to present a cheek for kissing. He said little, smiling, nodding, unaware even. Now and then he felt a small jolt of surprise when one broke with the conventions. Old Hurley, the transport man, whose firms boasted London, Manchester and Glasgow offices, said, in a hushed voice, but not shyly, 'That hymn you had, y'know. My mother's favourite.' The pair stood suitably grave over this information for a few moments before Fielding moved on. By the time he had completed his round, Hilda had appeared, and in spite of the lip-licking men had occupied a chair near Lady Rosen. Edward smiled but without acknowledgement in that she now seemed immersed, with hauteur, or close attention, in the aunt's saws.

Fielding shifted from the room.

The hall, wide and white, seemed only fractionally darker than the sun-splashed drawing room, for here all was light, banisters, treads, newel-posts, even the stair-carpet. A young man fiddling for cigarettes from his overcoat on the stand squinted guiltily.

The dining room was no noisier than the front. With the french windows open the air blew cooler, but the young ate, and grouped, and sipped like their parents. They needed, perhaps, a record player to encourage hip movement, foot-shifting, and thus to distinguish their youth.

As he entered, Edward saw his son Jeremy detach himself from a knot by the fireplace and move towards his father. The rest expected it, stepped aside, lowered their voices. Jeremy flicked back shoulder-length dark hair which he fondled with his finger ends.

'Is there plenty to eat?'

The boy nodded, smiled, eyes dark. He wore a sober suit, emphasizing his slimness. Twenty years of age, he stood two inches taller than his father.

'Ye'.'

'Good, good. There's beer, if you want it.'

The boy swooped to the sideboard, retrieving a pair of round, gold-rimmed spectacles which he put on to quiz the room before dragging them off and slithering them back to their place on the polished wood. The action had an irony about it, as if to suggest that the father had in some way totally misunderstood the situation, misread their wants, needed a rebuke, a chastening, though suitably modified for the occasion.

'Ye'. I know.'

'Are they eating?'

'It's only twelve o'clock,' Jeremy said. He spoke with a standard public-school accent, which up to now had been disguised by the strangled monosyllables of his replies.

'They'll be off for lunch.' The young man leaned forward, grinning, face slightly vulpine above the pointed chin, to tweak his father's jacket. 'At my age, you could have scoffed . . . I know, I know.'

Fielding felt affection.

The boy's eyes were dark-ringed, his skin pale, but he looked healthy, lively. In this room nobody smoked, while in the front, cigars, with the vicar's briar, darkened counsel. Fielding, son at shoulder, nodded to two girls, whom he did not recognize, noticing the pallid shine of their lipstick with distaste as they edged towards him.

Jeremy murmured names, Emma, Jenny, which meant nothing.

The girls lowered their eyes. In both cases the lids were painted light blue. The pair now smiled, but said nothing. Fielding, a non-smoker, wished for the social handing-round of cigarettes.

'Jeremy's looking after you?'

'Ye'.' Barely a sound, but the eyes opened wide, usurped the function of words.

'You're not cold, with that door open?'

'No.'

The two appeared to crane forward, as if they'd something to convey to him, some message of condolence, but nothing emerged. When Fielding moved, his son accompanied him, made necessary introductions, stood by for ensuing perfunctory conversation. On one occasion only did Jeremy inaugurate talk, and this to a fattish young man with a mop of long hair, when the two spoke about the Bach C minor Passacaglia which had been played as a preliminary, it seemed, to the funeral service.

'You'll have to give me a private performance.'

'Sure, sure.'

'Isn't the canned music at the cemetery bloody?'

'I didn't . . . I wasn't.'

'No. Of course not.'

Fielding deduced that the young man was the new organist at the parish church, an Oxford flier, his son had said, expected to land a cathedral.

'Didn't think you listened to anything but pop,' he said to Jeremy.

'I don't.'

'Pop's not your scene?' To the organist. Voice mocked phraseology.

'I hope not.'

'Cool jazz and Bach, this chap.' Jeremy. 'Messiaen on Good Friday.'

By the open door, staring down the brightness of the garden, Fielding took the boy's elbow, noting that he did not flinch.

'Have you seen Fletcher?' The lawyer.

'No. Nobody.'

'Your mother's left you a little.'

'What?'

'Oh, fifteen, twenty thousand. Enough to buy a house.'

'Is that what you suggest?'

'You've got to live somewhere.'

'I've managed so far.'

'With my assistance.'

Nobody listened to them; indeed they gave the impression of barely hearing each other, talking towards the glass, trying perhaps to mist it. Jeremy, at the university, lived with a girl three years older than himself in a flat by the Castle. They did not speak of marriage, conveyed no plans, offered little information.

While Jeremy had been at Rugby, he had lived in this place at holiday times, technically with his mother, though looked after by Mrs Makepeace. He had opted to study biology at the local university, two eccentric choices, in his father's view, and in early December had packed his trunks to join Linda Lawrence in the Castle Park. The Makepeace had played up, phoning Edward, writing notes two or three times a day, once summoning Fletcher the solicitor to do something. In the end, Fielding bullied the address out of the university authorities and turned up one evening with the boy's Christmas present.

The room was large, very clean, with shabby furniture, warm and comfortable. Jeremy sat writing at a kitchen table some distance away from the coal fire when Linda showed his father in. She – he had made little of her on the dimly lit, whores' kitchen stairs – now appeared a solid girl with a flattish, Slav face, long hair plaited severely, pulled tight from the straight whiteness of her parting. Both wore unisex jeans, striped jerseys.

'Hello.' Jeremy looked up from his work, pen poised, exactly as his father might face an interruption from his desk.

'Hello.'

No invitation to sit, but nothing inimical, mere quiet.

'I've brought you this.' He placed the Christmas-wrapped parcel on the table, actually on his son's sheets of writing.

'Thank you. What is it?'

'You can find out.'

'Now? Or do I wait for Christmas Day?'

'A radio.'

'Great. I'll open it now.' He did so, not neatly, ripping the paper, screwing it into a ball before extending the aerial, switching the set on. A burst of nondescript pop eructed. Jeremy grinned at the girl, who named a group. 'New Statesmen,' she said. He clicked for silence.

'Great. Thanks, Dad.'

He took up the card. 'With love from Hilda and Dad.' The wording, the bells and holly on the border, suggested, dictated his next sentence.

'This is Linda.'

She presented herself, moving out, big-breasted, hand stretched, a small hand, but hot. When she smiled, displaying regular teeth, she was almost pretty, with good colouring, warm brown eyes, straight brows. She did not speak but continued to smile at him, genuinely glad, unabashed. Jeremy rose from his table, stretched, yawned suddenly, and snatching his glasses made for the scuttle, mended the fire.

'Take his coat, Lin,' he ordered.

'I mustn't stay.'

'Take his coat.'

That was typical, with both sentences delivered *sotto voce*, unemphatically, but meant to be obeyed. Jeremy knew his mind from time to time. He sat opposite his father in one of the two armchairs, leaving Linda to drag up, perch on a hard dining chair, its leather seat discoloured and dented. Quickly he inquired after Hilda, and then his mother, saying when he learnt she'd be home for Christmas that he'd call.

'Have you enough money for her present?'

'I should think so.'

'Have you?'

'Ye'.'

Fielding passed over a cheque in an envelope which his son did not open. Soon they were talking about his course at the university, and Linda about her work in the path labs at the Midland Hospital. She was amusing with her anecdotes of error and miscalculation amongst the consultants, but unassuming, as flat as Jeremy; one needed to strain to catch the drift of her sentences. Fielding refused coffee; his son produced sherry, but that was returned to the veneered sideboard unopened.

'Aren't you on holiday?' he asked his son, pointing at the notebooks.

'That's when students work. Didn't you know?'

He'd stayed an hour, and learnt nothing because, though they were open with him, polite, baulked at no question, he could not bring himself to ask what he wanted to know. When they showed him out, as far as the landing, they did not touch him, distanced themselves, but showed, did not pronounce, real pleasure in his visit. It puzzled him, perhaps because he felt guilty towards Jeremy on his mother's account, but he feared the boy could only display this, this same shop-walker's polish of manner towards her.

Now staring down the bright garden Fielding asked:

'Is Linda here?'

'No.'

'You're ... you're still ... ?

'Ye'.' The mouth tightened. 'She's at work. She didn't know my mum.' Fielding had not heard that expression before from his son; perhaps that's what Linda called her.

'No.'

'Are you keeping this place? Open?'

'Open?'

'For Makey. She's got to live somewhere.'

'I see.' Fielding had now withdrawn.

'You can afford it.'

Both laughed, self-consciously. The boy had shown unaccustomed interest, and his father had interpreted it as conventional chat. From the next room Anna's sisters shouldered in, shook hands with Fielding, said that they needed to be on their way. Behind them, husbands disapproved, solid men who loved their wives. Edward was surprised that they had appeared at all; not that they had disliked him, or blamed him for Anna's condition. Their Christian charity demanded no contact. Lead us not into temptation. Hands were clasped. The hall filled. People made escapes. Cloud had blackened and wind cut northeasterly.

Fielding found Mrs Makepeace.

'Have you arranged for lunch?' he asked.

'Lady Rosen, and myself, and three others. Just salad. Snack. That sort of thing.'

'We shall leave without indigestion,' Olive said. 'You're not staying, Edward?'

'Not if I can help it.'

'That's not nice.' Mrs Makepeace's eyes were green and large in her brown face. One could see her among the roses with secateurs.

'Poor Anna.' Olive blew her lips out. 'And I thought she was a whole lot better. She really talked to me last time I saw her. Not about herself, I mean.'

'That's the danger period,' Ivy Makepeace asserted. 'When they have recovered enough to have energy to do harm to themselves.'

'What'll happen to Jeremy?' Olive asked.

'Happen?'

Olive's face puckered with fright, so that she put a pudgy hand before her mouth, appeared ready to suck a finger. Fielding took pity.

'I shall keep this place on,' he said. 'That's if Ivy will stay. So there'll always be a sandwich for him if he gets hungry.'

'Yes.' Olive sat straight, satisfied.

'It seems a waste,' Ivy averred, sullenly.

Edward patted her arm, brown as a glove.

'We'll talk about it,' he said.

Her eyes shone with tears. Hilda called across to him to come to the hall, where a further exodus prepared itself. Scarves and coats were donned, crumbs surreptitiously brushed down. Anna's brother, with doctor and vicar, muttered banalities to a brother-in-law. Companions moved away.

'I ought to say something.' The sentence rushed out, as if prepared, hidden amongst the clichés.

'Do so.' Fielding had no fear of this small man, who brushed his hand over his pate, whose spectacles had slipped low on his nose.

'It was a shame.'

'I won't argue.'

The hall was large enough to ensure the privacy of this low exchange.

'Not that it makes any difference now.' The half-apology.

'No, Charles.'

'I wish there were. . . . She was lost.'

The mourners swept out into new sunshine, while Fielding, polite and easy, mapped in his head the brother-in-law's later account of this conversation. 'I told him straight: "You didn't treat her properly. If you'd have looked after her as a husband should, she'd be alive today." He didn't like it. You know him. Didn't utter a word. Not a thing to say for himself. It's a pity, though. She was a beautiful girl, Anna. Clever.' And Charles's dyspeptic wife would screw her mouth under her incipient moustache, in disgust at her brother-in-law's flint heart or her husband's hypocrisies. Both would forget the mad woman.

'What did he say?' Hilda at his elbow.

'It was a shame.'

'Was it now? And how would he know?'

That's what kept him to Hilda, her *élan*, her spirits. This beautiful woman, this dominating goddess, sometimes pulled his leg, refused to make every crisis a tragedy, called out the same response in him. When they'd first met, five years back, it had been her physical perfection which had caught him. She had moved so that he had been riveted at the grace, had spoken easily, deeply, as if he were the only man within a thousand miles, offered him a hand, let it rest, sufficiently, perfectly, for a moment in his. The distracted, childless wife of a local headmaster, she had deserted her husband a few months later, had lived ever since with

18

Edward at The Orchards, his house out at Rempstone. Anna, by now in a mental home most of the time, had refused to sell this place, Marchmont, though she was no longer capable of caring for it or for Jeremy, so that Fielding had installed Ivy Makepeace, and, when necessary, a nurse, to oversee the property, the relicts. Anna had not objected; she had won her way in a moment of obstinate lucidity and that was enough. Now she could lie, talk her desperate pain, howl herself stupid, and know that her son would be cared for, her carpet swept, the garden weeded.

That was unfair.

Anna could no more have roused herself, pottered on with her bits of committee work, than she could have operated on her own brain, and yet he, unloving, not even interested now, wanted on the rare occasions they met to grab her by the shoulders, shake her into activity, curse her out of lassitude. When she was a girl, she'd been lively on the tennis court, at table, in argument, in love. His wife's contemporaries had rushed about the town, organizing their children's lives, their charitable circles, their refurbished careers, while his choice, the most vivacious, the richest, smartest, had slopped on her back, in volubility and tears. Fielding did not complain, merely shifted away. Why this should have happened he did not know; the rest blamed Anna's parents, a selfish pair of dummies, who'd neglected all but their pleasures and their investments. That seemed hardly enough. Fielding tended towards the medico's view: physiological deficiency.

He collected Hilda, said goodbye to the stragglers, mainly the young, pointed out again to Jeremy that there was beer and drove to The Whetstone where, at nearly two o'clock, a table and a meal awaited them. Over delicious turbot Hilda downed knife and fork, said:

'I'm exhausted.'

'Why so?' He hardly ceased chewing.

'One thing and another. I felt uncomfortable.'

'We agreed. I wanted you there. Did anyone say anything?'

'You're hopeless,' she said. They exchanged pained sentences, resumed the meal.

When they'd finished playing with their brandy, he asked:

'What do we do now?'

'Go back home, and if it doesn't rain, I'll work in the garden. You?'

They laughed and looked out over the lawn, the rough meadow where clumps of daffodils and narcissi threshed in the wind, and beyond to the grey silver streak of a reservoir. Above clouds black, grey dull, white skidded across flat blue. The trees in the distance, unleaved still, stood intricately patterned, a delicate dark.

'If I could paint . . .' Hilda began, sing-song, sharp, knowing.

'How did you guess that I . . . ?' He slapped his hands to his thighs in mock despair. 'We've waited for this long enough.'

'Don't make a thing about it.'

'Look, Hilda. You've not said a word since Anna died.' He swooped back to the table for his glass. She fingered to the hovering waiter to start clearing away.

'Lies, all lies.'

'We can marry.'

'We can.'

He felt no exasperation as they stood by the wide stretch of window, but saw himself bound to show temper, to exaggerate so that she'd recognize his concern.

'Don't you want to, then?'

'Yes.'

He groped for her hand. She pressed his, then side-stepped to pat her hair.

'A proposal and acceptance,' she said, genuinely amused. 'Let's have another brandy.'

'You're driving, my man.' She clutched the cloth of his sleeve. 'No.'

As they sat in the car, Fielding, composed because he liked the wheel, questioned her again. She replied drowsily, to the point.

'I never met Anna, Edward. I hardly saw her, even.'

'What of it?'

'She committed suicide. She's been buried. You need to think about her.'

'I don't.'

'You don't, then.'

'You sound cross.'

'I sound sleepy,' she answered. 'I've had a good lunch. It's warm in this car. I know you want to make something of this. I don't blame you. But I'm not going to help.'

'We must decide when we marry.'

'See the registrar. Let's get it over.'

He blew his lips out, disappointed, but she'd pander to him no further.

2

The day after the funeral Edward Fielding stood at one of the long windows in the drawing room of The Orchards at Rempstone. He looked southwards, over a terrace and balustrade, down thickly grassed slopes to a wood which fell away into the valley. In the distance, on its hill, he could see the little mining town of Underwood with its square-towered church, beautifully black against the bright arch of a spring sky. He could make out nothing of his own village, nor of its approach, which lay to the right and behind, but lower, straggling.

Hilda would be already in the garden at work, wrapped against the wind's swooping and the short spattering of showers. On the front below the terrace he could hear the gardener mowing the acre of lawn, his motor racing. A car appeared on the long drive, a tradesman's perhaps. Fielding, expecting nobody, returned to his armchair and *The Times*; if not exactly counting his bank entries, he checked his shares, as he did every morning. It meant little to him, for though he had considerable holdings his livelihood did not depend on them, so that he studied the figures as a keen schoolboy might work at the football league tables or the county cricket scores. He made pencilled notes on a large pad kept for no other purpose.

The front doorbell rang in the distance.

Surprised, he answered it, briefly greeting as he passed two women polishing the oak panelwork of the hall. A man holding yellow gloves asked to see Mr Fielding. Brisk, brusque.

'I've no note of an appointment.'

'It's inconvenient then?' The man shifted on his feet, a step backward, then flicked ill-naturedly at one of the pillars of the portico with his gloves. Fielding did not answer. The sun slid from behind a black disk of cloud. Until the visitor stated his business, the duration of the proposed interruption, he'd find no welcome here. The two stood in silence by the opened half of the heavy door, the sounds of scurry, muttered words from the cleaners oddly at ease in the depths of the hall.

'I'd like to speak to you.' Humbler.

'I see.'

'I'm . . . My name is Alan Gascoigne.'

Fielding looked again at Hilda's ex-husband in his good

tweed suit, his brogues, thickly striped shirt, wide decorated tie. To the best of his knowledge he'd never set eyes on the man, who was less formidable than he expected, with short fair hair, protuberant brown eyes, a small nose, a thin intelligent face, shaven close but darkly.

'Is it important?' Fielding looked out across the terrace where a cascade of aubretia topped a stone urn. He'd give nothing away, yield none of his privacy.

'I think so.'

Gascoigne tugged at his gloves, dragging them through the ring of left index finger and thumb, straightening himself to step inside, screwing his eyes in the paler light. Fielding pointed at the door; the other made for it, again with an effort, bracing himself. A whiff of after-shave touched the still air.

'Now.' Fielding indicated a chair, but remained standing.

'I'm sorry to intrude on you.' No answer to that. The man, crossing his legs, had laid his gloves on his crotch, was thinning his mouth. 'I understand your wife has died.'

'Yes.'

'I am sorry.' Silence again, but outside the sweet shouting of a bird. 'Are you going to marry Hilda?' Suave.

Fielding scratched the shirt over his chest.

'You aren't, then?'

'As a matter of fact, I am.' He sat down, at last. Gascoigne again puckered up his mouth, rabbit-faced, alert.

'I look on Hilda as my wife, Mr Fielding.'

'You divorced her two years ago.'

'In spite of that.'

They considered the situation, before Gascoigne sat upright, produced glove-play, spoke, easily.

'If you are not considering marrying her, I have a proposal to make. To her.'

'Yes.'

'That she remarry me.'

'I see.'

'I am putting this straight to you, Mr Fielding, in order not to waste your time. Your wife has died, and though you may not feel grief, and in the circumstances you may even be embarrassed, I've no wish to cause you unnecessary anxiety. There's no reason why I should. Nevertheless, I'd like to speak to Hilda, if she's here.'

The formality of the man's approach, the aura of quiet reason, derived, Fielding guessed, from the habit of addressing large numbers of children in his school. This voice would carry to the end of the hall, and yet gave no impression of shouting. A person spoke sensibly, rationally, as one to one, not as one to hundreds.

'I am going to marry her, Mr Gascoigne.'

'What does she say?'

Fielding did not answer.

'I would like to hear it from her own lips.' Wry smile. Variation on the mouth motif. 'You'd have no objection.'

'I'm not so sure.'

When Hilda had first left her husband, he had bombarded her with letters yelling blatant frenzy. In small, neat script Gascoigne had thrashed down his desperation, his despair, without balance or restraint. That such a man should have been director of an educational institution seemed unlikely, for he wrote with an adolescent, lacerating self-pity, immature and broken. If an infant's tantrums were translated into words, they'd shriek like these. These daily letters, often an hour's writing long, he had continued for six months.

Even now Fielding could hardly believe in the existence of these yelps of inked pain, gobbets of heart-flesh, though he had stored them all in his study, neatly tied in weekly packs. An impossibility of agony from this well-dressed, courteous man, with his mild voice, his comical mouth.

'She was my wife, Mr Fielding.'

'You keep saying so.'

'It means something.'

Fielding would not yield until Gascoigne explained himself.

'I want to keep this on a . . . a respectable course. You stole her from me. You had considerable advantages. Chiefly your wealth. Of course you might argue, justify yourself, by claiming Hilda could not have been happy or satisfied, at the personal level, otherwise she would not have left me. Now there's truth of a sort in that. But I know Hilda well.'

This man enjoyed uncontradicted assertion.

'Now for the first time you are free to marry her.' Pause. 'And that, if I judge wisely, will seem to her the only alternative.'

'*Alter*, one of two,' Fielding said.

The other sneered, put out a finger, left-handed.

'That,' ignoring the mischievous pedantry, 'is not the case. I, therefore, wish to propose marriage to her myself.'

'What makes you think she'll accept you?'

'If she does not, she'll see at least that she's not bound to you.' Again the finger. 'But that is not my reason. I want her back.'

Fielding noted the slightly northern vowel of the last word, the strength of the sentence. Hilda had been a member of Gascoigne's staff, at the beginning of her second year of teaching, when he had proposed marriage. A brilliant young man, with an Oxford first, an excellent book on the teaching of science, he had been appointed head of the Alderman Grant Hopewell Comprehensive School, Wentworth, at the age of thirty-one. This energetic, god-like figure had looked down at her, signed the form to certify that she had satisfactorily concluded her probationary year, and not many months afterwards asked her to be his wife. Shattering. Fielding nodded to himself. How could she refuse? Sparrows did not argue with hawks or men with earthquakes. He'd wasted no time here today. Plenty about him. Fielding approved of speed. 'Look, Mr Gascoigne, I wouldn't want Hilda upset.' He stressed the dull word.

'Our exchange this morning has not . . . '

'One minute. When she left you, you wrote a series of letters to her. They were, to put it gently, extravagantly expressed. I can barely think of them as the work of a sane man.'

'I was desperate.'

'I don't doubt it, but it was not one letter. The tally was near two hundred.'

'You don't understand.'

'I think that's untrue. You were a powerfully energetic man, used to his own way, at home and at school, and your vanity was hurt?' Fielding raised his voice at the end of the sentence as if to question the exactness of the vocabulary rather than the meaning. It insulted.

'She was my wife. For better, for worse; for richer, for poorer. You don't understand that, either.'

'Umnh. Arguable. Isn't there something about "love and cherish"?'

'I did that.'

'I don't think Hilda would agree.'

'You're a clever man, Fielding, and idle. In all probability you never exert yourself to look round the world, to feel as other men feel. Your money cushions you from that. You despise me, because you employ a dozen or a score of people who earn more than I do.'

'Mr Gascoigne. I may be a parasite on society. Your inherent importance may be greater than mine. You may work harder, or achieve more. I don't propose to argue any of these. All I am saying is that I'm very loth to expose Hilda to you, because, from what evidence I have, you are, well, unstable.'

26

'You think I shall attack her, or . . . '

'I suppose you deal out corporal punishment. I imagine you've a fairly sharp tongue. There seems no good reason why Hilda should . . . '

'You're afraid.'

'Not at all. Complacent, perhaps. Wishing to avoid needless trouble.'

'I promise you, Mr Fielding, that there will be nothing, nothing untoward. I merely wish to make my proposal to Hilda.'

Fielding looked again at the man, who did his best to appear collected. He did not exactly pity him, but imagined himself in a similar situation, without help, or resources, gesturing.

'I take it,' Fielding said, looking at his watch, 'that you should now be at work.'

'Yes.' Lip-biting; reddening.

'You're prepared to desert,' amusement cracked the word, 'your . . . ?'

'For an hour. Speed was essential.'

'I see.'

'Hilda must understand that there is this further course open to her. She is not bound by you.'

'Not in any sense you mean,' Fielding said, stood, walked to the window. 'However, I'll speak to her. She must decide. Just now she's out in the garden.'

'Shall I come with you?'

'No.'

Gascoigne half-rose as the other man left the room, but settled nervously back to examine the furniture, the newspaper neatly folded by Fielding's chair, the Peter de Wint water-colour just above his head. Bent trees, curling out from a cleft, a valley.

Hilda, gloved, was hoeing, hand-forking the earth of a small shrubbery hidden from the wind. With untidy hair, her slacks mud-marked, she straightened handsomely to wait for the message.

'You've a visitor,' he said.

'Who's that?'

'Alan Gascoigne.'

Her expression showed no alarm, no distress, only a mild ironical interest, as she consulted her wrist-watch.

'What does he want?'

'He's heard that Anna committed suicide. He's decided I might force you into marriage with me. He's therefore proposing to ask you to remarry him.'

'He didn't say that.'

Fielding nodded, lugubriously, overdoing it. She laughed.

'The silly sod.' She tugged at her gloves, throwing them into the trug. 'Well, I'd better see what he has to say for himself.'

'There's no need, if you don't want to.'

'You mustn't begrudge me my few minutes' excitement.'

He remembered her five years back in dread of opening the morning letter, but said nothing.

As she entered, Gascoigne rose to his feet.

'I'll leave you.'

Hilda took a seat, formally enough, settled her shoes together.

'His wife has died, has committed suicide.' He spoke in a low voice, gabbling the words, leaning forward almost double. 'I want you back. I mean I want to ask you to come back. There's no need for you to marry him.'

She did not reply, looked down her nose.

'We made mistakes, Hilda. I did. I was to blame. I had no sense then. Now I know better. Will you come back to me?'

'Go on.' No encouragement there.

'I didn't treat you sensibly. I know that now. But I'm convinced we have the making of a real marriage between us.' His hands writhed. 'You are my wife, Hilda. Whatever happens, you are my wife.'

'You always said so.'

'It's the truth. We were married.'

'For three years. You ask me back because that's what you want?'

'More than anything. I can't tell you . . . '

'Have you any notion why?'

'I love you. Forget the divorce. I shall never be a whole man until you are my wife again.'

'Why's that?'

'You think I'm a fool, don't you? To expose myself like this. To say what I mean. I shall not leave here until I've burnt it on your consciousness that I love you, that I am yours. And you mine.'

'This talk,' Hilda said briskly, 'about belonging to a person doesn't make any sense to me. We were married for three years. I was unhappy most of the time. You head-mastered it over me, took advantage of my ignorance, hit me, and when I left you your pride took a beating. I can see that in your mind I'm your chattel, that I belong in that sense. I'm your property. It is not so. It just is not so.'

'That's a lie.' He straightened. 'You've no right to say that.'

'Right or wrong.'

'You needn't marry Fielding.'

'What I need do is my concern. You talk about your love and your wants. Perhaps you'd be good enough to explain what are the advantages of return to me.'

'That's harsh, Hilda. I've admitted my fault.'

'Forget the confession. What's in it for me?'

He sagged into his chair, toppling a cushion.

'You're not coming back?' he asked, splaying his hands.

'I'd be a bloody fool if I did. With you.'

'This is life and death as far as . . . '

29

'You'll commit suicide? I don't believe it.'

Certainly he seemed overwhelmed, pale, drained of energy, thin with a thin sheath of flesh inside the smart tweeds, the polished brogues.

'You treated me abominably,' she said. 'I was a fool to stick it so long.'

'I didn't know how . . . I couldn't help myself.'

'You were mean and selfish. That's how I think of you. And brutal. When we married . . . Aggh. It's useless talking. I'm not coming back.'

He sat shrunken in this chair, as if he'd died, willed himself to death to punish her, but she was prepared to wait. She disliked his abject collapse, felt no pity, even exulted in her present strength. Now she must get rid of him, go back to the weeds, the fresh earth.

'I beg you . . . ' He rallied.

'No.'

'What can I do to make you understand? My whole body aches for you. If I see a woman in the street who resembles you, I'm jolted as if a bar of iron was thrust through my ribs. When you left I sat in my office for hours . . . '

'I read all this in your letters.'

'That's cruel.'

'Your treatment of me was a disgrace. When I married you I was an inexperienced girl. You broke my hope. I thought you were a marvellous man, who knew his mind, who affected hundreds of young people for good. You cut me with your tongue, until I could be hurt no more. You, the liberal, the progressive, fisted me. I was a disappointment to you, I'll not deny that. I'm ordinary as a tea-cake. You were deceived by my looks. I smile when I think about it now, that somebody who spends his working hours advising other people on their conduct or their prospects should make such a hash of his own private life.'

'Stop,' he said. The voice checked her; it carried power.

'All that is wrong. You possess me utterly.'

'I've said all I'm going to,' she said prosaically. 'I'll ring for Edward to show you out.'

'No.' Hoarse. 'One minute. Do you love that man?'

'Yes.'

'And feel no responsibility for his wife's death?'

'I'm not accountable there. No.' She enjoyed the frigidity of that.

'You had committed adultery with him before you left my house.'

She shook her head.

'Is it his wealth? Does that attract you?'

'It has advantages.'

'You loathe me.'

'When I think back on our marriage. But that's not often.'

'I am ashamed.'

She ignored that, neatly crossing her ankles.

'I was inexperienced as you, Hilda. I had to learn. I was frustrated and harassed.'

'You were cruel.'

'But can't you see why? I loved you. I wanted to impress. I sat in desperation, groping for you, blind for your love. It may not have seemed so. I must have seemed old, and collected, and calculating, but that was to you. I was a boy, showing off, making you look at me.'

She pressed the bell; they heard no peal.

'Hilda, believe me, believe me.' His eyes were red, wet. She sat, trusting the bell, mistress of a well-run house where gadgets and arrangements worked. Fielding entered, leaving the door ajar. His expression was quizzically good-humoured, as he turned from one to the other.

Gascoigne straightened in his chair, stood, hands behind.

'Will you come back to me, Hilda?' he said, grave, intense.

'No.' She spoke gently.

'I must take that as my answer then.' He spoke to Fielding as one giving a judgement, distantly, at ease. Now that he was on his feet, he looked almost foppish with his well cut suit, mod shirt, the fancy tie. 'Thank you for allowing me the opportunity of proposing what I did.' The ironical tone suited itself to the chairman of a hundred school councils, head teachers' meetings, educational debates. 'Goodbye, Hilda.' He did not hold out a hand. 'We may meet again. Goodbye, Mr Fielding. I feel this deeply.'

He made quickly for the door, shut it without further ado, not pausing, not speaking. His brogues spanked the flagstones.

Fielding, returning, linked his arm through Hilda's, led her to the window where they waited until they saw the car skim along the drive.

'What sort is it?' she asked.

'Triumph 2000. Three years old.'

They giggled at the inappropriate conversation.

'Sit down,' he said, in the end, 'and tell me how you got on.' Rain, hard as pebbles, rattled the window.

'He was different,' she answered. 'His temper was there, but he'd mastered it. I tell you one thing, Edward. He convinced me he wanted me back.'

'How's that, then?'

'It's not so much what he says as his way. He makes you feel, this sounds silly, the whole man behind a simple sentence. When you say something to me, or I to you, for that matter, then I feel you've just been thinking about your golf or your next meal or your day's work, but he seems, conveys it to you, that he's thought of nothing except that sentence for the past twenty-four hours, that it's boiled out of him like molten rock. He was the same in staff meetings. He'd carry fifty or sixty people with him by just an ordinary sentence.'

'Well done.'

'It's the truth.'

'I'm not arguing. He didn't strike me like that. We were very formal. I can never remember what I've said, but it was like an exchange of notes.'

'He only impresses women and schoolmasters?'

'He impresses where it pays, I'd guess. Otherwise he sits still.'

They did likewise, watching the progress of the shower. The sun was out when she spoke again.

'Were you afraid of him, Edward?'

'Not really. He didn't match up, for one thing, with those letters. Who is he? Where did he come from?'

'A poor boy. West Riding. Father a railwayman. He won a scholarship to Oxford.'

'What sort of woman was his mother?'

'She died before my time. He had one older brother. A bank clerk. He came to our wedding. A Methodist local preacher. Well-spoken, but nothing like Alan, in looks or temperament. He's dead now.'

'They die early?'

'Not the father. I'd never thought of it. He'd mentioned an old grandmother somewhere. You've never asked me about him before.'

3

Hilda and Edward were married within weeks.

They decided against a honeymoon, asked two business associates of Fielding to act as witnesses at the register office, briefly lunched with these, drove straight back to Rempstone. Jeremy and his girl did not show up.

That evening the newly married pair took a walk through the village, past the reservoir, called in at The Mason's Arms. In the almost empty bar, sitting to the counter, they drank one brandy and soda.

'Well, Mrs Fielding.'

'Don't say that. I shall cry.'

Disconcerted, he raised his glass.

'Marriage is something,' she mumbled. 'I can't help it.'

He patted her hand. She touched new, resplendent rings.

'I'm sorry it's been so long.'

They walked back in May twilight, arm in arm, moving swiftly against the chill. He at forty-five had not put on fat, could leg it still, delighted in doing so.

'We ought to have invited Mrs Makepeace to the wedding,' Hilda said.

'And about fifty others.'

'Will she mind?'

'We'll have her up for dinner at The Orchards. She'll like that.'

'Will she? She was Anna's close friend, wasn't she?' He said nothing. 'How old is she?'

'I can tell you that exactly. She'll be sixty in September.'

'Is her husband dead?'

'Yes. He was a bank manager. Quite a bit older than she was.'

'I can never make her out, Edward. She dotes on you. She does, really.'

Now Hilda laughed, joggled his arm, but under the trees of Safety Wood, gently crackling, rasping above, he considered Ivy Makepeace and his first adultery. He'd no idea how his wife would have taken a brash announcement, and untempted did not risk it. It seemed too long ago to bother with. Besides, that stocky matron, with the untidy hair, the county voice, had nothing in common with a thirty-four-year-old mother of three daughters who'd jollied him into

34

her bed one afternoon in the summer before he'd gone off
to national service. It appeared extraordinary now, as it had
been a portent then.

No sooner were they back in the house than Jeremy rang
the doorbell. His congratulations did not prolong themselves.

'You couldn't make it this morning?'

'No. Linda was at work.'

'And couldn't get time off?'

'Suppose she could. I was busy. I'm writing some stuff
up. There didn't seem much point.'

'You could have phoned to say you weren't coming.'

'Ye'.'

'Ye'?'

'That wouldn't have made it any better. Besides, we're
having trouble.' Jeremy dawdled at points of crisis. 'This
morning Linda's parents turned up with her husband.'

'I didn't know she was married,' Fielding said.

'No? She is. When she was nineteen.'

'What's he do for a living?'

'Lab technician. They worked in the same hospital in
Birmingham.'

Jeremy rarely developed conversation. Meticulously
polite, he answered questions, but worked on the assumption that his bare account was enough, that no interest would
be roused. Now he waited for his father to begin direct
interrogation.

'What did they want?'

'Linda to go back.'

'When did this happen?'

'This morning. About eleven.'

'So she was out?'

'Ye'. At work.' Pause. Fielding snorted annoyance.

'Let's have less of the village idiot, Jeremy. Get on with
it.'

'They came. I'd no idea who they were. They asked for

Lin. They explained themselves.' The boy laughed, nervously, at his father's impatience. 'I'd guess that the parents had been on to Rob to get Lin back. That's how it seemed.'

'You mean he didn't particularly . . . ?'

'I should think he did. He's twenty-six or -seven, but he didn't look older than me. I expect he did, but they pushed him into it.'

'He was . . . ?'

'The parents did the talking. Lin's mother.'

'Oh. And who was she like?'

'Big woman, with glasses, and fierce, really. Lin had no right. She was married to Rob. If I'd anything about me, I'd know all this, without her telling me.'

'Did she resemble Linda at all?' Fielding asked maliciously.

'A bit. In colouring. But coarser.'

'That's age.'

Jeremy grinned, in rapport with his father, acknowledging they were of the same mould.

'And the upshot?'

'And the consequence was,' the boy intoned, 'they instructed me to hold Linda in this evening, and threatened that they'd get after you if they had no joy from her. Flashed your address, The Orchards, Rempstone. That's why I've come.'

'That's not like you.'

'Tkk, tkk.' Noise of mild reproof on the palate. 'That's the reason.'

'Leaving Linda to the family.'

'What she wanted. So I escaped. And straight back any minute to mop the blood.'

'What else are you after?'

'I came to warn you.'

'You know damned well, Jeremy, that they're not likely to get any change out of me. And if they did, what difference would it make? You'd go your way.'

'Ye'.' Mournful smile now. 'I felt guilty about this morning. I ought to have turned up. I should have missed them then. Did Hilda say anything?'

'No.'

'Sure? I don't know why I didn't come. I dressed up for it. Cleaned my shoes. I was in my glad rags when they arrived.'

'That prevented you?'

'No, Dad. I ought to have been away. I'm sorry. I dithered. Don't know why.'

'Because of your mother?'

'Don't think so. She didn't do much for me lately.'

Hilda opened the door, striking in green velvet with a small lace collar.

'May I come in?' she called. Invited, she stretched both hands to her stepson, fingers pointing down, a stage queen. The movement was histrionic, and utterly successful. She kissed the boy, who took her hands, held them.

'I hope you're both happy,' he said.

'Thank you.'

'I should have turned up, Hilda. I'm sorry. I wanted to come. I'm a bloody fool.'

'Just like Father,' she mocked, pointing. 'Do we have a drink, Edward?'

'I'm driving,' Jeremy muttered. 'Have to dash.'

'Matrimonial trouble.' The father.

'What's that, then?'

Her husband explained, succinct and lucid, and when he had finished she tucked her arm through Jeremy's, pulling him towards her.

'Poor boy.' Again, it was stagey, but warm; a parody; sincere. 'Does Linda ever talk to you about them?'

'No.'

'Not even when she's upset?'

'She might say the odd thing. But by and large, not. I think she was glad to get out of Brum.'

'What sort of girl is she, Jeremy?'

'What sort of question's that?'

'Sorry.'

The boy took Hilda's hand.

'Mum,' he said. 'And a mum-type question. I ought to have turned up this morning. It's not good. I think you'll be happy.'

He delivered his sentences simply, like riddles, standing with his feet apart, arms flopping.

'What sort of girl's Linda?' Fielding asked.

'She's sane enough.'

'Oh?'

'Among other things.'

'Marriage?'

'I think so. Not that it's so important.'

'Well, Jeremy Tactful,' Hilda said. 'On our wedding day.'

'You're oldsters.' He laughed outright, straight at his father who disliked the word. 'I've offered my apologies.'

They both accompanied him to the front door, across the flagstones to the gravel of the car park where he waved an arm, flicked hair handsomely back, and doubled into his Mini.

'What did he want?' she asked.

'Exactly what he said. To apologize.'

'He's nice. I don't understand him.'

'Don't start that,' Fielding growled.

Indoors they drank whisky, sitting apart in armchairs in a silent house. The radiators, on against the chill, ticked and creaked, while outside through the one uncurtained window they could see the tall spiraea jerking, dashed by the wind.

'Let's have some music,' she said.

Obediently he moved to the cabinet.

38

'Name it.'

'I think I'd like the slow movement of the Brahms' Second Piano Concerto, the one with the cello.'

'Rum wedding-march that,' he said, pleased again that she'd decided immediately.

'Pick something else, then.'

'No. That will suit me.'

He consulted his index, found and cleaned the record, turned on the machine, at a kind of attention. Hilda, lying back, enjoyed these preliminaries which he'd learned from somebody else, Jeremy perhaps.

'From the beginning, or the third movement?'

'*Andante,*' she said.

Brahms's cello settled to its rich cream of rise and fall. All sang balanced, suffused with autumn warmth. Now as the orchestra spread with fuller weight Rubinstein's piano plunged with trill and steadied rise, a millionaire's romance, a squandering of beauty not yet cloying or faded. Fielding conducted with absent-minded vigour, but as the piano set about the finale, he poked the set into silence.

'Middle-aged music,' she said.

'Suitable.'

'I heard that first when I was eighteen and I thought that was the sort of music I'd like to write. A marvellous lush tune, all swelling like an atom bomb, and declining with no harm done.'

He pulled a sour face.

'I expect Brahms was like the rest of us. Uncertain what he managed. Blind. Struggling. On the edge.'

'That's right,' she said. 'I've never heard you say anything like that before.'

'Wedding-day.'

'All right.'

'That's my equivalent of Brahms's composition. He practised his counterpoint so he could make this out of his

39

inadequacies and his yearning. All I can do is find the best woman and marry her.'

'Thank you.'

'He never managed it.' Fielding tonelessly, breathily, began to sketch the cello tune, whistling. 'Poor sod.'

'And which would you rather, young man?' she asked.

'No choice.' He refilled the glasses, stopping her side to palm her cheek.

'Let's have it again, love.'

The telephone shrilled. Fielding swore, made for the hall. In five minutes he was briskly back, miming annoyance.

'Linda's parents,' he said, into his whisky.

'Come on, then. You're worse than Jeremy.'

'They wanted to see me. I asked them why. They'd no idea. Her mother. They'd failed with the girl, who'd pretty well pushed them out of the flat, and presumably they thought I might do their dirty work for them. I explained that they were quite right to argue it out with Linda, but that it stopped there. The woman insisted she wanted to see me. I said I saw no point.'

'Was Jeremy back?'

Fielding glanced at his watch.

'Can't be.'

'From a phone box?'

'Yes.' He sipped, then turned his glass, held it at arm's length to the light. 'She made no attempt to blame me. Sounded tart.'

'But you're not going to see her?'

'No.' He smiled at his wife. 'Suppose she comes here, she might get the impression that her daughter's made a good catch. Then she'll start to elbow Rob out of the way.'

'And that's immoral?'

'Natural.'

'What would you say, Edward, if Jeremy had told you

tonight that he was going to marry Linda. I know she's not free. But suppose she were. Would you mind?'

'I hardly know her.'

He seemed pleased with her harrying, as if she protected him by showing him the worst.

'I'd point out he was young, that he probably didn't know his mind. I'd warn him I wouldn't pull any of his chestnuts out of the fire. Financially, I mean. No buying him houses. I don't think I'd lose my wool.'

'He seems so good.'

He whistled. 'Nobody makes judgements like that these days. Are you serious?'

'Just talking to please you.'

She shook her head in the warm light of the room, and picked an onyx paperweight from the table, laid it flat on her hand.

'When Jeremy gets back,' she asked, 'what will they do?'

'Make love, I should think.'

'Because they're troubled?'

'Because it's their style. When I was their age there was nothing I could do. I'd no independence, no judgement, no scope.'

'No affair, either.'

'There, now. Yes, I had. Not with a girl of my own age. It all seemed outside my proclivities, if that's the word. It made no difference to what I was going to be.'

'How did you know that?'

'I didn't. It was earth-shattering, but trivial. My thing was to go into the army, Oxford, then join the firm.'

'That meant more than your woman?'

'I like to talk to you, Hilda. You don't ask important questions.'

'If you told me her name, I mightn't know her.'

'No comment. Curious?'

'Bursting.'

41

He laughed.

'She was older than me. I was terrified and shaken that she'd seduced me. Couldn't make it fit. Though she wasn't the only one. I knew it would pack up. Even then I was certain that in ten years' time my property would matter more than she did. But when I come to die, when I'm on my death bed, I don't know what will be important.'

'You poor old thing,' she said.

'Yes, love. Fielding in the evening. That's why I swill my whisky until the wallpaper's fuzzy, and then I can just about bear life.'

'You don't mean that.'

'No. I've plenty I can manage. But now and then, on important days like this, I look about, and by God my ignorance appals me.'

'Of what?'

'That's it. Every bloody thing. Except office blocks and flyovers and shopping centres.'

'You're not blaming yourself for Anna, are you?' She sounded sharp.

'No. She was a poor bet anyway. The doctor told me years ago she was incurable. I didn't do her any good, mind you. I abandoned her, but it wasn't bad sense. And yet she left me pretty well all her estate.'

'Why, dearest?'

'Damned if I can say. If I'd have been in her shoes, I wouldn't ... '

'What was she like when you married her?'

'Just as you would expect. Pretty. Lively. Spoilt. She broke down in the middle of the wedding ceremony and howled.'

'You wouldn't be pleased.'

'No.' She fingered his tie. 'It seemed unnecessary. And I wasn't sure I'd done right.'

'Nor was she.'

'I grant you.'

'Do you think,' Hilda asked, 'that she would have been all right with someone else?'

'No. She was abnormal. She was bound to crack. I think her parents knew. There'd been trouble. But they hoped with marriage and a family that she'd grow out of it. They were to blame. They knew next to nothing. It was hard on Jeremy, with his mother being packed off to hospital times enough, when she wasn't creating scenes around the house.'

'You're worrying about him, aren't you?'

'I don't think so.'

'Truth?'

'No. You'd like me to be. That's nearer. He can look after himself. I don't know what he'll make of his life, or what he and Linda will do. But he's energetic. He can kick and scream.'

'Will you see Lin's parents?'

'What do *you* say?'

'Yes.'

'Yes, then. That's easy.'

She kissed him, and they stood together, arms embracing. In unembarrassed silence they listened to the small sounds of the room.

'I wish I'd known you at nineteen,' she said.

'You'd have been six years old.'

'And you?'

'Bloody awful. Wet. Knock-kneed. Full of the Holy Ghost.' He stretched his arms above his head, wrists bent aping a cartoon phantom.

'Not like Jeremy?'

'No.'

'I shall have it out of you who it was dragged you struggling into bed with her. So watch it, my man.'

He wondered if it mattered, saw again Alan Gascoigne in the room, neat and tormented, felt the grotesque comedy.

43

'It's the uncertainty,' he said. 'I don't know how long I shall keep you.'

'Or want to. Put Brahms on. There's a good boy.'

This time he obeyed immediately.

4

The flower of the county shuffled round the floor of Marcroft Hall.

Under a wall wild with horned heads of beasts, Fielding shrugged as he watched the passing figures, landowners, farmers, financiers, a lord lieutenant, two or three provincial mayors, colonels, a bishop, doctors, vets, solicitors, golfers reduced to uniformity in evening dress, pushing women before them. By their wives ye shall know them. The youngsters were best flailing into this waltz, as if to break its sobriety, trip it into the hammered frenzy of rock or reggae. His wife floated by in the arms of a baronet; she stared past the red cheeks, over the black shoulder, her face waxen and serene.

The Countess of Marcroft touched his elbow.

'Is Jeremy here?' she asked.

'I haven't seen him.'

'Is he behaving?' She coughed, a nervous habit. 'These days?'

'He's living with a married woman. I don't know how that counts. You'd gather this was the habit of people his age, but I doubt it. He seems to work hard at his biology. It all seems respectable.'

'And disappointing?'

'No, Elizabeth. I don't care what he does, but he's coming

44

into a fair amount of money one of these days and I'd sooner it went to somebody who'd show a sense about something, even a degree. I don't make much of him. A bit of a sobersides.'

'Tom always asks.'

Tom was the heir, Lord Ravenshead, now studying in an agricultural department.

'Does he?'

'Don't be so prickly, Edward.' She clutched his arm, a small dark woman, digging her nails in. 'They get on well. And Anna was kind to him.'

He did nothing about that.

'I like Hilda,' she said. 'That's the truth. I wanted you to marry her.' The band blazed to a halt; with a whisper of applause couples moved to their seats. Hilda's fiery-faced partner returned her, blustered belching politeness, wiped his head, sought the bar.

'I'm trying to get information out of your husband,' Lady Marcroft said.

'And he's not forthcoming?'

'I want to know about Jeremy.'

Hilda did not answer, but nodded, expression radiant.

'Tom asks.' Lady Marcroft spoke almost in supplication. 'He and Jeremy got on well.'

'I'm sure they did.'

'You're as bad as he is.'

The MC made a booming announcement over a totally inefficient public address system. Sound thudded from the marble staircase at the end of the hall, from the Victorian mahogany, the military pictures, the cases of uniforms, the ghastly trumpets, the antlers.

'What did he say?' Lady Marcroft asked.

'Something about a prize draw in the ante-room.'

'That'll be me.'

The Countess moved diagonally across the hall, straight-

45

ening a black shawl on her shoulders; two or three officials converged on her expected point of arrival to escort her to her duty.

Hilda suspected the trouble. Anna's friend, benefactor, Elizabeth Marcroft believed Fielding responsible for his first wife's breakdown. A woman of little moral sense, she had convinced herself that he had deliberately set out to exacerbate his wife's condition. Fielding had warned her not to make mischief, at which she had twittered surprise and disparagement. Oddly she had invited Edward and Hilda to visit her, even though Anna still lived. She had also made several aristocratic descents on the mental hospital, where she had been received with ceremony, which she expected and disregarded. This small woman had no misconceptions about her husband's place as the largest landowner in the county, and the richest. Perhaps it irked her that she could not drive Fielding back to his wife.

'It's not as if she had any interest,' Hilda said.

'She said she wanted you to marry me.'

'How odd. Does she ever think what she's saying?'

'God knows.'

They danced together, drank punch, made bitter, she gibed, from the Countess's bath water, before a military solicitor claimed Hilda for a quick-step. Fielding's aunt, Lady Rosen, waddled across, done up white and pink as a sugar mouse.

'Edward,' she murmured.

'Olive.'

'You didn't invite me to the wedding.'

'You wouldn't have come. And if I invite one, I have to call the rest. And some of you would have accepted.'

In her plump, sluggish way Olive Rosen was not without a certain prettiness. Years younger than his father, she'd seemed mischievous to Fielding, without qualms, shocking. One day in their bathing hut near Filey she'd slammed the

46

door shut as she and the young Edward had come in from a swim and peeled her bathing dress straight down. She'd been attractive then, with small well-shaped breasts, a pouting belly, curly pubic hair in the green light. Nothing had come of it; at the time he'd committed faithful adultery with the Makepeace, and that had been enough. Now he was certain that Olive had known all about the affair and had signalled her knowledge or approval or envy in this curious way. She was married to Frederick Rosen, a Jewish solicitor, property dealer and city councillor, a dry old stick, knighted for services to the Conservative Party, had presented him with three sons, all clever, and had eaten her way through a mountain of puff-pastry and cream in good causes. Though Fielding had much to do with Rosen in the last years of the old man's life he'd never made anything of him. Stiff, old-fashioned, with a ripe Edwardian pronunciation, the man had hovered like a stage butler sniffing out tips. He'd made a pile, done his stint as Lord Mayor and Sheriff, but had never come alive, been a cardboard cut-out to the end of his days. After his death, one of the sons had taken Fielding to an attic full of lead soldiers, toy cannon, camouflage. The place was spotlessly clean, but young Frederick claimed he'd never known his father spend any time there.

'Were they here when you were a boy?' Fielding asked.
'I imagine so.'
'He never showed you, then?'
'No. The room was locked.'
'So you didn't know?'
'I found out when I was twenty or thereabouts, and in the army. He sent me up there for a book on some military matter, regimental badge, we were arguing about. As soon as I came down I mentioned this lot, and he said,' here his cousin looked slyly at Fielding, not unlike his father, about to disappear into a pinch of dry dust, ' "I started to collect

47

for you boys when Adrian was a baby, but I could never get round to letting you play there. You were too destructive." '

So presumably, once or twice a week, Sir Frederick had crept upstairs like a maidservant to dust the present he couldn't bring himself to hand over. The son saw nothing odd in this; his own children were wreckers.

'Would you have come, Olive?'

'Certainly.' She laughed. No, she was ugly, not pretty, triple-chinned, pork-handed. She would not have worried her head about the undelivered soldiers upstairs. If she wanted something, she asked bluntly and her husband coughed up, no demur, and such behaviour more than paid for minor eccentricity. And yet she'd pulled her bathing dress down to flaunt herself in front of a boy not much older than her sons. 'Has Elizabeth said anything? About Anna.'

'The right platitudes.'

'You're a close devil. When you were young, you looked so helpless. Like Jeremy. All the women wanted to mother you.'

'Good or bad.'

'Good. Denis says what a nice boy Jeremy is.' Denis, her second son, was a mathematician at the university, another dry man, with rimless glasses and a thin-skinned bald head. Clever, people said, in his abstruse corner, fecund, but what his judgements of human beings were worth, even those noncommittally flat as this, Fielding did not know. 'He'll get a good second, they think.'

'Most kind of them.'

'Where's Hilda?'

'Dancing.'

'A credit to you,' Olive said, following the unmatched couple with her eyes in malice. She paddled away to collapse in a chair nearer drink and gossip. A hand touched Fielding's elbow. He turned to find Alan Gascoigne, whom he did not immediately recognize in the shadow. The man reintroduced himself, said:

48

'We might as well be friendly. Now you are married.'

'I see.'

'They make me do some of their charitable work and I get invited here as a reward.' No disgruntlement, almost pleasure in his servility.

'They being Lady Marcroft?'

'No. A bit further down the scale. Whalley, the party king, and Brooks, her solicitor. That sort of man.'

'You don't mind?'

'Why should I? Brooks and I see to it that it's efficient.'

The quick-step completed, dancers left the floor, but Hilda did not appear. She'd spotted Gascoigne, didn't seek trouble, and had detained her partner in talk, or perhaps ordered him to find her a drink.

'Can I do anything for you?' Fielding asked.

'No.' The man had started. 'No. Thank you. I find my way round in time.' Suddenly he touched Fielding's arm again, as if lining him up to punch him. 'I don't bear you ill-will.'

'No?'

'No. I don't. Hilda would have left me, you know. Without you. It could easily have been somebody else. Somebody worse. We did not know each other. And we hadn't the means to learn.' He spoke quickly, spluttering his words out, his energy concentrated in the furrow between his eyes. 'It was a disaster. Could not have been otherwise. I see now. We should do better today. That's why I asked her back. The incompatibility derived from the circumstances not the personalities.' The last sentence took Fielding aback. The man had prepared that, comforted himself, oiled his wounds, wined them with that summary of unreality. 'I accept all this. I could not then. She's been lucky with you.'

Now the listener wanted to push him away, vilify.

'It's odd to you, Mr Fielding, that I can talk like this,

49

isn't it? It's what I have been trained to. Talk. Discussion. Explanation.'

'Yes.' He reminded himself of his son with monosyllabic politeness.

'I hope you don't mind my raising the matter.' Irony. 'No.'

Lady Marcroft, shedding satellites, made for them.

'Now, Edward,' she called. 'What was it I was saying to you when duty called me away?' An excellent middle-class comedienne, all teeth and lunatic ceremony. 'You'll never talk to me. Yes. No. Thank you. All he'll say.' She flung this at Gascoigne. Fielding introduced them. She swapped roles. Victorian aristocrat descends on deserving poor.

'Mr Gascoigne is one of your charitable assistants.'

'I know that. I know that.'

'Good. Hilda's first husband.'

He made himself say it, to wound himself as he thrust her off.

'Men of taste,' she said, but she was surprised. 'I want a word with you, if Mr . . . er . . . Mr . . . will excuse us.' She took his arm now. 'I feel terrible.'

'No need.' He thought she meant about Hilda, was dashed as she looked up in surprise.

'Absolutely down. And none of your optimism. Your wife died.'

They sat.

'Go on, Liz. Let's hear you.'

'Everybody wants something done. Willy's complaining about money. I'd like to stay in bed and sulk.'

'Do so.'

'No wonder Anna hated you. It's not that I feel old. Often I might be sixteen. But everything looms like a last chance.'

'You're forty-two, not eighty.'

'Friends die. I grudge it. People who have been there all my life. Not just one.'

'I know what you mean.'

'I doubt it. I run my charitable chores, look after the estate, pet Sarah and the baby, visit London, abroad. It's nothing. I'm not desperate yet, but I can guess what it's like.'

'Doctors?'

'Before long, but I don't want medicine yet. I ought to be able to cure myself.'

'You'd better spend a day or two with us at Rempstone,' he said.

'Doing what?'

'Lying in bed. Eating toast, drinking white wine and worrying about all the things you should catch up on.'

'That's . . . You make it sound good. Anna always said that. "He'll make it sound like heaven." We wouldn't get anywhere. Not walking in your little wood, three of us. This isn't a fairy-tale and I don't know why you should think it is. I'm frightened. I'm depressed.'

'Not sensible.'

'You don't understand, either. It won't be long before I'm properly old. Incapacitated.'

'Or dead.'

'I shan't mind that.'

'Look, Elizabeth. You're an energetic woman.'

Her lip trembled, as they sat in chairs, slightly apart from the crowd. The Earl stumped past as if his boots were clogged with clay and he raised a heavy hand in their direction; three underlings pressed close to his shoulders.

'Am I normal?' the Countess asked.

'I imagine so. Why don't you try the doctor? He'll give you something.'

'I don't want drugs. I want to be myself.'

He did not argue. Because she was who she was, nobody approached now; they were left in isolation. Small, dark, lively, she bunched herself together, the eyes bright, the nose beaky, not large, the pallor of her skin beautiful still. Fielding knew that she did not regard him highly, nor like him, but he was the only one near enough in age or status or friendship or qualification to be burdened with her confidences. His wife had found living too hard; perhaps he'd noticed it before he'd greased off to his adultery.

'You're not like me.' Now she was vehement. 'You've got something to live for.'

'I'm glad you think so.'

'Why don't you give me some advice? Really say something?'

He thought as the band struck brassily into a military two-step. The middle-aged stomached it forward.

'We ought to dance,' he said.

'No.' Incisive. 'You say something.'

'I think you should take one matter at a time. Enjoy it if it's to be enjoyed. Do your best to put up with it if it's nasty.'

She considered, head craning forward, breasts white.

'That's true,' she said in the end.

'But you can't manage it? Your time of life?'

'How do you know? At Easter we were at Castergates and I came across a bed of narcissi and daffodils and the scent was so beautiful I burst into tears.'

'There's not,' he said, 'much wrong with that.'

'I distressed myself,' she spoke with a detached insistence of one used to laying down the law, 'when I should have been delighted.'

'You didn't approve of your manner of showing pleasure, that's all.'

'It was uncontrollable.'

'And socially unacceptable. You should be pleased. Feeling's alive in you, not atrophied.'

'If I weep, Edward, because I smell flowers, what should I do about Anna's dying or a war or an earthquake?'

'Grin. Abide. Cry a bit more because you've spilt some

tears on your daffodils. I don't know. We can only go so far. I don't expect you to decapitate yourself at a major tragedy because you made a bit of a fool of yourself in front of the gardener.'

'There was nobody there.'

'Do you not find it odd,' he gave her each word separately, 'that we have a conversation like this here in the middle of . . . ' He spread his hands.

'I didn't expect it, certainly.'

Two elderly ladies hovered, heads together, perhaps three yards back. Elizabeth smiled now, grimly, but settled.

'You're wanted,' he said.

'So I see. Thank you, Edward.' She touched his arm. 'Now, Mrs Harcourt-Smith. I must have forgotten something.' She swept forward, queen-secure, chattering.

Fielding did not shift from his place, watched Hilda furiously poised in the dance. Gascoigne romped not many paces behind her, pale-faced and grinning. The floor vibrated with the thump of feet, boiled with the flashing light from silk or flesh, amongst the Victorian weight of the furnishings. Why had he no pleasure here? He had.

Twenty-three years ago he'd first come as a young husband. Anna, typically, had never mentioned to her fiancé that she'd been a close school-friend of the new Countess of Marcroft until they'd received a wedding present, ugly silver trays, and an invitation to the Hall. The young woman had been cool, as if she recognized, or wished to make plain, the social gulf between them, though they called each other by Christian names. The Earl, whom Fielding knew slightly, hobbled down for ten minutes, laughed awkwardly jovial, drove off to London.

Elizabeth, already a mother, for she'd married within months of leaving school, had conducted them along this hall, with little conversation. She did not approve of her husband's slaughterous ancestors, but did not say so, nor make fun. Here was a place big as the hugest non-conformist chapels, built in the same stone and style, with gothic windows, but decorated not with pulpits and pews but with armour, banners, military relics and trophies from the sporting field. A pipe organ in one corner did not seem unduly ostentatious. They'd walked along, dimly in a sun-bright afternoon, mounted the stairs towards a fireplace, on the landing, rich with armorial carving and mock-medieval andirons, rather breathlessly, ducking as if the stags' heads would topple off the walls.

'What did you think of her?' Anna had wanted to know, at home.

'She made almost no impression.'

'That's what I think.' Anna grabbed his sleeve; she loved to touch when she was excited. 'When she was at Wenlock she was full of life, always thinking something up.'

'She's learnt the new role.'

They'd taken high tea from a small table in a huge dining room, with servants in attendance. It might have been a film, so artificial were the sentences exchanged. Even the sandwiches seemed stage-props. At the end of the uncomfortable hour and a half, Elizabeth Marcroft had said, in the same imperious, withdrawn voice:

'Please come again. You're the only people I know.'

They saw Anna was weeping. That seemed, later, beautifully apt.

The Fieldings often discussed the Countess together until it approached a game, with rules. One tried to state the axioms in new ways, to decorate their reality. Exaggeration was allowed, but within limits. They would make up conversations in the bedroom between the Earl and his wife; imagine what Lord Marcroft, whom they knew very slightly, would say to his baby daughter. They'd make the butler report below stairs on some act or adage of Elizabeth's.

'We're snobs,' Edward concluded.

'Do you think we are?'

'We don't talk like this about our other friends.'

Then they'd be silent, not quite comfortable.

Anna visited Marcroft almost daily for some periods, seemed caught up with the schemes her friend worked out, acted as chauffeuse, but after Jeremy was born she truanted. The Earl stood, by proxy, as godfather to the boy; relatives were impressed.

Now, this evening, in the thump and glare of the dance, Fielding remembered the small, dark woman who hardly had a word for him until Anna's illness, when she'd turned up, demanding satisfaction. Frightened by his wife's condition, he'd talked, and the pair flowed in words together, in half-accusations, concerned quarrels. Their relationship was close; they did not meet often, but needed no preliminary sparring.

He'd taken relief from his wife's illness by working. His grandfather's firm of building contractors had now become enormous, with national and international projects, and he slaved in his office. Anna unable to shift from her bed was cared for by nurses, by Mrs Makepeace, so that a short visit of perhaps twenty minutes or half an hour in the evening was all he devoted to her. He had no understanding of the illness, in spite of talk with psychiatric experts, and excused his callousness by exhausting himself at his desk. Now he saw those exertions as time-wasting. Though skilful enough at planning, he'd made much more money recently with purely financial transactions, but he'd kept himself, moralistically, from his wife's bedside.

At first he'd considered his wife's indisposition as temporary. When he'd realized that she was incurable, against the protestations of specialists, he'd had several casual affairs. Only one of these threatened to be serious, but he had extricated himself sharply, having a fine sense of self-preservation. Mrs Makepeace had already 'reasoned with him' as she put it, though she assumed no privileges from her former intimacy, and rightly. At thirty-five he was nothing like the boy of nineteen, and let her know it. But she'd spoken on that occasion.

'Alma Fleetwood's not the woman for you,' she'd said, blunt, outright.

'Have I said she is?'

'She'll do you harm.'

'In what way?'

'She'll want to marry you. She'll press for it. She's not interested in your wife.'

'Why should she be?'

'I've said enough, then, have I?'

Mrs Makepeace withdrew, in a rough embarrassment. Nearly fifty then, she'd looked older, lined, saurian-skinned, tweedily untidy. How the scented matron of sixteen years earlier had changed to this dry, not stick, bole, puzzled him. Her husband's death and consequent shortage of money had perhaps been responsible, but when she had been recommended to him as an efficient housekeeper he'd been shocked at the interview by her appearance. Neither had been anything but business-like, these ex-lovers, but she bore little resemblance to the careful beauty who'd seduced him.

Soon after this he took up with Hilda.

Anna was in hospital, but Fielding had immediately sent for Mrs Makepeace and offered either Rempstone or the town house for his wife's use when she was discharged. Makepeace chose the smaller place; it would take less keeping, but there was plenty of room still for Jeremy and his friends. He told her that he intended to live with Hilda, but she'd said nothing in reproach. Not long afterwards she'd touched his arm at the hospital bedside and whispered:

'You've done the right thing.'

She meant, he thought, Hilda, and he shrugged. He did not need her support.

Oddly he'd enjoyed the furore he'd caused.

People talked in Beechnall. Here was a man whose own wife was prostrate, an attempted suicide, a desperate case, and he'd stolen a young beauty from this schoolmaster without a qualm. They hinted disaster. She must be a bitch. Women loathed the idea, but liked him. The men openly approved. He could afford two women, and if one incapacitated herself, then it was no more than sense for him to choose a better.

He'd chosen to tell Anna himself.

First he'd seen Makepeace about the interview, then Anna's GP, who'd stroked his chin, looked wise. Finally the man advised him to bother the psychiatric consultant. By this time Fielding had argued himself into a mild fuzz of anger.

'This,' he said, having explained, 'is what I intend to do. Now is there any reason why I shouldn't tell Anna?'

'You realize, Mr Fielding, that she is utterly insecure, feels unloved, unwanted, and that seems to stem to some considerable extent from her parents' lack of concern when she was a child.'

'People get over that.'

'Some. To some degree.'

'What I want to know, Dr Newton, is whether or not I tell her. I've taken action. Now do I tell her myself, or do I leave it to you, or shall we let her hear gossip?'

'All will have an adverse . . . '

'For heaven's sake, man. Is one worse than another?'

'Mr Fielding.' Newton's face had reddened. 'You are acting entirely selfishly. It's not for me to dictate your morality, but I cannot help pointing out to you that this course of action is, in this case, medically speaking, quite reprehensible.'

57

'Are you going to cure her?'

'I can't guarantee that. I'm hopeful.'

'More than I am.'

He had no anger against the physician, but a whim, a velleity to goad him.

'I can't wait,' he said, 'for you to set her right. I'm not that sort of man.'

'Does marriage mean nothing?'

'A legal contract. What use is Anna as a wife? You'd have me at her beck and call, her bedside, year in, year out, wouldn't you? And when I'd ruined my life, worn myself out, you'd be prepared to praise me.'

'Suppose, Mr Fielding, you became ill, and society took a similar view to yours?'

'I'm not talking about society. I pay to be looked after by doctors, nurses, skilled people who can do their work and go home at the end of an eight-hour stint. That's sensible. That's what my taxes provide. Moreover, I'm rich enough to buy private services over and above that.'

'Your wife is deprived of love.'

'I blame the chemicals in her synapses, and hope you'll come up with a corrective drug. You think I'm hard. We've been married for eighteen years, and over the last eight Anna has been nothing like a wife to me. I am perhaps responsible in some small way. But as a human being she is deficient.'

'She is a human being, Mr Fielding, craving affection.'

'Which she has from you and your staff here. She's safe in hospital. She can demand and get. She'll never be any use to me again, or I to her. I'm talking plainly to you. You can judge me as you wish. I guess from your expression that you hope I fall into similar straits. So be it. But Anna has had ten years from me. Ten years of hope, encouragement, service. And it's enough. She will never be right.'

The psychiatrist was taken aback, unbelievably so.

Fielding imagined that the man must have seen wide ranges of human conduct, from extreme to extreme, but truth had shocked him, caused him to purse his lips like some tut-tutting old aunt, because this husband spoke his mind without heat, as if from calculation.

'You must do as you think best, Mr Fielding.' Medical experts feel none of the pain.

'But?'

'How can we help when you are prepared to do so little? She loves you, admires you, but cannot feel anything in return. Does your life together mean nothing, the years of marriage?'

'They've killed any feeling on my part, if that's what you mean, except distaste. I've nothing to say in my own favour. I might act differently if I were somebody else. But she's been a burden too long. She's . . .'

'Go on, Mr Fielding.'

'There's no need. You know exactly what I mean. In terms of money I shall do my best for her. But as for time, life, affection, I'm not prepared either to give or to pretend.'

'That's straight enough.' Newton sighed.

'Isn't it better to be so?'

'In my job, Mr Fielding, I find it very difficult to judge whether a person means what he says. People change their minds from minute to minute.'

'Am I speaking the truth, do you think?'

'You sound like a man running out of patience, certainly.'

Newton, his rimless glasses sparkling clean from a silk handkerchief, relaxed on his elbows.

'Am I to tell her then, Dr Newton?'

'Please yourself.'

'I don't want to add to your difficulties.'

The psychiatrist smiled sarcastically.

'We've our line of action here. It won't be until she is out that you'll be able to make your announcement.'

'Wouldn't it be better if I did it here, so she could have the benefit of any medical, chemical adjustments?'

'No.'

That was it without argument.

When Anna emerged, Fielding approached Mrs Makepeace to prepare his wife, but she was adamant.

'It's up to you,' she said. 'She's asking why you don't visit her, and I expect that means she suspects something's wrong. But you must tell her. I'll do what I can afterwards.'

'You don't think much of me, do you?'

She eyed him, up and down, up and down.

'We'd all like things to be different. I don't blame you.'

He visited his wife after a few days, preceded by a barrage of flowers. Anna sat in bed, pale, slightly lined, alert. When he inquired after her health she answered steadily, claiming improvement, but her hand fiddled with the coverlet.

'You haven't been to see me, Edward.'

'No.'

'I wanted you to come.'

Uncomfortable, he'd have to be out with it.

'I have to say something,' he began. 'It's rather unpleasant.'

'Bad news?' she asked, listlessly.

'Yes. In a way. Yes. This is the finish.'

She lifted her head, once, a swift glance, then composed her features to wood. Her bottom lip protruded, trembled already.

'I'm living with somebody else.'

She might not have heard.

'At Rempstone. A girl called Hilda Gascoigne.'

No answer. The mask; the lip; the hand picking.

'I love her, Anna. She's been married. She left her husband.'

Incomprehension, outwardly, visibly.

'I can't go on living with you any more as your husband. We've . . . we've . . .' He groped for a kind word. None existed, appeared. 'I'm sorry, Anna. Especially as you've been ill.' The long hiatus. 'I shall see to it that you don't suffer on account of this.' Big promise, broken already. 'Financially, I mean. I'll see that you are comfortable.'

She had turned her head slightly away from him, but he did not remember her doing so.

'I'm sorry about this. I didn't want it.'

What did that convey? A miserable sentence without truth, a tube of Secotine to mend an earthquake's havoc? She did not, could not, reply.

'Do you understand what I've said, Anna?' He asked gently, repeated the question. Still she looked away from him. A spurt of anger thrust meanly in him.

'Anna, can you hear me?' Louder.

Then her face podged itself into putty, into dough, un-human shapelessness for some seconds before she clapped her hands to her cheeks, turned, smacked herself down on to the bed away from him in a howl of tears. She wailed, like a bellows, almost rhythmically, a siren sounding weird distress. He hated the mechanical insuck of breath, the gulp, the slobber.

She had heard. She understood.

'Don't distress yourself,' he mouthed, putting a hand limply to the crooked back. 'I'm sorry.'

He allowed her to cry on, as he'd prepared himself to do, imagining his own misery. In a kind of hedgehog comfort he crouched there, waiting for the next development, ready to snatch the knife from her wrist or throat. All she managed was this crying, this feeble energy directed to wetting a few square inches of the sheet.

'I'm sorry, Anna,' he said again.

She lived, unhealthily.

61

'Is there anything I can do for you?' Sobbing. 'I mean this. I honestly mean it.'

She must have heard, for she put a hand out, from in front of her, to jerk the sheet higher up her head. He looked out of the window, at the greenness of lawn, shrub, lime-trees, a still place, under a fair sky, between high walls. If only the wind would thrash about there, whip leaves into sound, dash the branches, liven.

He left the room, reported to Mrs Makepeace, who listened like a servant without comment or expression. Within two days Anna was back in hospital.

Now as the dance ended in a burst of brass and the couples scattered he recalled this without revulsion. Nothing could have saved his wife; he'd convinced himself. Gascoigne had seated himself nearby, watching him. Bored, ill-tempered, Fielding walked across.

'Do you enjoy this sort of thing?' Gascoigne asked, after Fielding had carefully avoided speech.

'No.'

The band had been replaced by deafening record player and near-darkness which had cleared young people from the side-rooms. Two beams of light, one red, one orange crossed near the centre of the floor and in the surrounding dimness bodies jerked, but slightly, almost delicately, hands spread, apart from partners.

'We have this in school at lunchtime.'

'Do you approve?'

'You mean, "Would I prefer them to be reading Shakespeare or playing or listening to Mozart?" I would, but they won't, or not many.'

'Is that bad?'

'Yes. I prefer high art to rubbish. But I can't judge it morally. These children will grow into respectable parents or wage-slaves.'

'You don't force them ... ?'

'Yes. Of course. I'm a little dictator. I lay the law down. That's what I'm paid for.'

'But you waste your breath?'

'Difficult to say.' Gascoigne pulled a wry, attractive face. 'One doesn't know what's rubbing off. I sometimes think I should have moved back to the private sector, into a public school. That's where I started. Something of the old ethos still there. I don't know. I keep trying. And my school's in a good catchment area.'

'Does that make any difference?'

Again the facial contortions.

'Very much so.'

'So you're not very influential, really?'

'More, I'd say, than if I were in a council estate. Hard to judge. We keep at it. I talk more about university scholarships than cases in magistrates' courts, and this suits me. But come over and have a look at us.'

'No, thanks.'

'You're paying rates.'

Fielding stretched his legs, squinted about for Hilda. He'd enjoyed this exchange, appreciated the modest sentences Gascoigne had offered him, but felt that an outsider would have claimed more for the man. He'd ask Hilda.

'One doesn't know.' Gascoigne stared away from him, but his voice was pitched with intensity. 'I passed examinations with extraordinary ease at school. I worked hard, I was quick, with a good memory and did as I was told. But I'd been a year at Oxford before I became alive, educationally speaking. I went to Italy. I'd seen historical ruins before; I'd been round art galleries; I'd been abroad. But I came back a different man. Alive in the world I was writing words about.'

'Why was that?'

'Hundreds of reasons. I'd won a college prize. I was in love. I'd come into money; not much; but unexpected to a

63

poor boy. And there for my benefit were these monuments of classical antiquity, of the Renaissance, all of which I knew something about, and suddenly working on me. You remember Wordsworth. The sounding cataract haunted me like a passion. That's as near as I can put it. It amazed me then. It does so still. I did not expect it. But my tutor had been there to advise me to go to Italy, to look. That as a schoolmaster is what I hope to do for some of my pupils.'

'How many?' Fielding, interested, cynical.

'I don't know. More than you suspect. It may not be Italy, of course.'

'Is that,' Fielding said, 'the aim of education, then?'

Gascoigne leaned back, approvingly.

'It is not. There are a dozen other things I put before it. But it must be there for those who want it, are capable of it.'

'How d'you manage that?'

'When I appoint staff, I look for the man or woman who is not only well qualified, can keep discipline, will give his or her best in the classroom, I try to find those who'll go that mile further.'

'Don't you make mistakes?'

'More often than not. Schools tend to breed mediocrities. But sometimes . . . '

'How do you know?'

'Talk. Time's short, but if a candidate can fire me with a touch of enthusiasm, then I'll have him.'

'At the expense of these other virtues?'

'No. I tell you the system militates against rashness. Not that the two things are incompatible. All this strikes you as pretty airy-fairy, I take it?'

'I'm interested. I've never had one of these eye-opening moments. So you wouldn't appoint me.'

The record player thudded for the young jiggling groups.

'This is not the bread-and-butter of education,' Gascoigne

64

said, playing with the crease of his trousers, 'but it's neglected at our peril.'

'But is it neglected?'

Gascoigne now gave him full face.

'Yes. It is. I wouldn't mind you on my staff, Fielding. You're sharp.'

'You don't pay my sort of money.'

Fielding moved away, friendly, effrontery put into its place. He made for the bar, drank with Hilda who questioned him about his recent tête-à-tête, danced with her, did a turn with the Countess, was invited for a private gin in an office, arrived home in Rempstone at two in the morning. On the way back he and his wife barely exchanged a word.

He made his way to the kitchen to brew coffee, unusually, uncertain why he did not leave the chore to Hilda. She, white, exhausted, sat in an armchair unspeaking. When he returned, she had not moved. 'Now what is it?' He sat wearily. With a handkerchief she shielded her grief from him. 'Here, take your coffee. You're tired.'

She pulled herself squarer, sipped; could not staunch trembling.

'What's the trouble?'

'Nothing. It's nothing.'

At least she could talk. A mildness of anger touched him as he remembered that Anna's illness had begun like this, in unreasonable silence or tears. He checked himself quickly. Everybody felt down; most shook free of the depression. Only the Annas, without necessary physical resistance, succumbed. As he touched her arm, she looked gratefully at him, eyes brimming.

'What is it, Hilda? Anybody said anything?'

That sounded unnecessarily gruff.

'No.' She shook her head. The question seemed to have settled her. 'I just felt done in. And when I heard you clumping about in, in here . . . '

'Drink up, then, and let's get you to bed.'

Now she sat sullenly, plainly, hunching herself while he stirred his coffee. He'd pulled his bow-tie loose, sat uncouthly, shirt unbuttoned from his chest. In the low light he could have been a workman in his tea-break, sprawling, easing limbs, steeped in inaction.

She finished her drink, put her cup from her. He'd hardly begun; the liquid scalded.

'Have another,' he invited.

This time she edged upright, composed herself, twisted a smile. They sat.

'You think I'm silly.'

He was surprised to hear her speak, immersed as he was in his unease.

'Tell us about it, then.' He made himself speak gently.

'I don't know,' she spoke very slowly. 'It all seemed so unnecessary. All that preparation, and money, and finery, and all for nothing.'

'You were disappointed?'

'Yes. There's nothing in it. It's not worth doing one thing or another. I can't put it into words. If you don't know, you don't know.'

'I don't.'

She hung her head at his curtness.

'I can't stand it.' She stood up.

'What?'

'Everything. Everybody.'

'So there was something?'

'There wasn't. There wasn't.' She staggered towards the door, dragging feet, scarecrow in ball dress.

He let her go.

5

Next morning Hilda slept late, but apologized for her outburst. Now she spoke rationally, describing her fatigue,
blaming herself for overworking, overthinking when neither
was necessary. She convinced him utterly, so that both
enjoyed the careful examination of her symptoms which they
made, calling on similar experiences, crediting the body with
a kind of commonsense that the higher brain sometimes
lacked. She even quizzed him about his conversation with
Alan Gascoigne, and when he described how the Italian
visit had awakened the man, she laughed, sat down to do so.

'Now what's up?' He feared hysterics.

'The proof of the pudding.'

'Come again.'

'He's just a hypocrite. He'd no taste at all for pictures.
The reproductions he chose for the school were conventional. Lord Clark's top twenty.'

'But wasn't he choosing for a community, not for himself? So he'd do well to follow some lively expert.'

'Have you,' she asked, 'known anybody who cares, who's
made his mind up for himself, to choose in that way?'

Now she was beautiful, large, serene, sure of herself, a
woman whose balance of mind, whose weight of judgement,
was reflected in her bodily poise. In every way she differed
from the shrivelled, pallid thing of the early hours.

'I was rather impressed with the man.' Pompous because
of pleasure.

'Oh, he's impressive all right. But not on aesthetics. He
wishes he were.'

'How, then?'

'Looking after number one. He's ambitious, and selfish.
That's where he scores. And all this talk of art, and educa-

tion, and opening vistas, and opportunity for all, merely translates into "I am outstanding. This'll prove it to you." ' She laughed again, tartly. 'You don't believe me?'

'Oh, no?'

'Now if I'd said something like this to Alan,' he disliked her use of the name, 'he'd have been posturing like mad, strutting and flashing the jargon, to prove he was better than I was at this sort of judgement.'

'God bless him.'

'You've not had to put up with it.'

Reassured, he turned to the City pages as she moved to the garden. In half an hour she announced that Linda Lawrence, Jeremy's girl, wanted him on the phone. She sounded brisk. Could she see him? At once? Yes, important. Never mind about lunch. Thank you. He finished his papers, rang the office, rearranged an unimportant interview for four, helped fix a date for a directors' meeting, made the manager's mind up for him, as usual. Doing this by phone gave him satisfaction, in that it was carried out against time, over obstacles, with slight risks in that he hadn't his fingers on all information here. Linda would come by the country bus which passed the gates at twenty to twelve.

She clapped along the terrace sharply, her coat-hem swinging with tassels, her jeans patched, but the bright orange, pocketed shirt-blouse laundered. As she entered the room, she pulled off sunglasses, shoving them carelessly away.

'Now what can I do for you?' he asked.

She crossed her legs; these also were heavily fringed.

'It's a nuisance,' she said, without emphasis, so softly that he was not sure he'd heard correctly.

'I see.' He'd wait. The hair was less tidy than usual, frizzing from its constricting bands, though there was nothing restive about her. A big girl, not stout, strong-boned

68

she sat, eyes dark in the wide face, choosing the exact words to begin with.

'My parents have been down. You know that.'

'They threatened to visit me.'

She grinned companionably.

'They, my mother, pressed me to go back to my husband. You know all about it.'

'And?'

'Jerry thinks I should go.' They paused, examined shoes.

'May I ask why?'

'That's it, really. That's why I've come here.'

'Aren't you at work?' he asked.

'I've taken the day off. I've got to talk to somebody.'

She looked by no means desperate, hugging her knee to her chest, casual, large-handed.

'Does Jeremy know? You've told him?'

'He advised me. "My dad's objective," he said. "Doesn't get hot under the collar. Ask him what he thinks."' She stopped again; her eyes were big, shapely and she knew it. 'We've been married for four years. I left him a year ago. Rob, my husband.'

'I don't know anything about him. How old is he, for instance?'

'Twenty-seven. He's a lab technician, like me. Very good at it. He ought to have gone to university by rights, but he left at sixteen. He's qualified himself. The consultants respect him. He's a worker. Loves courses, and facts. But he's not there.'

'Not all there?'

She laughed.

'Not forceful. If you ask him about something in the lab, he answers as if he weren't sure. Drops his head, won't look at you. You'd think he was ashamed of being ignorant, even when he's giving you a perfect explanation.'

'And this doesn't suit you?'

'I think,' she said, still without emphasis, 'he came to me on the rebound. Somebody threw him over, and he proposed to me.'

'At least he proposed?'

She frowned, perhaps at his levity.

'We worked in the same lab. He explained things to me. He was miles better than the doctors. They'd got medical qualifications, but he knew much more than they did.'

'Why did you accept him?'

'I was fed up with everything. Home, mainly. And he was so good at his work. Once you'd seen through it.'

'And the marriage wasn't successful?'

'Not really. Boring. He was only interested in the hospital.'

'Sex?'

'Not bad. A bit tepid.'

She giggled on her word. Her voice was never raised, but there seemed a care about what she said, a taste, a respect not so much for the phraseology as for the fact. He confessed himself puzzled, saw no attraction in the girl, wondered what she offered Jeremy.

'That sounds like most marriages,' he said, matching his face to hers. 'Why did you leave him?'

'Two things. I applied and got a job here. He said it was silly, that I could become better qualified where I was. But I think he didn't like my getting promotion so quickly. He was a bit jealous of my "A" levels. And the other reason. He began writing to this girl again. There wasn't much in it. He used to hide the letters, but I knew where, and I looked at them. All about their jobs and what they read, or, rather, she read. She wasn't married. He used to go upstairs and write. Miss Susan E. Belchamber.' She raised her eyes at the name. 'I saw the envelope once.'

'And that . . . ?'

'No, it didn't. We never mentioned it. It was the job. I

70

said I was going, and he moaned so much how wrong it was for a wife to go off that I told him I'd pack him in. I wasn't serious. Not then. But the rows got worse, and I got part-share in a flat here, and left him.'

'Didn't he write to you?'

'Yes, he did. He tried to make them love-letters. Full of "darling": he never called me that once.'

'And all to no effect?'

'I went back to see him. His letters must have . . . You know. But he was the same. All buttoned-up. Mumbling. And I was comfortable. Four of us shared a flat. And we did the meals, went to the laundry, between us. With him, I did the lot. His mother had spoilt him. And we had to save. Never went out. To buy the house. When I'd done a day's work, there I had to stand ironing his collars and cuffs, while he sat with his head in an article on the chemistry of the bloodstream or something. I knew when I was well-off.'

'But you shacked up with Jeremy?'

'In time.' She blubbered her lips, wetly.

'Why's Jeremy want you to go? You've not quarrelled with him, have you?'

Linda stroked her legs, as if to move them by some small amount to a more correct posture. Fielding watched the workmanlike hands, nails too long for their shape but scraped clean, thumbs hook-shaped, at their unhurried task.

'No, we haven't.' She stared, judging him perhaps. 'He's a funny boy. He's mad-keen on fairness. "That's unjust," he says. It seems to mean more to him than anything else. You've noticed this, I expect?'

'No, I haven't.'

That stopped her. She'd been ravelling this out, had come up with a satisfactory hypothesis, and now had found the clinching evidence merely subjective.

'Well, it's true.' Aggrieved, surly, aggressive, not to be proved wrong.

'I see.'

He considered this view of his son. As far as he could tell the boy was selfish, like all young people, bent on his own way. But, then, he never discussed principles with his father, merely received presents or advice politely, so it was unlikely that the older man would have heard of this concern for fairness. Yet. All yets. Why had it not been obvious from Jeremy's behaviour that he'd based his life on this abstraction? Fielding had failed to notice? Likely, likely.

'And he thinks,' he began again, 'that you should go back to your husband?'

She considered him, frowning, did not answer.

'Does your husband know you're living with Jeremy?'

'Of course he does. He came over with my parents.'

'And what line did he take? Was he prepared to overlook it?'

'He didn't say.'

'That's not a very sensible reply, Linda. You surely considered the matter?'

'He wants me back.'

'Do you think,' Fielding asked, 'he'll forgive you? That's what I mean.'

'Yes. He will. He won't forget it. It's happened to other people.'

Fielding held his breath, then expelled it slowly.

'You see, Linda, you're asking my advice. I hardly know you. I don't know your husband at all. And your description of Jeremy doesn't tally with my own observations of the boy. And you won't help. That's the predicament.' Kindly.

She pouted her lips.

'Oh, well. Never mind, then.'

He smiled, politely, in middle age.

'There's one thing I'd like to say, ought to say. This may just be rather cruel. Has it struck you that the reason Jeremy wants you to go back to your husband is that he, he doesn't think your relationship is, is successful?'

'He's tired of me?'

She burst into laughter, harsh, coarse, scorning him.

'That's the first thing I did think of,' she said. 'And told him. "You're fed up." But he shook his head. He's not a great talker about himself. I don't think it's right.'

'He convinced you, did he? Why was that?'

'I don't know why. I just think so. That's all. We don't go into every bit and piece. He hardly says anything. You know what he's like.'

'You are convinced, though.'

'Yes.' She made a convulsive movement, lightly slapping her thighs, half-jack-knifing upwards before crossing her legs. 'Well, thanks very much.'

'Have we finished, then?' Amused. She returned his smile.

'Yes. Ye'.'

'Have you made your mind up?'

'Oh, no.'

'You've wasted your time, then?'

'I don't think so.'

'You're just as much in the dark?' He felt he must press her. She pushed herself forward in the chair, arching her back.

'Jeremy always wants to know the whys and wherefores about other people. Never tells you anything much about himself.'

'And I'm like him?' Humble father.

'Ye'.' Exactly the boy's intonation.

'And that's not good.'

'I'm prepared to take people as they are.' Cool. The lady.

'But how do you know how?'

'Everybody has some idea. I mean you don't need to have the names of their ancestors, do you?'

'Or their blood group?'

She looked up, surprised, intelligently awake.

'I see what you mean. You do sometimes.' She chewed on that. 'It'll all come out, I expect, in the wash.'

'Did you and Jeremy consider marriage?'

'Well, y'know . . . '

'The reason I ask is that it's said to be a matter of no importance to people of your age. With us, we could commit adultery, or beat our wives, but the institution was important.'

'I should like to marry him.'

He waited for her. She went no further.

'I thought perhaps you would.'

'He's not bothered, though. I'm not the right one for him. And as I'm married to Rob, he's covered.' She spoke dolefully, but without spite.

'It mightn't develop,' he asked, 'into lifelong partnership?' That seemed pompous, wounding, pointless.

'No. He'll marry somebody else.'

'That's not the trouble now? He's not met . . . ?'

'No. I keep telling you. We get on all right. He's come round to thinking it's not fair to Rob, since my mum and dad come, came.'

'What about fairness to you?'

'He thinks it's easier for me.'

Fielding scratched his head.

'Would you like a cup of coffee?' he asked.

'If it isn't any trouble.'

When they had sipped and stirred together he asked:

'Do you want my advice?'

'Please.' The word was courteous.

'If you don't want to leave Jeremy, don't let him bully you into it. Please yourself for once.' He coughed. 'I find

young people cover their emotional snags with fancy principles. Perhaps it's a good thing they do. But if you want
Jeremy, fight for him.'

She screwed her face as if biting a lemon.

'Do you think,' slowly, 'that I'm the right sort of wife
for him, then?' It was a pathetic, childish appeal. She wore
no wedding ring.

'I've no idea. He'll have to choose for himself.'

'He said,' she began, with voice normally dull, 'hinted
that you chose wrong.'

'How do you mean?'

'His mother wasn't, y'know, suitable, he said. He feels
sorry for you, because it led you to act,' she hesitated,
'badly. You didn't pay much attention to her. When she was
ill, y'know. He said that when you were married she was,
was normal.' Hesitant, she squinted in expectation of punishment.

'He knows nothing about it.'

'He thinks he does.'

Fielding put his empty cup carefully down, rubbed his
hands drily together, said:

'I've thought about this for years, and I never got to the
bottom of it. I ought to feel guilty, but I don't. Or not much.
Perhaps I shall. I did what I could for Jeremy's mother, but
it was useless. All this talk of sacrifice that saves life is so
much nonsense.'

'But your present wife?'

He was amazed that this diffident girl could advance the
argument. The language was oblique, almost tenderly so,
but the accusation stood blunt enough.

'I didn't drop Anna to take up Hilda like that. We'd been
married seventeen, eighteen years when I met Hilda for the
first time. By then Anna was lost. I doubt whether she cared,
really, whom I lived with, or where.' He knew that for a lie.
She'd begged him to come back, howling her distress out

75

loud. 'Her depression was so deep that it latched on any matter, however trivial, to make a tragedy. She'd be driven to suicide because I called her "Annie" and not "Anna", or because I wore a fancy tie and not a plain one.'

'Why was this?'

'You mean,' he asked, 'was I in any way to blame?' She did not change her expression. 'I suppose I was. But her illness was all set up before I knew her. Parental neglect, chemical deficiency. Oh, God knows. Marriage might have set her right, but it didn't.'

'I see.' She sounded like the boy, and thus his father.

'You think I didn't treat her properly, I expect. Didn't love her. That's possible. Jeremy's a cold fish, sometimes, isn't he? But we don't know the results of our actions. We can do something utterly wrong or mad, and get away with it, while at another time we do an action without thinking and somebody dies, or crumples up mentally. That's why I say please yourself.'

'You're like him.'

'In what way?' He grinned.

'You say things, odd things, I'd never dare.'

Hilda knocked on the door, demonstrating she knew about the visit, walked in.

'Is Linda staying for lunch?' she asked.

'Oh, no thanks. No.'

'We'd be glad if you could.'

'I don't usually eat lunch. I'm slimming.'

'We're on salad today.'

They persuaded her, took her round the garden, talked easily. They ate together rather silently, and he left at three for the office. Linda travelled in his car, claiming that since she'd had the day off she must be back to prepare Jeremy's dinner.

'You've given me ideas,' she said to Hilda, laughing, a sociable being.

6

In the next weeks Hilda Fielding became friendly with the Countess of Marcroft.

A phone call, a visit, further telephoning and Lady Marcroft had failed to attract Hilda to one of her committees. Uncharacteristically she contacted Fielding to know why.

'You must ask her.'

'I've done so. She's very reserved, Edward.'

'You surprise me.'

He enjoyed teasing, but promised to quiz his wife, who said that as Alan, her ex-husband, was a member she'd no intention of joining.

'Why didn't you tell her so?'

'She should have known.'

'Perhaps she didn't think it mattered.'

'Perhaps she didn't.' Hilda spoke tightly, did not like it.

He passed the message on to Elizabeth Marcroft who arranged to call again, was apparently perfect in apology, took Hilda back with her. They discussed shrubs so that his wife returned home flattered and suspicious.

'What does she want?' she asked her husband.

'A playmate.'

'Somebody else at her beck and call?'

'I shouldn't think so. She's enough of them. A confidante? That's a good word. Don't you like the idea?'

'She was Anna's friend.'

'I see.'

'She can choose anybody she likes, pretty well.'

'I doubt that.'

They posed and answered questions mildly. Though Hilda seemed uncertain, over-sensitive, she quickly fell into

77

the habit of visiting Marcroft for an hour, or arranging lunch at Rempstone for the two of them. Fielding, pleased, mocked.

'Have you found out what she's up to?' he asked.

'No. Have you?'

Now and then he worried in that Hilda, his wife, seemed unsteadier than Hilda the mistress, more capricious, nervier. Before she'd acted with pride, a dominating cynosure, dismissing all question of her right to be there queening her occupation. Now that persona had disappeared, and she seemed uncertain of her status. If she'd donned an apron, or gardening gloves, become a domestic nonentity, Fielding would have been slightly puzzled, even annoyed, but this suspicious woman, who was only at ease with her plants, or consulting her catalogues, harassed him. He could see no reason for it, unless this was the real Hilda, and the one he'd loved and admired for the last five years mere disguise. He could not have misjudged so wildly. He thought back to the beginnings of Anna's illness, but found no similarity. Perhaps the change was in himself, in that now he possessed her legally his own personality had been jolted into more accurate judgement. To put such questions to her seemed impossible, a demand for real trouble.

He proposed a holiday. She did not object, so that they flew immediately to the south of France. Here Hilda revived as she swam and sunburned, gambled a little, was lively at night. After five days the board of the property company called him back for an important meeting. Annoyed, because he knew exactly what the trouble was, how it should be handled, and at the same time suspecting that the other directors were equally competent to solve the problem, he arrived in London to find the meeting merely needed to rubber-stamp a decision. He complained to the acting chairman, Sir Benedict Arnold, who brusquely said they'd needed his vote. 'And, Ted, you know what they're like. As soon as they knew they'd be outvoted, they caved in. You miss three days of your holiday. So do I. You and I have got the decision we wanted. If we'd have left it to September, it would have been harder. Time well spent.'

He knew Arnold was right, approved of his action, but feared his desertion might have affected Hilda.

Curiously, on his return, she showed, for the first time, interest in the transaction that had caused the rift. Her questioning was fierce; she'd be a tartar in the classroom, he guessed. At the same time she seemed quite ignorant of his business, and he enjoyed his explanations of the mathematics, the guess-work, the jockeying for position. They seemed closer, as if she'd admired him now with justice, for his real worth, his proven achievement. Again, he found himself surprised in that he'd never noticed before her lack of grasp of what he did. She'd always proffered the correct cliché, the expected questions, and he'd taken her interest, her knowledge for granted.

Now as they sat over dinner after a sea-baking she'd begin, and he'd decorate the menu, and the sheets of paper he'd put ready into his pocket. It became a ritual, and this with her liveliness on the dance-floor, the casino, the bar, bed last, comforted him. Men admired her, but she'd come alive for him. He lost his fear. She stood beautifully, with pride amongst other handsome women, with supremacy. Her diffidence had gone or developed into a correct pleni- tude of calm. She won; she compelled admiration.

Perhaps, he decided, and in his present content he was willing to analyse past discomforts, she'd been uncertain whether he'd marry her on Anna's death. She'd never voiced such suspicions. He glanced at her as they sat on their balcony, her face pale and composed, superb under the great splashes of the stars. The sea hardly moved, heavy with ease, listless, tideless and phosphorescent in the warm ease of the Mediterranean night. Or perhaps she'd feared the marriage would come to nothing, would start without impetus, peter out. He touched her hand. She would turn nakedly to him, inside minutes, master him there. She perhaps felt guilt about Anna, whom she had never met. Whenever she'd spoken of his first wife it had been with sympathy, which he had dismissed, to himself, as hypocritical. Now he was not so sure. Out there the sea turned to scented oil; his wife, this new perfect woman, pointed at the lighted streets, the clumps of palm and described her childhood holidays in Torquay, chuckling.

She now spoke of her parents, something she had not done before, and with affection. Her father had been a regular army officer who had retired to a bungalow in Hampshire, where his wife, daughter of a police superintendant had raised fowl, built greenhouses, bossed the wives of brigadiers and full colonels, spent her time and her husband's energetically. Fielding had seen their photographs, a thin, serious, balding man and a woman with an imperious head, the expression humorous but unsoftened by thick-rimmed glasses. They had died, unexpectedly, in the winter of Hilda's first year of teaching, he with bronchitis, she after a minor accident, a fall, in the orchard.

Now as she described those early holidays, she explained something of herself. Her mother rushed them about, organizing expeditions, making certain that every place in the guide-book had been investigated for interest, and visited if found worthy. Her father tailed along behind, smoking cigarettes, unhurrying in what now appeared to her as a quiet show of irony because he knew that after the first week his wife would be fretting to return to her estate, her plants and creatures, and could only disguise this from herself by a more furious pursuit of the instructive. In the same strenuous manner, the three of them bathed in the sea, every day, whatever the weather, because Mother said so. Her father swam as he lived, slowly, quietly, smoothing the wisps of hair across his head, constantly chided into a different activity, while Mrs Kennedy dug deeply, efficiently into the water, thrusting it, Hilda recognized the exact description in *Julius Caesar* at school, aside and demanding equality of effort and progress from her daughter. When, finally, it became clear that Hilda was the stronger swimmer, she'd no idea whether or not her mother was pleased. The older woman struggled to the diving board, the buoy, designated as their goal, gave her daughter a race, blew heavily in distress at distress, issued when she'd the breath a further challenge to be attempted singly by her daughter, or an order to her husband to restore the *status quo*. Hilda was entered for the swimming gala, where she gained deserved prizes. She never forgot the silver cup she won at the age of nine; to own, for good, this silver egg-cup, on its ebony plinth. She rushed to her parents, where her mother turned it about, commented unfavourably on its size and lack of baize, then commandeered it so it would come to no harm, while her father stood greyly, thinly, by, in civvies, smiling grimly, touching her briefly with a bony hand that trembled, and defying his wife as he bought the child a second ice-cream that day.

Though Hilda laughed now at the pair, her husband could not decide whether she approved of one rather than the other. She said once, by the hotel pool, that they'd met neither Alan nor Edward, and she wondered what they'd make of their daughter's choices. He pressed her.

'Mummy would have been suited with Alan. She could see the effort and the result. With you she'd have seen the results, and been impressed, but not the work. She wouldn't have liked that. She thought she'd got everything taped.'

'And your father?'

'God knows. He didn't ask much. Perhaps he wasn't very energetic. But I think he got what he wanted.'

'In your mother? I thought like usually married like.'

'Are we similar?' she asked. 'I don't believe it.'

He took her into his arms.

They spent another week, came home suddenly when she saw that he'd had enough. He argued with her, but she knew she'd won.

'You're just like your mother,' he said.

'You didn't know her.'

Hilda, pleased beyond expectation, had received a curious letter from Elizabeth Marcroft. It described what was happening socially in a formal and distant style, recalling reports in a school magazine so that Hilda wondered why an adult could bother with such fatuity. Soon she saw. After two or three sides, tenor and temper altered. Lady Marcroft begged her to return, in a manner that was hectic, overwritten, even blotted on the paper. The world was dull; Willy acted awkwardly; young Ravenshead played nothing but the fool, and she needed someone to confide in, to hold on to. Then, feverishly, she described their last meeting, an hour with boiled eggs and brown bread that Hilda remembered as pleasantly bucolic in her own kitchen at Rempstone, as a meeting of hearts, as a revelation of beauty in which Elizabeth had wrestled with temptation, had barely kept her hands to herself. This half-declamation of love, Hilda could not think of it otherwise, neither amused nor frightened her. It had happened before.

She did not show the letter to Edward, replied with a postcard which, she knew, might well arrive after she did.

Their flight was diverted so that they arrived home an hour and a half late. They could not grumble, but did so. They were dog-tired. As soon as they sat to a cup of tea, the phone blasted out.

Jeremy.

'Is my father there?'

Hilda explained that they'd only just got in, but the boy's exasperation was evident.

'I've been trying for a fortnight to get you,' he snapped at Fielding.

'We've been to St Tropez.'

'I want a job.'

'For the rest of the vac? I should think we could manage that.'

'No.' The boy shouted, stopped. 'I'm not going back to university.'

Edward said nothing, waited for explanations, heard none. They breathed heavily, together, in a clash of angry wills, but the boy broke first.

'It's no good, Dad.'

'What isn't?'

'Going on there.'

'You did well in your exams, if I'm to believe you. You've put some time in at your studies during the holiday, again if I'm to believe you.'

'What's the use? I'm at the end of my tether.'

'Your what?' He'd make him repeat the cliché, drum its banality home.

'Tether.'

'I'm in no state now to discuss this, Jeremy. We've just got back. Hilda and I are going out for dinner because we've had nothing to eat all day. You'd better call in at the office tomorrow morning.' He fiddled wearily with his engagement diary. 'Quarter to twelve.' Pencilled in.

'I want a job with the firm.'

'Yes.'

'What do you say?'

'Eleven-forty-five.'

Fielding put the receiver down, blasted it, closed the diary. Resuming his chair, he outlined the conversation to his wife, swore at the cool tea, cursed his son.

'Does he mean it?' she asked.

'I always thought he was sensible,' he replied.

83

'That worries you?'

'I'm tired. We've got to go out to eat.'

'Let's not bother. I'll make an omelette.'

'You bloody well won't.'

She liked him when he jovially bullied her, but carefully did not press him. Over dinner he said little, sat pre-occupied, claimed half-jokingly that he couldn't turn his back for a holiday without somebody going gaga. At home again, they stood by one of the long windows at Rempstone to watch the night. Here everything moved; tree-tops ruffled, small winds twitched, dabs of cloud smudged cold stars. She put her arm awkwardly across his shoulder, re-newing the intimacy of the holiday.

'I ought to do something for the boy. I don't mind taking him into the firm somewhere. At the proper time. I don't know what he wants.'

'He'll tell you tomorrow.'

'I shall lose my temper inside ten minutes. I'm fond of him. I thought he'd make his own career, and I'd leave him well-to-do.'

'Is that what you want, Edward?'

He turned to her, spreading his hands, monkey-faced.

'You think I don't care to be bothered. Isn't that so? And it's right.'

His voice denied the comical gestures.

'When I married Anna there was nothing wrong with her, that I noticed. And we weren't in any desperate hurry. We were engaged for six months. I'm told that she'd al-ready been treated for nervous trouble, but I saw no signs of it. She was normal, lively, ordinary. Her family hoped so. Marriage was going to set her right.'

'It did, didn't it?'

He started at the sharpness of her voice, jerking his head up.

'I suppose so. But she was ... tainted.'

'And you think Jeremy's the same?'

'Why the bloody hell can't he go through university like anybody else?' Demotic common vulgar sense. 'He chose the course. Get his degree, then come along and talk about jobs if that's what he wants when he's shown he can apply himself.'

'He got good "A" levels.'

'He's not without brains. Neither was his mother. Then there's this girl.'

'Is that the father's side?' she asked, slyly, pressing his lapel.

'I'm not claiming to be a saint.' He drew away, huffily.

Next morning he left early for the office. His mood was cheerful, because he faced a difficulty more confidently than his anticipation of it. Brusquely he said he'd no idea when he'd be back, but his Rempstone housekeeper, Mrs Shacklock, would be in, to see to dinner. Hilda did not much relish this dismissal of herself to a subordinate womanly place, but the weather, after morning mist, was fine, and she made for the garden.

Halfway through the morning Lady Marcroft's secretary rang to see if Hilda were back and able to attend a committee meeting. Yes, Mrs Tenby said, her ladyship was at home, but very busy. The woman sounded aggrieved, middle-aged or dyspeptic. Hilda, slightly put out that Elizabeth had not rung herself, went back to the borders. The letter probably meant nothing, then, was the result of an afternoon's frustration. No, she could not believe that. She surprised herself with the violence she applied to cutting and clearing. She shifted dead flowers, wrenched out weeds; overgrown plants were thinned, marked for moving, uprooted with personal vindictiveness. It was perhaps half an hour before she noticed this.

Not much after three Edward called out, came smiling into the garden.

'You're soon back,' she said from her knees.

'Not a deal to be done.' He rarely spent a whole day at the building firm's headquarters, only liked to be called in to Thomas Fielding, Hallam & Co. when there was a very large contract under discussion. Directors and managers were excellent, knew what they were in business for. He liked to be consulted on purely financial matters, because there his advice, he considered, was expert, worth having. Otherwise, he sat in his office, a small out-of-the-way hole, six or seven hours a week. They knew what he did, respected him, reported regularly to him. The contact pleased everybody, kept management on its toes, did not impede or restrict. 'Quiet time administration-wise.'

'Is there plenty of work?' she asked, naively.

'For the next twenty-five years.' He laughed, puffing his chest. Silly, she thought.

'And Jeremy?'

'Ah, Jeremy.' That must have gone well or he wouldn't be posturing. 'He came. He'd put a suit on.' They smiled together. 'I asked him to sit down and talk.' Fielding pursed his lips in the sunshine, screwed his eyes. 'What it boiled down to was this. He couldn't see much sense in completing his degree. He'd nothing against them at the university. They did their job properly, looked after him. But he wasn't too involved with it. He wasn't blaming anybody. It was his own fault. However, as this was the case he might just as well make a start on his life's work, and could the firm etcetera, etcetera?'

Hilda listened to the slow exposition, relishing his enjoyment.

'I heard all this out. He put the case well enough, but he never stresses anything. Anyway, when he'd done I just said that he'd never be short of money, and he answered straight off, "You'll need to leave it to Hilda." I was a bit taken aback. Touched.'

'It's our marriage that's upset him?'

'I shouldn't be surprised.'

She didn't relish such bluntness.

'I told him that there'd be plenty for him to go at. He shook that off, and said he couldn't see much sense in completing his university course. So then I had a dip at him. "You chose the subject," I said. "I didn't." And do you know the young monkey replied, face straight as a yard of pump-water, "I admit to my mistakes." '

'And you were cross?'

'No. I don't think it's a matter of money or zoology. I let him blab on for a bit. Did him good. I was surprised because he usually hardly strings two sentences together to me. Then I had my piece. "Work in this office is just as boring as work in your lab. And less justifiable, morally. I appreciate your point," I said, "but I'll be better pleased if you show me you can finish the job you've taken on. Never mind 'another two years'. Get it finished, and then if you still think that's not your line, we'll take you on here." Oh, he argued, huffed and puffed, claimed I was encouraging him to two years' idleness, but he was relieved. Poor kid needed somebody to tell him, order him what to do. "You go back to your bench," I said. "That'll please me. And yourself. I'll see you're all right," I said, "when you've shown yourself you are so." It convinced him.'

'Are you sure?'

'No. He might easily change his mind. But there he was. He's no real objection to university, but he feels restive, wants to make a gesture. Time he started to earn a living. We're all like that.'

'You speak for yourself,' she said.

'Then I asked him about Linda.' Fielding smiled. 'I'd no business to, but I was pleased with the boy. He'd been so reasonable. I'd expected him to be obstructionist.'

'He's no mind of his own?'

'Don't be bloody awkward, Hilda. I don't think he's got any real objection to university. It's just that our marriage made him think he might have to fend for himself.'

'By asking his father to get him a job?'

'There's nothing very logical. Didn't expect it.' He waited politely, perhaps for further condemnation, eyes wide. When she said nothing he continued, 'I was telling you about Linda.'

'Yes.'

'She's still there. He wants her to go back to her husband, he says. I don't know.' Appropriately solemn. 'Do you know what I'm supposed to have said to her? That she'd better make her mind up for him, because he was incapable of doing so.'

'Did you not, then?' Amused.

'I told her to do what she wanted. The other's his gloss, I imagine. He sees himself as feeble. Shouldn't be surprised.'

'He admires you. And he's a bit afraid.'

Edward went off to look at a piece of land in the north of the county. There was no need for him to do so, his firm had already acquired it, but she guessed he'd agreed to the trip in his euphoria after Jeremy's capitulation. She found the trait attractive.

When she'd completed her day's stint, contentedly peeled off her gloves, kicked out of her boots she was called to the telephone.

'Ah, Hilda?' Elizabeth Marcroft. Hilda tugged at the discoloured sleeve of her blouse. The nail of her little finger was rimmed with dirt; presumably she'd holed her glove. 'Can you come over?'

'When?'

'Later in the evening?'

'I'm sorry. Edward won't be back until eight. It will be past nine before we've finished dinner, and then he won't stir.'

'I don't want to see him.'

'No. But I do.'

The rudeness collapsed conversation.

'Oh, well. Never mind then.' Rebuffed, diminutive voice.

'Mrs Tenby rang this morning,' Hilda said, contrite if amused. 'Welfare Committee, Friday. I'll see you then.'

'The woman's a bloody fool. I told her I wanted to speak to you myself, but nobody's efficient except her. She must do it.'

'You could have rung me. You've more than one line.'

'I wouldn't have thought of it.' Her ladyship would not demean herself. Noblesse.

'You could have used a call-box.' Hilda could not resist the gibe.

'You had my letter? When you were in France?' This small, breathless.

'Yes.'

'I must see you.' Gulping. 'There's so much on.'

'Elizabeth,' she spoke coolly. 'We've done without each other for nearly a month.'

'I've had time to think. I meant what I said in that letter. I need you.'

'I wonder,' slow speaking, not without cruelty, 'whether I shouldn't show it to Edward.'

'Do what you like. It makes no . . . '

'He'd be furious.'

A pause, Lady Marcroft incapable, Hilda winded, uncomprehending.

'Will you see me?' Choked through ravaged throat, in the end, at the end.

'Tomorrow morning, then?'

'What time will Edward go out?'

'I don't think he will.'

'Come here, then. Come to . . . '

'No, Elizabeth. He needn't be with us. We can talk in

the garden or up in my room. We shan't be disturbed. Ten-thirty.'

'You don't hate me, Hilda, do you?'

'That's silly.'

Hilda rang brusquely off, found herself trembling, in-secure. She sat in front of her mirror, not seeing the face she dabbed at, fingered uselessly. After half an hour she dragged herself up, forced herself to grin, bathed, changed. Down in the kitchen she could hear Mr and Mrs Shacklock preparing dinner, in a constant rumble of conversation. The husband, who had a job in a nearby plastics factory, helped his wife on the two or three occasions a week when the Fieldings dined at home, and the pair spent the time in a low, strong, uninterrupted chatter. When one met them elsewhere, separately or together, they appeared taciturn, but in the warmth of the stoves, the rattle of baking tins, the chunter of knives, they spread themselves, expanded into communication. What they talked about Hilda did not know, and when she asked Edward he'd not even noticed the transmogrification of the two.

At her open door Hilda listened, drew comfort. Both spoke equally, sometimes together, but Mrs Shacklock burst into high neighs of laughter so that one gathered that her husband was something of a wit. From there one couldn't make out a word, merely the patterns of intonation, and not clearly, at that, but one felt, guessed, hoped that every sentence had its interest as Shacklock described the machines and moulds and workshy workgirls and his wife outlined the busy, worrying idleness of the Fieldings above stairs.

Edward passed, shirt open, cuffs flapping. His expression questioned her presence by the door.

'They're having a high old time down there,' she said.

He listened with her, made nothing of the sounds, shook his head.

'Decent couple,' he said, moving on to his dressing room.

For the moment she stood desolate, envious of the cooks, wondering if she and Edward would take to talk again as they'd done at St Tropez. But, no fool, she shrugged, certain that if she heard the inconsequentialities below she'd be less impressed.

Mrs Shacklock served an excellent meal. Hilda asked after her husband.

'Oh, he's here, in tonight, helpin' me,' the woman said. 'He always does, y'know.' Why did she think them so stupidly unobservant? Or her affairs so unnoteworthy?

'Isn't he tired?'

'He's not one for goin' out, if you see what I mean. Pubs and clubs.'

Edward didn't much like these exchanges, she guessed. He'd been brought up to servants. Once her father had retired, lost his batman, her parents had done their own dirty work. Perhaps Shacklock, stirring the gravy, spread dissension, arguing no trade union would stand for cooking and serving dinner at eight at night without heavy compensatory payments. And those treble glissades of laughter were the answer to such a bass of heresy.

Over coffee she said Elizabeth Marcroft had rung.

'What does she want?'

'Didn't say. She's coming over tomorrow morning.' She disliked her evasion, wished to be open.

'If she's coming around, making a point of it, she's got work for you.'

'I see.' She waited, got nothing. 'You don't approve of her?'

'I never really know. About people. Not about my own colleagues. Except within limits. One doesn't know what'll break them. Elizabeth has always been friendly, but she's used to patronizing. It's second nature. You go easy. And have your engagement book conveniently filled up.' He straightened the seams of his trousers. 'She's got her head screwed on.'

'She complained about her son.'

He sipped whisky-and-water through the evening, talking easily. His passage with Jeremy had pleased him, and he wanted her to share the joy. Over her one brandy the world brightened, became warmer; together in this long room, with only the wall-lights on, they did a Shacklock, occupied each other with talk. But the conversation was marginal. Hilda wanted to ask about Elizabeth's proposal of love, dared not do so. They had achieved her wish only to discover her desires had shifted.

Hilda next morning found herself incapable of work, and once she'd finished breakfast, discussed lunch with her husband and Mrs Shacklock, she hid herself in her room, sitting, jumping up to pace, trying to pass a few minutes with a book, eyebrow tweezers, a nail file, a duster.

Lady Marcroft arrived late, was received by Edward, who held her in conversation for ten minutes in the hall.

Frightened, breathing fast, Hilda edged below. As she entered the room, Elizabeth, who was thumbing a coffee table book of archaeology, leaped up. She was small, and under a hat of feathers stood fierce as a tomahawk. Her face was lined by the eyes, her mouth tired, but her shoulders were back, her legs beautifully shaped in inaction, elegantly muscled. She'd dropped her gloves so that her small hands, fingernails pointed, hard, sea-beach polished dark stones, poised themselves to point, or emphasize or strangle. Both were now held out for Hilda to touch, but immediately, carelessly withdrawn. Elizabeth subsided into her chair, easily, as if the sight of Hilda had soothed her.

'You're looking well,' Lady Marcroft said, smiling socially.

'We had a good holiday.'

'I'm glad I could come to talk.'

'Oh.' Hilda sat nervously. 'Are you, are you, all right?'

'You can help me.' Schoolmistress's lash, sharp, to the point, know where you are. 'This last month or so has been ghastly.'

'Tom?' Hilda felt bound to join in.

'Amongst others. Things have got on top of me. Willy's worrying himself stupid about a new road through Ancaster Park. It can only make him money, but he's frantic. Grouses on, and on. It's senseless. The estate manager's ill. Just when we've had trouble with a major alteration at Marcroft. Always so. People won't do what they are bid. And committees, committees. Then we had a bomb scare at the London house. Caused trouble with the staff; two of them were Irish girls.'

This was delivered without haste, every word enunciated sharply, but with a kind of weary good humour, as if one expected these snags as part of the aristocratic burden. Hilda was relieved, relaxed into her chair, preparing to enjoy the visit.

'And the thing is I'm getting too old for it all. I can manage one upset . . . '

'How old are you?' Hilda, flatly.

'Forty-three.'

'Prime of life.'

'You won't say that when you get there.' Elizabeth narrowed her eyes, so that her face hardened, coarsened. 'And now there's nobody I can turn to.'

'Has there been somebody?'

'Willy's useless. He's nearly sixty. Bates, the estate manager, has gone into hospital. I hope it's not serious. Yes, I had a friend. In London.'

Hilda waited.

'She was divorced. Fifteen years. Made her own career again, as a solicitor. Beautifully straight mind. Incisive.

93

Do this, because . . . You know. Then she suddenly announced, by letter, she was about to marry again. I'd seen her only three days before.'

'And she said nothing?'

'No.' A glance of searing suspicion. Bitterly. 'We were as we'd always been. Do you understand that?'

Hilda shook her head, baffled by question, by answer, by herself.

'We were as we'd always been. And yet she knew. She said in the letter she knew. She was the cleverest, most truthful woman I ever met, and yet she couldn't bring herself to tell me.'

'Intelligent people feel things strongly, sometimes,' Hilda said, stumbling to comfort.

'She did. She knew where she loved. That's what's so damnable.'

'Was she beautiful?'

'Not particularly.' Dry voice, ice in a glass. Hilda felt, stung by the half-rebuke, that sanity was restored.

'When did all this happen?'

'Not very long before you went away.'

'You wanted me in her place?'

'That's not possible.' Pride spoke. 'I'd like a friend. Because I'm so isolated. I decide everything, do it all, and I have nobody. . . . You don't know what it's like.'

'I see. I don't . . . Perhaps.'

'If you'll let me come and grouse to you, Hilda, sometimes. I'm demanding, I can tell you. But if you'll listen.'

They talked for some minutes, with appeals and qualified answering comfort, until it seemed at first only a meaningless patter, useful merely in its repetition. Later, when she described Tom's poor showing in estate management, or Bates's surgery, she spoke clearly, with brevity unchanged. These things happened, could not have been avoided by her. At the same time she outlined her campaigns to cope with

94

contingencies, and here again she conveyed an impression of capable energy. To Hilda it seemed that the exercise of particularizing these misfortunes had set Lady Marcroft on the way to sanity. As she spoke, she became not more relaxed but more imperious, in command of herself and her world. To watch this change, hardly to believe it, fascinated Hilda.

'I feel better,' Lady Marcroft announced. 'You've done me good.'

'I'm glad.' Hilda smiled. 'Let's have coffee.'

'No. I've a call to make, on the estate. I hate it. Will you come with me?'

'Now?' She considered lunch, her husband, herself. 'All right. I'll tell Edward.'

Elizabeth stepped across, grasped the cloth of the other's sleeve, pulled her, kissed her on the lips. Immediately she broke away though Hilda did not draw back. The kiss had been short, yet unmistakably placed, slightly wet, full. It was not unpleasant, in its warm certainty, and yet Hilda trembled, shocked, pleasurably embarrassed. She felt as if she had been summoned from parade to receive a decoration she had deserved but not expected. Elizabeth now had turned her back, was arranging her hat in front of a mirror.

'I must tell Edward.'

'Of course. We shan't be long. I'll bring you back.'

Fielding, at work with a slide-rule, smiled mischievously, rose to kiss her, but on the forehead.

'Don't get too involved.'

As they drove Elizabeth explained. The daughter of one of the gamekeepers, a child of eight, was dying. She had caught influenza a week ago; this had become pneumonia which affected her heart. The local GP, consultants, had fought for the life, but now it was over, a matter of hours.

'Didn't they take her into hospital?' Hilda asked.

'It happened so quickly. They had to see to her at home.

She was too ill to move. I don't understand these things, but that's what they say.'

They knocked at the door of a neat, semi-detached estate house, in orange-red brick. The front garden was bright with tall dahlias. The father, a pale, strong man with an open-necked shirt, answered the door, stared for a minute at them, mouth open, young face haggard. He waved them inside to where his wife stood, back to the fire in the heat. The room was dark behind small windows; the garden outside brilliant, shaggily alive with the riot of late summer.

'Her ladyship,' the husband said, mumbling.

'How are things?' Elizabeth asked. She spoke without hauteur, comforting, moving across to take the mother's hand. The woman looked upwards, with adoration, eyes big with tears.

'She's better.'

The words were whispered, and then, as in some blasphemous pantomime, the mother bent her knees. Elizabeth accepted the gesture, circled the head, pressed it. The tableau with its feudal overtones appealed to Hilda as serious; one saw nothing absurd in this. The satirical spirit withered.

'That's good. What happened, then, Jones?'

The man stepped, stood by his wife, clumsily took her arm before he spoke, signing himself as a human being, fit for any company.

'After you called yesterday, your ladyship, and went up to see Judith. . . . The specialist came in, as you were leaving, you remember. He said he was going to try one more thing. He'd discussed it by telephone, he said. A new medicine. It worked like a miracle.'

'What was it?'

'I don't know, your ladyship.'

'Judith was immediately better?'

'Well, you know, not quite. He came before two. I looked

in at about four. Dreading. And Mag was sitting in with her. "How is she?" I asked. "I'm sure she's better, Bob," she says.'

'She was sleeping easier. I could tell.' The mother butted in, excited.

'I couldn't tell any difference, but she could. She's sleeping easier, she said. The doctor, our doctor, saw her after seven, and he confirmed it. "It's very encouraging," he said.'

'And today?'

'She's eaten a spoonful or two. Slops. The specialist came in again. He was pleased. You could tell.' The mother.

'You don't know the name of the drug?'

They shook their heads; names meant nothing. Mr Jones tucked his arm more comfortably into his wife's, smiled crookedly, long teeth white.

'She says,' he began, ' "It's since her ladyship called in to see her." ' His eyes twinkled. His wife dropped her head, abashed.

Elizabeth shook off the tribute.

'I can't say how glad I am.' That was more distant, but warm still. 'It's very good, very good.'

'She'll have to go into hospital.'

'Would you go up and see her?'

Husband and wife spoke together, so eagerly that they, Hilda included, all laughed, in relief, in a swell of delight. They went upstairs, the visitors ushered forward, followed heavily. The child was asleep, her face so small that she seemed little more than a baby in the subdued light behind the drawn curtains. With a couple of fingers Mrs Jones edged the sheet away from the chin, then smoothed it back. The furniture, Hilda noticed, was modern, veneered, bought in the local town, but on the wall hung an oval frame with an enlarged photograph of some buttoned-up granny, fading to brown now. Hilda glanced down again to the small, sleeping face, and the hair which was smoothed flat, tied with a ribbon. That mark defied death in the close confines of the room. Outside great trees spread, green still, heavy in the bright air, and the shouts of children squealed at play. Elizabeth was leaning across the quilt, one hand down by the body of the child, lightly supporting herself. The parents had moved together by the bottom of the bed in the foot or two of space, approving, subservient. A minute later the mother had straightened the bedclothes.

Downstairs Jones thanked Lady Marcroft.

He spoke now with a kind of fervour, almost aggressive, as if to punch his words into unreceptive ears. His wife smiled, sure of her mind. Elizabeth listened, acknowledged, did not pause, left quickly without rudeness, upright and splendid, but once the two had reached the car, she sagged limp, virtue gone out of her, over the steering wheel. It was as if the hint had become fact, that Elizabeth by her aristocratic presence had cured the child, and knew this, had felt its toll. Impressed Hilda said nothing, waiting, in thrall, until the other tapping with a gloved hand on the column said, briskly, mundanely enough,

'This won't get you home for lunch.'

'They were very grateful.' Hilda had to speak, and that was noncommittal.

'They are good people.'

'The hospital's taken a lot of trouble over them.'

'Of course.'

The two words lifted Elizabeth away, reducing Hilda to the ranks. Why should hospitals not? The Lord, milady, gave the word. Jump.

They chatted about the countryside as they drove back, cheering each other. Elizabeth had a sharp eye for agricultural matters, but this morning she was more intent on praise than blame.

'That man's improved his place several hundred per cent.'

'Is he a tenant of yours?'

'No. But his uncle is. He learned with him. Took over here from his father who wasn't much good. Nor did he get on with the boy. Spick and span, now. Got a head on him.'

Hilda had passed the farm dozens of times without a glance.

When they arrived back, she invited Elizabeth in.

'No, thanks. I've a busy afternoon. You've done me good.'

'We can give you lunch.'

'No, thanks.'

She leaned across to kiss Hilda's cheek, sisterly.

'I'll call on you again,' she said.

She drove off without so much as a wave, a turn of the head. Edward who'd arrived at the door ironically waited.

'A good time had by all?' he shouted.

She explained briefly and they parted until lunch, when he sat gloomily chewing.

'Something's wrong?' she asked, shyly still, in pleasure.

'Ye'. We've slipped up over a contract, which'll lose us money. Not serious. We can stand it. But it ought to have been spotted. I ought, myself, to . . . '

'I see. Is that it?'

He had to be bullied into grumbling.

'I feel guilty,' he said. 'I leave you rather a lot, one way and another.'

'You always did.'

'Before we were married.' He looked abashed; handsome and in trouble. 'Since this Jeremy thing I've . . . The boy agreed with me; he raised no objections; he saw the sense in going back to the university. I was pleased. But he said something on the way that's harassed me.' He handled his hair like a film-father. 'I was pressing him about Hilda,' he stopped in surprise at the name, 'Linda, Linda, I shall forget my own bloody name next, and I crackled on about

99

a stable relationship, and obligation and the rest, and he suddenly stopped me and said, "Dad, you make too much fuss about sex." He seemed not to be arguing, expected my agreement, silly sod. I gave him the length of my tongue, and he turns cool as you will. "Sex is sex," he said. "No more." "What's that mean?" I asked him. "Because you say 'A murder's a murder', that doesn't give you leave to go round committing mayhem." He argued then, shifting values, human sacrifices, legal homicide, road deaths, but he thinks quite differently from me. His generation takes sex as I lick ice-cream.'

'Are you sure?'

Her simple question, high in the register, signalled laughter out of them both so that they gestured without words, tears gushing from her eyes. Mrs Shacklock bringing the pudding tried to organize her face into suitable joviality.

'It isn't ice-cream?' Fielding asked. Hilda rocked, hugging herself.

'No, sir. You said crème-caramel.'

'Don't listen to him, Mrs Shacklock.'

The fit had passed; they addressed their plates solemnly.

'Is it, he ... ?' Hilda gave up.

'I shouldn't think he's very experienced,' he said, guessing her drift.

'All talk?'

'That I don't know.'

'You'd scored over him, and so he gets back at you. He's intelligent. Shocks you. Knows he can.'

'It's not him,' Fielding said, in the end, wiping his mouth. 'It made me think of us. Are we all right? I'm as casual as he is. With you.'

'To all intents and purposes,' she spoke slowly, smiling at him, relaxed, comforting, 'we've been married for a long time.'

'We haven't.'

'And you haven't done your duty by me, young man?'

'Damned if I know.'

'So you want me to tell you? Is that it?'

He stood up, turned his back on her.

'You're very good to me, Edward. I think you understand me.'

'I don't.'

'You appear to. Now, you tell me what's wrong.'

He sat again, gently moving spoons, plate, cruet.

'On a bad day, like this, when I feel like death, I wonder what we've done. You're going your own way. Do you remember how upset you were after the ball at Marcroft, edged off from me?'

'I was tired.'

'Do you know what I thought?' Rabbit-faced. 'You'll hate me. '

'Go on.' She was frightened, disturbed at his lack of balance.

'Here's Anna all over again. That's . . . Now that's not the truth, but I believed it for a time.'

'And today?'

'I felt bloody awful,' he said, 'because of this boob, and it made me want to get into your mind. There's Hilda and she might be desperate and I haven't considered, properly, her for days.'

'That's nice,' she answered. 'Bless you. But there's no need to worry about . . . '

'If there were?'

'Well, now . . . '

'I shouldn't notice.'

'You would. Or I'd attract your attention.'

'Anna didn't. I shut my mind to her. I bought people to look after her.'

'You forget, Edward, I expect.'

'I don't, you know.'

'You're thinking of the end, when there wasn't hope, when she was hopelessly lost. You used to chase about after her. You've said as much yourself. And I've heard what other people. . . . '

'Why don't I remember it?' Voice near a shout.

'You don't choose to do so, dearest. Your method of charging the batteries.' She waved at him, ironically now, as if to check he was awake. 'It's not very sensible. Is it, now?' She waved a hand. 'I love you, Edward.'

His face screwed.

'I love you,' he said, arms about her. 'Upstairs.' Gentler. 'Shall we?'

'What about my garden?'

7

That afternoon they made love, and on others, but it altered Edward's style very little. He liked his own way, allowing her half an hour's conversation at breakfast, and three-quarters at lunch when he was at home. Then he was pleasant, but concentrated on her affairs rather more than his own, rarely telling her whom he'd met, what he'd managed. In the evening he liked to lay on treats, but made it clear that she must insist when she wanted to see something at the theatre or hear an orchestra. They'd discuss the plays; listen to the music again on the stereo, comb the *Radio Times*.

'I'm learning,' he said one evening. They'd listened to the Berg violin concerto. 'I never saw the advantages of marrying a teacher.'

She hummed him the Bach chorale, mentioned whole

tones, reached him pictures of Manon Gropius, Alban Berg, handsome as Oscar Wilde. Delighted, he kissed her, walked the room fast.

'I didn't know any of this,' he said.

'Did you and Anna never go to concerts?'

'As I remember, we did. I heard the Water Music, once, and Sibelius's Second. We never said anything about it, though. Except who we'd seen; what they'd said. This is new.'

She warmed to his naivety.

'There are books. In the public library. The BBC publishes pamphlets. The record sleeves are packed with information.'

'All wasted on me.'

Sometimes he made demands.

'I want you to descend on Jeremy,' he said.

'That expression shows you're embarrassed.' Miss Classroom. 'Why?'

'Invite him up here. And Linda. If she's still with him.' She raised eyebrows. 'I've not heard a peep since our interview. There he is, meek as milk, agreeing with me, and then not a blind word.'

'You want me to go? On my own?'

'If you would.' He gestured round with his hands for words. 'You'll make it pleasant. He'd wonder what I was up to. I'd like to be invited out by you.'

'Compliments.' She knew what he meant, saw his sense, did his bidding. The hour she spent in Jeremy's flat she enjoyed.

'What's he up to?' the boy asked.

'You never come.'

'He doesn't want us. Edward lives his own life. I think perhaps he shut himself off when my mother was so bad.' He looked up, fearing he would hurt her. 'I don't know, he's . . .'

'I don't think he's straightforward with us,' Linda said, equitably.

Taken aback, Hilda waited for an explanation which she did not get.

They produced coffee. Linda smoked. She seemed heavier-handed, coarser than Jeremy, nearer some blunt truth with the small hole in the calf of her tights.

'You're changing him,' the boy said.

'A little. Very little.'

'I think he's improving. When he had me up at his office, his line was exactly what I'd expected. "Don't play the bloody fool . . . Finish your degree." But he looked at me, listened, as if he'd some interest. Before, he'd say his piece as if he'd read it in the paper. This time, he's a human, and I s'ys to myself, " 'ilda. She done it." '

Linda laughed loudest at the Cockney.

'Perhaps you've tamed him, your man,' Hilda spoke to the girl, pleased with hilarity.

'Jerry's dad doesn't think about me,' Linda said.

'He's invited you.'

'He perhaps thought Jeremy wouldn't come without me. And he'd be wrong there.' She waited, belligerently, for contradiction. 'Ah, well.' Disappointed with placidity she kicked her heels on the frayed carpet. Now they began to talk about a professional tennis match they'd watched, but as they'd described they seemed not far from open quarrels. Or Hilda was not quite sure; perhaps she was misled by their certainty of opinion, their strength of assertion.

'Do you two ever row?' she asked.

'No,' Jeremy answered.

'We do nothing else.' Linda.

Again the uprush of laughter, its ferocity.

'Who am I to believe?' Hilda asked.

'Linda,' Jeremy said.

'Jeremy,' Linda, slightly late.

That was self-conscious, with rabbit-teeth smiles. For half an hour, now onwards, the three chatted as if they knew one another well. Jeremy who'd been caught that afternoon in a shower and soaked suddenly described a patch of sky he'd been watching, cloud with bright curled edges, overlaid with smoke, like a Victorian illustration of a poet's cottage or Doubting Castle. He spoke attractively, not fluently, sometimes groping even with his hands for words so that one began to imagine the complexity of his world behind the handsome orthodoxy. Linda's approach was simpler; she knew one or two things about one or two, and said so.

'Why don't you listen to weather forecasts?' she asked.

'Not accurate enough.'

'They'd have saved you today. He was saturated. You and your pretty textures.'

Linda seemed not disgruntled, merely emphasizing her presence, so that Hilda was surprised, on a pause, to hear the girl say,

'I don't think we should go, Jerry.'

'Why not?'

'He doesn't want me.'

Jeremy shrugged, said diffidently, politely,

'We're going. And we don't discuss it here.' In front of Hilda. Here. Something of Father. Linda's lip drooped sulkily, but no more was said.

When Fielding asked for a report, she took pleasure again.

'He's a charmer. And the boss. She does as she's bid.' They discussed it. Then, 'Why does she think you'll not make her welcome?'

'God knows. Perhaps she can't live without her bit of drama.'

'You don't like her, then?'

'She wouldn't be my choice for the boy. No.'

On the evening of the dinner, the two arrived by car almost at dark-hour, an autumnal chill in the air. Jeremy insisted on a turn along the terrace.

'You can't see a thing,' his father said.

'Nevertheless, in spite of all this . . . ' The boy used this expression of his mother's without self-consciousness.

'You go on in where it's warm.' Fielding to Linda.

'Oh, if you've got secrets.'

'This,' said Jeremy, 'is, in my view, the most pleasant place in the whole county.' The pedantic sentence sent her indoors to find Hilda of her own accord and complain.

'In the cold and dark. There's no sense.'

The meal was admirable. The Shacklocks had excelled themselves, while their married daughter, a beauty queen, served, smiling whitely, quick as a surgeon with her fork and spoon, from the silver dishes.

'I envy you,' Linda said to Hilda. No aggression there, she spoke like a deprived child begging reassurance. Edward would be eased. They settled in the long room, round a wood fire.

'How do you keep all the house so warm?' Linda asked.

'Oil. God knows what'll happen when supplies run out.'

Fielding enjoyed prophecies of doom, brandy glass in hand. He knew what he was talking about, Hilda thought, had bothered to store and sort this information.

'I'm enjoying this,' Jeremy said, winking. He looked about sixteen, wicked, ready for them. They discussed Tom Ravenshead, cricket, the taste of apples, skirt-lengths, before his father coughed chairman-fashion.

'You can imagine,' Fielding said, portentously. They all laughed, and Linda's glass was replenished. 'I haven't got you here for nothing.' They sat in uneasy silence, only Fielding grinning. 'Are you satisfied with your flat?'

'Yes,' said Jeremy.

'No.' Linda.

'I'm wondering what to do with the house on Magdala Avenue. Marchmont.' Anna's house. 'Do you want it?'

'Want?' said Jeremy. 'What's that?'

'Do you want to live there?'

'Ah.' Jeremy sucked his thumb. 'Well, ah. I can't afford it, one. Two, Mrs Makepeace's there.'

'There are,' said his father, with cross patience, 'six bed-rooms. Plenty of room for her. I'd provide the money.'

'Why?' Linda burst out.

'I'm not short of a penny or two, and if I'd like to spend some of it on my son, then that's not unnatural, is it?'

'She wouldn't stay.' Linda.

'Mrs Makepeace?'

'Not with me there.'

Nobody spoke for a moment. Fielding threw a log on the fire back, rested his chin in the large palm of his left hand.

'Jeremy?'

'With Mrs Makepeace to look after it?'

'Of course. Unless, as Linda expects, she's pensioned off.' Fielding rolled in his chair. 'The house is there. One day it'll be yours. I don't want it. But it's better than that poky hole where you live.' Chin to collar. 'What do you think?'

'Thanks.'

'And m'lady?' Rudeness, overt, slapped at Linda who, ignoring it, sipped. 'Mrs Makepeace made the suggestion, actually. Didn't she, Hilda?'

His wife hummed confirmation, knowing nothing.

'Does she know about me?' Linda asked.

'Everybody does that, love.' Jeremy spoke so gently, but the girl grimaced, clenching her fists.

'We shared before,' she said.

'That's silly,' Jeremy said. 'I'd no money then.'

'If I won't go?' Linda's face, plain, unlined, clear of the handkerchief now, was turned to him.

'I can't see your objection. It's a big place. You'll have all the help you need. No housework. Meals. Fussed over.'

The boy's voice, flatter than ever, ran over the conventional phrases as if to take the edge, the soreness away from the proposal.

'You know,' Linda said.

'What?'

'They don't want me.'

' "They"? Who are "they"?' Jeremy clasped hands between knees as if his question posed a real problem. 'My father? Hilda? Mrs Makepeace?'

'All of you. You don't want me.'

'Does that include me?'

'You know it does.'

The pause struck lengthily, silence vibrating as a gong-beat. Hilda, with a pang, vividly remembered her rows with Alan, when words mattered no more, only the pain, the suppurating wound inside, the inconsolable weakness, the mad dumbness. She'd learnt to fight back with taunts, with insult, with vulgar attack on her husband's motives, his culture, his pride. But now and then, without warning, she'd be stripped of energy, not by his cold sarcasms, but by some lack within herself, some draining of resources, which left her tied to her chair able only to sob, or gasp, or choke, or shift her face away from his accusatory eyes. The pain killed, then, scourged, as she sat naked to his gibes, emptied of pride, full of windy, weak anger. So sat this girl, this Linda, slumped, red-eyed, ugly and whipped.

'That's not true,' Hilda said.

Linda's mouth opened, fish-like, wordless. Hilda knew now she must talk, 'Mary had a Little Lamb', 'Onward, Christian Soldiers', 'Much have I travell'd in the realms of gold', until the block shifted, humanity seeped back. She began.

'It's a beautiful house, but it's convenient. Just think,

now, of the parties. And Magdala Avenue's so quiet. You'd think you were miles out of town.'

Linda took no notice until the third time round with parties when she said sullenly,

'The furniture'll get scratched.'

Hilda had won, and Fielding was smiling at her.

'I tell you what,' he said. 'I'll take Linda round myself.'

'Push my nose out.' Jeremy understood.

'You were there as a child. We had a Christmas tree in the hall,' Fielding said, pleasing his wife.

'And a garden party in the garden,' Jeremy said. 'My mother supported good causes.'

'When did you come here?' Linda spoke normally.

'When my father died. It was his house,' Edward answered.

'You were married into Marchmont?'

'Yes. It was a wedding present. I was for a bungalow in Redcliffe, but Anna talked to my father. She wanted a house to entertain in. I wasn't earning too well. My father was a hard case, paid me what he thought I was worth, and that wasn't much. But he indulged Anna. It's the only time he gave money away. He paid, and he made her an allowance. But he never said a word to me.'

'He'd know Mother would tell you?' Jeremy.

'He'd know that, certainly.'

'You never said anything?'

'No. I was afraid.'

'You'd been to university, and in the army.'

'I wouldn't have mentioned the allowance. For one thing, he might have stopped it. And I couldn't keep the place going. Jeremy's not afraid of me.'

'I wonder,' Hilda said.

'And I.' Jeremy grinning, handsome copy of his father, unbroken.

'What do you say now, Linda?' Hilda asked.

'I shall go round with,' she struggled, 'with Edward.'

'And so the whirligig of time brings its revenges,' Hilda said.

'We can do without that.' Her husband, in small suspicion.

Fielding had already outlined his plan to Mrs Makepeace who had the house in full polish on the evening the two paid the visit of inspection. Linda was handed into the Rover, then to the outer bar of the Quails Club, so that she, in a fiery trouser-suit, pillar-box-red coat belted, had sipped unaccustomed sherry, stood proud, face matching scarlet.

Mrs Makepeace handled more wine. Edward, Linda saw, drank tonic-water, seemed dry, wry, ironically distant, as if there were no substance inside his suit. After suitable minutes of introduction, the housekeeper led Linda forward so that the man hung back. They moved from room to room, but not with the rapid patter of the stately-home guide. Mrs Makepeace sketched this as a place to live in, its comforts, its drawbacks. Once or twice she remarked on the age of a piece of furniture, and named the painter of a huge gold-framed classical landscape in the upstairs drawing room, a Frenchman Linda had not heard of. The rooms on the third floor were empty, carpeted but empty, except for some large trunks.

'My wife Anna had bursts of clearing out,' Edward said.

'We had bonfires in the garden that went on for days. Sometimes,' the housekeeper looked at Fielding, 'I thought it was the only thing she cared about. Clearing up. Burning it.'

As they followed her downstairs, Mrs Makepeace opened the door of the main bedroom again, ushered Linda inside. With drawn curtains, radiators, the bed ready for occupation, the place, in spite of size, seemed cosy, furnished with sheepskin rugs, big mirrors, comfortable chairs, traces of perfume. The housekeeper switched on the lamps above the mantelpiece, and opened a wooden box on the dressing table. Linda had noticed it on their first round, wondered at its light colour. It seemed oriental, with the lid a carved writhing of snakes in leaves, not well done, almost machine-turned, and Mrs Makepeace had to shake and rattle before she managed to wrench it open.

'There,' she said.

The box flashed with jewels, necklaces, rings, bangles, chains and brooches pushed into the blue velvet of the under-side of the lid.

'Look,' Mrs Makepeace ordered. 'Look at them.'

Shyly, Linda lifted a string of ugly blue beads, bean-sized, bean-marked. A silver bangle, caught up, dropped loose, bounced to the floor. Edward stooped.

'They're very good,' the girl managed.

'Imitation jewellery,' the woman said, lifting a topaz ring to the light. 'Dress jewels.'

'Are they?'

'Would you like them?' Edward asked. The girl said nothing, made out she had not heard the question. Very simply he repeated himself, not emphasizing a word.

'Oh, no. I can't . . . '

Mrs Makepeace had picked up the box, it was large, two feet by one, in her arms and proffered it. They'd planned the gift, Linda thought, decided, talked, discussed, to be nice, to humiliate, to win, to put her wrong, to buy her out, these two conniving, scheming old Judases.

'Mr Fielding would like you to have them,' Mrs Make-peace said. 'They were his wife's.'

Linda stared into the profusion of the box, pantomime pirate treasure, a rich glitter, unlike the bits of stone in her hands, then fell to her knees, and wept into the coverlet of the bed.

The housekeeper shoved the box back to its polished place without ceremony, clapping the lid shut.

'Now, now,' she said. 'There's no need for that.'

They put Linda into a chair, dabbed at her face, touched her until her crying stopped and she sat with lowered lids, mouth sternly thin. When she, fit now, moved, she muttered, away from them. 'I'm sorry.'

'Not another word,' Fielding said. 'I'll put them into the back of the car.'

Linda howled again into tears.

'Edward,' Mrs Makepeace said, surprisingly. 'Edward, now.'

This time the girl recovered quickly, was made to sip wine in the wide front room, with velvet curtains, huge furniture, dark pictures. Fielding disappeared, and the housekeeper sat, disapprovingly, opposite, saying nothing, touching the glass, waiting for the close of the incident. Fielding, on his return, seemed equally put out, brusquely refused drink, said he would not sit down. Mrs Makepeace did not accompany them beyond the door, but Linda turned in the drive to stare at the lighted stained glass, scrolls and floral calligraphy, in the huge front door. It seemed important to learn something from that, as if it encoded the character of the house or revealed it. When she reached the street, Fielding stood on the kerb, ready to open her door; he spoke kindly, not hustling her. While he drove, he talked about the traffic, pointed out a new hotel his firm had built, told her an odd story about a former Lord Mayor whose house, an undistinguished shape in a row of dark humps, they passed, explained, as they waited to cross a main road, what the City Council had done about pedestrian precincts.

'She didn't like me, did she?' Linda interrupted.

'What makes you think that?'

'She wouldn't speak when you went out.'

'I don't think that's because she didn't like you. She's not much of a talker.'

'She wanted the jewellery.'

He braked gently as if to rebuke her.

'I don't want you to upset yourself again, Linda. What will Jeremy say, now, if I hand you back in tears?'

'I shan't.'

'That's good.'

'Sometimes,' she began, choked on it, 'sometimes . . .'

'Go on.'

'It doesn't matter.'

They drove quicker again, very smoothly. Inside the car the air warmed them. He pointed out his old school, explaining that his father had no time for boarding establishments.

'You sent Jeremy away.'

'I did. I always intended to. I expected trouble from my father, but in fact he died before it happened. He knew, of course. "The High School was good enough for my father, and for me, and for you. What's so special about him?" In fact it was necessary when his mother became really ill.'

'That wasn't because you sent him away?'

'Not at all.' No ill-will; rational certainty.

'You think I am childish, don't you? Crying because you gave me that box? You've never known anything like that, have you? You don't understand.' She spoke in a desperate small gabble, but clearly enough, as if through clenched teeth at her window.

'I see.' Soothing.

'You don't see. You don't know why I did that, do you, Mr Fielding? You don't know.'

'I don't suppose I do.'

He drove on in silence, unmoved, ready with soft-soap, she felt, if needed, imposing his big silent manly comfort in the warm interior.

'I won't come in,' Fielding said, 'if you don't mind. Tell

Jeremy what you think about the house, and he'll make his mind up.'

He left her at the street door.

Their room stretched shabby with chipped paint, faded curtains, carpets worn to the backing, a ragged hole by the scuttle. It was warm, but knocked about, uncared for, nothing matching, undusted, scruffy; under the light, ridiculously hung by the window not in the centre of the room, Jeremy sat at the unpainted trestle table where he worked writing away. On the other table, a veneered, scarred, folding affair, splinters knicked out of its ugly legs, he'd arranged three cups on a tray, a milk jug with a beaded cover, and a pot of Nescafé.

'Where's the dad?' he said, laying pen square.

'He wouldn't come up.'

'I see.' He wore round reading glasses which he now pulled off, flourished. 'You been crying?'

'Yes.' Sometimes he probed your soul. He waited. 'Your father wanted to give me your mother's jewel-box, from her bedroom. They said they were imitation, but they looked so beautiful, that it all boiled up inside me.'

'Where are they?'

'I don't know.' She hadn't thought. She wanted them, needed them now. 'He said he'd put them in the car, but he didn't say anything when . . . ' They could be sorting now, touching, she trying them against the mirror, he recalling his mother. 'I think your father was angry. He didn't understand . . . '

'He's seen plenty of mental illness,' Jeremy said. That put her in her place. 'He looked after my mother for years at first.'

'I thought . . . Did she tell you?'

'She did. "He'd lie awake all night with me. He was the only one who could soothe me. With his hands, they were so big and smooth." She never forgot that. I think she looked back to that time as the best. When she was ill, and he knew it, and tried to cure her.' He spoke without emphasis, leaning back at his ease as if to underline his mastery of the material. 'I think he tried. Don't say he knows nothing about mental disturbance. Your little tantrum . . .'

'He didn't do anything for me. It was Mrs Makepeace.'

'You were sufficiently aware to notice who looked after you, then?' The sentence had a snake's coldness, the chill eye of the biologist, blank from the microscope. She didn't answer that. 'Make us a cup of coffee, Lin. The kettle's boiled.'

He picked his pen up, knuckled his glasses into place and began to write, puckering his mouth, noiselessly whistling.

She obeyed.

8

In the brightness of an early October morning Lady Marcroft hurled herself into Hilda's room.

One of the cleaning women had answered the front door, been brushed aside as soon as Elizabeth had discovered Mrs Fielding's whereabouts, and the clatter on stairs and passage after the fierce aristocracy of the raised voice had warned half the shire who'd arrived. Hilda disliked people, retired army men, friends of her father, know-all admirals, scions of county families who talked as if on the parade-ground so that twenty yards away one could not fail to be battered by their harangue. They must live openly, she thought; she'd no wish to advertise her business, would as soon have inserted a paragraph in the newspapers. But Elizabeth had the public style; she did not waste herself on conversation, she broadcast.

The door was rapped, pushed open.

Hilda, dumb with a cold, moodily closed her book. The bedroom chair was comfortable, the sun, the radiators warm, the view of tree-shaped slopes, the elegant far fence, the gleam of a lake, and blue woods on little hills conventionally beautiful, admirable for the idle eye to cover, to rest on. She stood. Lady Marcroft ran the room, reaching her before the door had shut, flung arms about her, kissed her cheek hard. Hilda toppled, as if from an attack, but Elizabeth held on, steadying her, fixing her so that she could herself droop, rest her face on her friend's shoulder. It happened quickly; it was ridiculous. Elizabeth Marcroft had never been in this room before, had no idea what she would find. Hilda wished she'd been making the bed, or pushing the vacuum-cleaner; not that she did often, but it would have reduced these histrionics, regulated them somewhere near sense. As it was one highly perfumed lady lay across the bosom of another. Hilda had neither the energy nor bravado to giggle.

'I had to come,' Elizabeth said, to the world.

'Sit down.' Hilda had soothed hysterical pupils in her time, but Lady Marcroft refused to release her hand, hung on for life, face red, eyes over-bright.

'It's all so bloody, bloody.' She snapped the words together. Hilda rose, managed to seat her guest, but could not disentangle herself; the hand held. 'Tom's in hospital now.'

'Why?' How to sweeten the air in one word.

'Crashed into a tree with his motor-cycle. After all the trouble he's had this summer, we persuade him back to the university, and he comes home for a weekend and does this.'

'I'm sorry.'

'It serves him right. It's what we could expect. But it's one more damn thing, one more responsibility. Will's in

London; Bates's not back yet; nobody will move or take a decision.'

'If,' said Hilda, emphasizing her words by moving Elizabeth's hand up and down, 'some understrapper took it on himself to make his mind up, what would you say?'

'I'd say, "Thank God". You think I love laying the law down. I've a thousand public duties and functions, and the estate, and the charities . . . '

'You've a secretary.'

'She's away in Canada. And the deputy's an idiot. She can barely type a letter.'

'How's Tom?'

'What?' Near shriek, parrot-like.

'How badly hurt is Tom?'

'Bruised. Shaken. Sorry for himself.'

Hilda gripped Elizabeth's wrist hard, wrenched her hand clear.

'What's set it all off?' She put her back towards the other, spoke clipped.

'Everything. The estate accountant's been in for a week. Upset everything. Now he advises some legal move. There's a property company . . . What's it matter? I decide. I, I, I. Why won't anyone else make his mind up?'

'Look,' Hilda said, reasonably. 'You've done all this before, without too much wear and tear.'

'There comes a time . . . '

'When you take a holiday. Yes. Right.'

'How can I? Nobody'd do a thing?'

'If you dropped tomorrow, the world would go on.' The words sounded dead inside herself, sensible but inert, lifeless. This woman wanted power, wanted to lord it, but required an hour's refreshment, no more. She needed no schoolroom mottoes.

'How you can be so beautiful and so stupid?'

'Birth. Practice.' Hilda would yield nothing. Elizabeth

marched across, like a battalion with bayonets, stamped both feet to a halt, stood straddle-legged in front of Hilda, who purposely fiddled at her dressing table.

'Why don't you kiss me?' Elizabeth said.

'Christ.'

'Kiss me.' She snatched at Hilda again, hard as iron, a woman in armour stiff as a trap. 'You hear what I say.' They struggled ineffectually for a few seconds, then more strongly, upright, one to run, one to thrust down, but neither knowing the aim, both elusive but unmoved. Hilda stood taller, younger, more lissom, but Elizabeth fought for herself, in a subconscious dedication, willing the other's collapse as she willed the servitude of the underlings at Marcroft. They swayed, staggered a foot, banged Hilda's hip on the sharp oak corner so she cried out and at the short squeal both suddenly realized the seriousness of their actions, the foolishness, the exotic quality of women in sober finery scrapping like urchins. And yet this intellectual grasp meant nothing, eased, cured nothing. They wrestled on, Hilda for herself, her self-love, her morality, Elizabeth out of untamed lust or greed to win another soul into her own, which itself spoiled her strength, because she took pleasure in the fight, in the limb locked to limb, the heaving breast to breast.

'Stop,' Hilda whispered.

Still Elizabeth thrust her back, dominating, hard, harsh, without love in this moment, or winning it with blood.

A tap on the door.

They heard, heaved on, though both knew this was the end. Now the rap was peremptory, and Hilda dropped her arms, shouted an invitation. Elizabeth groaned, a small sound, stepped back, still wearing her hat, polished straw, bright, half-veiled. Mrs Shacklock, smiling vaguely, bundled herself across the room, in a flowered apron and slippers slit for bunions.

'Lunch, today, Mrs Fielding?' She nodded or bobbed towards Elizabeth, muttering 'y'r ladyship', smiling still, unaware. Hilda sat on a brocade-covered stool, her legs trembling, breath fast, noisy, near sobs.

'What's my husband say?'

'Roast lamb, if you'd no objection.' She held out Edward's suggested menu. Hilda unable to read it, tumbled it in front of her face, handed it back. Mrs Shacklock gave no sign of recognizing distress. 'Will her ladyship be staying?'

'No, thank you, Mrs Shacklock.'

The imperious voice of ten minutes back, under control, directing the plebs.

'I see. Thank you. Shacklock's going into the town if you want anything.'

'I don't think so.' Hilda's voice stretched, sagged like worn elastic. 'Is he not at work, then?'

'No, he's owed a few days that he has to take before January or he'll lose them altogether. He's having them now while the weather's fine.'

'But you're not going away?' Lady Marcroft.

'No. A fortnight a year at the seaside's enough for him. He can have a bit longer in bed, and a walk down to the Drum at lunchtime, a run out to town, a sleep in the afternoon. That's what he calls a holiday.'

'And you?'

'You don't hear me complain.' The smile was wiped from Mrs Shacklock's face, replaced by a look of obstinate set malice. Lady Marcroft, interfering, needed rebuke, indirect but plain. 'I'm well suited here. If that's all, then, Mrs Fielding?' Pleasant again, vague, hands at apron pockets in proper subservience. She left, closing the door quietly.

Hilda, steadier now, did not look, but twitched her foot up and down from her shoe.

'I'm sorry,' Elizabeth said, as from a distance, so quietly

that Hilda was unsure. In any case, she had to answer in words. Sorrow met by silence; if she were assailed again, she'd knock her stool over, thump with her heel on the floor for help. 'You don't feel anything for me?'

Nothing there. In the shock what rationality? Where does it hurt, darling? She wished she could indicate. Instead she sat, crouched, as it were, round her gut which was shrivelled with cold, taut in fear, a frozen fountain round which her whole being hunched, in rags.

'Look at me, Hilda.'

Elizabeth must have moved over, unseen, now spoke in an unfrightening tone. Hilda raised her eyes, large now with fright. Elizabeth bent, touching the upturned face, with a small handkerchief, rubbing hard at a smut, homely.

'Darling. I'm sorry. I frightened you.'

The tone steeled Hilda, so that she thought of Mrs Shacklock's defying her ladyship.

'You're a fool,' she said. Her voice was steady, cold, detached from herself, furious. She sat afraid still, shaking, muscles flabby, but thrust her voice out like a spear.

Elizabeth frowned, eyes in pain.

'Hilda, you don't understand.'

'You may not think so.' For a moment she nearly blundered into abuse, but checked herself, in a puff of triumph, knowing this was her moment to stop. She stood, found she could manage it, picked her handkerchief from the dressing table, clenched it in her fist and walked, shoulders straight, to the door. She did not look back, but half-expected an appeal she could ignore. Slowly she closed the door behind her, walked theatrically, queening it, down the wide stairs, made her way to the drawing room which, thank God, was empty. She wondered where Edward had gone. With serious mien, she chose her husband's armchair by the fire grate, eased herself into position, picked up his newspaper which seemed neatly folded still, the Business

News without a crease. Walls were too thick in this house to betray sounds outside.

The door clicked open.

Elizabeth Marcroft stood, hands behind her, leaning on the thin of the door. Hilda stared at her, then allowed her eyes to drop to the paper on her lap. 'Canal Flare-up. Heavy Fighting in Sinai.' A pictured tank flung back a cloudy horn of dust. Elizabeth moved the door behind her to and fro, like a small girl publicly embarrassed, wagging her trunk.

She stopped, said, 'Can you forgive me?'

'No.' Hilda felt better for that, angry, on her high horse.

'I'm in trouble.'

Hilda turned over, held the newspaper out, at arm's length, shook it to straighten the sheets, failed in that.

'May I come in?'

Hilda did not answer, knew she must not.

'Nobody does anything for me.' No self-pity there; no trembling, no plea. 'Your Alan Gascoigne, he's the only man with anything about him.'

That seemed ludicrous to drag in that name at this minute. The woman couldn't be sane. Panic. Momentary painful panic.

'He's really helped me on the Festival Committee. He can organize. He thinks really fast.'

She offered these titbits as apologies, pushed out tentatively, little saucers of sacrifice, peace offerings. Hilda wondered whether, if she made for the door, the other would check her physically, decided to sit. Very slowly she refolded the newspaper, laid it on the table, and sat, cold again, near-terrified, waiting. Elizabeth no longer wagged at the door. Hilda rose, walked to the far end of the long room where three huge windows overlooked a hedged lawn, bounded with slabs of stone. An aeroplane laid its trail across the sky.

'This is childish,' Elizabeth said, still not advancing. 'Why don't you speak?'

'That was beastly.'

She turned as she spoke, and now back to the windows, one hand upon the thick white casements, she crossed her legs.

'Why must you be so silly? You know what I'm like.'

'I do now, certainly.'

That was as infantile as the scuffle upstairs.

'I'm sorry if I upset you, Hilda. I was too impulsive. You obviously don't realize what you mean to me. I'm sorry.'

There must be no exchange of slander, no slanging.

'I've got nothing to say to you. If you want help on your committees, your secretary can explain.'

'Personally, it's personally.'

'You heard what I said.' Now she was high-aristocratic. 'I shall tell Edward what happened.'

'He'll laugh at you. He knows what the world's like, what goes on. And if you go shivering up to him . . . '

'Don't be certain,' Hilda said, and then more slowly. 'The fact that you claim something does not make it the truth. My belief is that Edward will forbid you the house.'

'That's what you hope.'

'Certainly. And if he doesn't, I shall. I don't want you.'

'Why not?' Nothing hangdog about Elizabeth.

'I value my peace and quiet. And now, if you don't mind going . . . '

Hilda returned to *The Times* again, salvaged the sports page, footballers in floodlight. Lady Marcroft stood by Hilda's chair.

'Don't be a fool,' she warned.

'I'll try not.' Silly to reply childishly.

'I'm doing my best to speak gently.' Succeeding, with rat-trap mouth. 'I know if I leave here without making this up, between us, I'll never have another quiet moment. Believe me that that's the strict truth.'

'I don't believe it.'

Elizabeth turned away. She should have carried a riding crop to crack across her calf.

'Say you'll speak to me again.'

'I'll speak to you again.'

Lady Marcroft dropped to her knees beside the chair, quickly, down, without difficulty, a lithe movement, as if practised, often performed. The speed and silence impressed. She laid her hand on Hilda's, squeezed it, bent her head as if praying, then rose as quickly, as powerfully to stride from the room.

Hilda felt the pressure upon her hand still. She looked for a change in it, found none. No rings melted nor blood flowed. She ought to loathe that last contact, that woman's flesh on hers, but she did not. Elizabeth Marcroft was a personage, lived out of the ordinary, ruled a not inconsiderable empire; to be chosen by her for love complimented. Now that fright had disappeared, that her limbs recorded mere vestiges of former pain, she was excited, stirred by the encounter. What would have happened she did not know, but she felt no shame. If Elizabeth had stripped herself to a womanly naked lust Hilda might not have recoiled. The violence, the rough seizure, the wrestling had unnerved her. With a delicate frown she realized Elizabeth's gaucherie. She'd been like a schoolyard bully, whanging with fist and boot, to win love. If she had entered quietly, not pleading, but easily, as in right?

Hilda pushed herself from her chair, afraid now of the direction of her thought. She raced upstairs where not a mark in the bedroom recorded the tangle. Outside October sun brightened the fields, on which trees and walls launched purple shadows. She laughed, prepared to go out into the garden.

'Liz's car?' Edward called at the back door. In gumboots and raincoat he'd been walking the vegetable garden. 'What's she want?'

'She's in trouble. Needs a shoulder to cry on.'

'Did she get one?'

Hilda averted her eyes from the sun.

'She threw her arms round me.' In this version it sounded commonplace.

'Why?'

'To impress me that . . . '

'What did you . . . ?' He spoke too mildly, too slow, as if he did not notice the hotness of her voice.

'Broke away. Went out of the room. I'm against brawling on principle.'

'Disguised Lesbianism,' he said, laughing. 'Watch it.'

'I've never heard anything like that about her.'

He left her soon, after a few sentences. He did not believe what he said. There was a vulgarity about such conversation, though it was not untypical of her husband. Sometimes, unserious, he talked to her as if he were some old gossip squawking over a garden wall, without sense, a mere collection of maliciously collected clichés. She suspected he took his tone from hers, judging what she wanted, providing it.

The rest of the morning she spent in the borders, exhilarated by the sun and the swooping wind. Warm inside her anorak, face chafed into colour, she enjoyed cutting down, weeding, throwing out, carting away, head alive with plans for the spring.

Over lunch, Edward said:

'You weren't exaggerating when you said Liz Marcroft embraced you?'

'She had her arms round me.'

'What was she trying to do? Throw you over?'

'That's what it seemed like. For a moment or so.'

'Was she all right afterwards?'

'Apologetic. She knew she'd been a fool. Kept saying she was sorry.'

'Why did she do it? That's what I can't understand.'

They kept this conversation alive for a quarter of an hour, varying the questions, elaborating the answers, decorating the lack of conclusion. Both found pleasure in the exchange, in its virtuosity, but she wondered if she roused his suspicions.

'Was she like this with Anna?'

He hadn't expected that. His face showed it.

'They were at school together.'

'I know that. Doesn't answer my question.'

'She was a dominating girl, as I understand it. But she made a fuss of Annie, who was pretty. They weren't much better off than the Lathams. Minor county family, some stockbroking. You know the sort of thing. Then suddenly here she appears as the Countess. Anna said it didn't surprise her. Liz was special.'

'And?'

'She learnt the trade. She needed to. Will's no genius.'

'Has she been happy?'

'She's a highly energetic woman, drives herself, lives on her nerves. Here she's found a place with plenty of scope. She's organized and chased and chafed. It suited her, and she's grown into it. Whether that makes her happy I don't know, but I guess she's had the chance to do what she wanted.'

'You sound quite shrewd,' she said, teasing him, meaning it.

'You'll be good for her. She's middle-aged now. Doesn't relish the hurly-burly quite so keenly. And here are you, a big, beautiful, calm pussy-cat for her to stroke into purring.'

'That's no way to describe it.' She enjoyed his ambiguity, sure that he did not intend it.

'Be nice to her.'

'Why should I?'

'An important person.' He rose, as if the conversation grew dangerous. 'Please yourself.'

'Do you like her?'

He aped the baffled schoolboy, scratched his crown.

'Yes. Ye-er. I suppose I do. Really. I never thought about it. She's been on the landscape so long I'm used to her. I do like her. Yes.'

'She scared me.'

'Uhnh, I can understand that. She's high-powered. Slipped the traces. Unnh.' He let the fatuous phrases mumble. 'You're quite sure?'

'Do you think I don't know when anybody goes for me?'

'Well . . . '

'Hysterical women, Edward? Out of proportion?'

'What do you want me to do?' No answer.

He kissed her quickly, though on the mouth, and left the room for his office in town. He seemed intemperately cheerful at her account. He played the pander? Pimp? That was impossible. Now her imagination did riot.

That afternoon she was fetched in from the garden to answer a phone call from her former husband. Mrs Shacklock loitered genuinely embarrassed, face comical as a St Bernard's.

'It's Mr Gascoigne, ma'am. Headmaster of the Wentworth Comprehensive.'

Alan was in his study at his ease; she could imagine him, legs outstretched, leaning back in his leather chair. Certainly she could hear him stirring his coffee, making the spoon ring on the china.

'Ah. Hilda. I want the whereabouts of George McHenry.' The poet. 'Do you still keep in touch with him?' No introductory inquiries, apologies.

She fetched her address book, dictated, said she was not sure if he still lived there.

'I want to get hold of him for a weekend conference I'm organizing.' She said nothing. 'That's most kind of you. I thought you might know.' Stuttering George, her cow-eyed contemporary at college, now of television and the Faber poets. 'Is all well with you?'

'Thank you.'

'Good, good.' She waited. 'Well, very many thanks. Most kind. Oh, you'll be interested to hear that Lady Marcroft often speaks of you.'

Hilda hummed down the phone; Alan gave up, galloped through thankfulness again, hung up.

She listened to the efficient voice, dabbing sweat from her forehead.

9

Linda Lawrence rang Edward in his office to announce that she was a burden to Jeremy.

'What else did she say?' Hilda demanded.

'Nothing.'

'Said that, and rang off? I don't believe it.'

It appeared she'd cried, mumbled, claimed in the end somebody was outside the phone box.

'How did she know you were in the office?'

'She'd rung earlier. They said I'd be in that afternoon. She claimed she was ringing for Jeremy.'

'I see.'

'I suggested she saw you.'

'When?'

'At the weekend, Sunday, some time. She's at work.' He looked contrite. 'I didn't know what the hell to say. I wish to God they were on the phone, then I could get at the boy.'

'They'll be in the house, soon.'

'That's part of the trouble. She went up again on her own. Makepeace and Olive Rosen were there, and were unpleasant.'

'Is that likely?'

'I don't know. Find out, darling, if you can.' He did not use endearments often, so that she wondered what this one conveyed.

'I'll put my brass plate up,' she rubbed her hands. 'What about Mrs Makepeace? Is she ... ?'

'Yes. Not surprised.'

'And you don't mind?' Hilda asked.

'Why the devil should I?' That showed he knew.

'You wouldn't consider giving her the sack, now?'

'She's useful. And I'm grateful to her. For seeing to Anna. The girl's done nothing for me.'

'But you offered her a box of trinkets?'

He pulled a sour face, satisfied.

Hilda wrote to Linda who by return proposed coming up on Sunday morning.

It rained, blew cold so that when she arrived, anorak hood tied, her face was ruddier, hands almost purple. Jeremy, it seemed, had brought her in his Mini, but had turned straight round, scuttled off, saying he'd be back for lunch when he'd done an hour or two at work.

Hilda doled out coffee, demanded an account of the visit to Magdala Avenue. As she expected, the Makepeace, if not exactly hospitable, had been correct and any snubs were inferred, not delivered. Linda had determined to find enmity, and with fluent doggedness repeated the housekeeper's remarks until she'd worked herself into sullen anger.

'What did Jeremy say? Have you told him this?'

'He doesn't care. Tells me we're going in, and that's that.'

'He's not sympathetic?'

'No. He listens, then says I'm making mountains out of molehills.'

'You don't think so?'

'You do.' The words flashed, before she could still herself. Now she smiled apologies. 'Well, you do, don't you?'

'What I think's not important.' Hilda felt mature, judicial. 'You're lucky. You'll have this big house paid for and looked after for you. Not one in a million young people has anything like that.'

Linda burst into tears, behind a man-size handkerchief.

'I'm not his wife. I've no security.'

Hilda considered the paradox, not unconvinced. The other sobered herself.

'It's not so bad in the flat. I pay more towards it than he does. He couldn't live there without my help.'

'You can't buy him, Linda.'

The girl dashed her handkerchief from her face, screwed it in her hands, thumped her lap.

'What about you?' she asked, hoarsely. 'You lived here. You weren't married, not then. Weren't you . . .'

Hilda pursed her lips, waited for the storm to blow out into words, and when the sentences broke, became curt beginnings, intervened again.

'I don't know now what I felt,' she said. 'I'd be lying if I said I did. Probably, I altered from day to day, minute to minute, if I know myself. But, at first, if I felt anything at all, it was relief. I'd escaped from a man I was frightened of, who could hurt me, and did so to please himself. I didn't walk out because my husband bored me with his chemicals or whatever. He terrified me. He beat me.'

'But you'd come to a man . . .'

'I'd come to peace and quiet. I'd no job. I was shattered. I was applying in London when I spat it all out to Edward.

It seemed like chance. He brought me here. I didn't know what was happening.'

'And you . . . ? You . . . ?'

Hilda cast about in her head for an answer. She remembered her flurries of tears, a ferocious outburst when she'd fisted Fielding's chest, her hysterics, and then the warmth, the physical comfort of this house, this haven Alan knew nothing of, from which he couldn't ferret her out.

'I came because I had to.'

'You didn't love him? Mr Fielding?'

'No. He offered me something I needed. Protection, perhaps. He looked capable of taking my husband on.'

'Did he?'

'It never happened. Alan wasn't half the man I thought. I'd got it round my neck.'

'What about sex?' The question came – in rough innocence.

'I was no more capable of that than sky-diving. It came later.'

'Thank you for telling me,' Linda said, her demureness approaching irony. 'I don't know what to do.'

'Will your husband divorce you?'

'He says not.'

'He's a Catholic?'

'Him? He's not anything.'

'Except your husband, Linda.' Why did she not bite that back? Malice had no place here with this sullen supplicant.

'And if he did, Jerry's not certain he'd marry me.'

'He's said so?'

'Not in so many words. He doesn't know his mind. He's got his father on his back, the big boss-man, who doesn't care but plays hell if you fail. And then there was his mother. Depressed until she couldn't move out of bed. And when she'd the energy she killed herself. That's my choice for you.'

'You love him?'

'I hate him sometimes, when he won't come to a decision, and I've got to mother him and pat his back to fetch the wind up and change his wet little nappy. All he's fit for is to make bloody biological diagrams. He's worse than my husband. At least, somebody's life depended on him and his knowledge, now and then. He could advise the doctors, and they listened. Jerry's bigger and handsomer and speaks better. You're lucky. You get men who know what they want. I get babies, one dull, and one pretty.'

'At least you get somebody.'

Linda lashed herself. Hilda allowed her the necessary minutes to regain composure, then said,

'I don't think Mrs Makepeace has anything against you. Try to live your life as comfortably as you can. That's my advice. And never mind searching for insults.' She felt constricted.

Linda's tears had dried, and her eyes, round, were open and dumb. Then intelligence disappeared. 'Thanks.'

Jeremy returned for sherry and lunch. Linda had spent the rest of the morning in the library with *The Times Atlas*, concentrated, crouched, smoking cigarettes, and, whenever Hilda poked a head in, apparently happy. The young man wore a dark suit, white shirt, small-knotted tie, highly polished shoes, and his thick hair was brushed back from his ears. Linda's corduroy skirt, home-knitted pullover, untidy hair, scuffed sandals seemed to make a proclamation, 'Outsides don't matter; God looketh upon the heart; *à la lanterne*; I hate the rich.' And yet she spoke more lively now, fussed round Fielding, suggested to Hilda that she might be old.

In this atmosphere of conviviality, Edward expanded, talked of the golf-mania of two of his colleagues, laughing at human oddity, and then insisted on showing Linda round the glasshouses while his wife got at Jeremy.

The boy was, rightly, suspicious, answered in the slurred monosyllables that so riled his father.

'You realize, don't you,' Hilda had outlined her case, 'that she feels inadequate?'

'Ye'.'

'She needs love.'

'Ye'.'

'And she needs telling that you love her.'

He didn't answer that, stood apart, as it were, from her, handsome, unsour.

'I don't want to interfere, Jeremy. It won't do any good. But I've been dragged in by your father, and so I feel bound to say something, however stupid. She needs love, especially now you're putting her into a place where she's no claim, and whose door you can show her to any time you think fit. She's got a share in the flat. She's nobody in that house, except a kept woman.'

'I suppose so.'

'Do you ever talk about marriage?'

'No.' He looked surprised as if she'd asked about bull-fights or cosmic black holes.

'Don't you think you should?'

He shrugged, peevishly, brushed imaginary crumbs from his jacket. Hilda, angered, said:

'If she were free, would you marry her?'

'I don't know.' He hesitated, mumbled, not looking up.

'She's right then. It's no wonder she's afraid you'll throw her out.'

'We don't think so highly of marriage as you do,' he answered, humbly, though.

'She does. She wants status and love, and all she gets is your mumbling. Do you love her?'

'Ye'.' He didn't argue, didn't justify himself.

'She's not perfect, Jeremy, but she's a human being. You've shacked up with her.' She liked that word, ramshackle, shoddy, shabby. 'She deserves something. You can argue that she's not your father's choice for a wife, that she's not mine, that you don't know yet what you think, that she's older than you and went into this with her eyes open, but it makes not an atom of difference. She needs your love, and she wants notices announcing it posted up in every street in red six feet high.'

'Charming.'

'You're not prepared to do it?'

'I don't know what you're talking about. What you describe's nothing like us.' Puzzled, hands spread.

'Don't you believe it.' Hilda stepped across, took his hand. 'She needs you. She's going through a bad spell, and you ought to have noticed.'

He looked at her, not hard, but quizzically, as if the holding of his hand had changed the relationship, not bettered, but altered in some way. Perhaps he read it as a sexual overture, and she'd be hard-pressed to deny it. She liked bullying this boy as she caressed him.

'She's the sort,' he said, speaking dully, without grace, 'that if you give in to one demand, she's back straight away with another.'

'That's right.'

'It's useless. She's not a bad girl in some ways.'

'But you've had enough of her?'

'I didn't say that.'

'You've had enough of her,' she pursued, 'but haven't the nerve to tell her so? Is that about it?' She twisted his hand over so that it lay palm upwards, tiny sparkles of sweat among the tracery. 'That's a man's hand,' she said, 'a grown-up man's hand.'

He snatched it away, child-quick.

'There's not much I can do for you,' she said, at length.

'I don't suppose there is.' He laughed, not unpleasantly. She sat down, studied him as he held up for his own inspection the hand she'd fondled. 'There aren't many like you.'

She did not care to answer that.

'My dad,' he said, slowly, like grit under a door, 'had Mrs Makepeace. As a mistress. Started when he was my age. That's why he keeps her on. Not after he was married. My mother let it out. He'd told her.' He stopped, shied as if he realized he spoke of this woman's husband. So immersed in himself, in her rebuke, he'd forgotten, lost sight of Hilda as a human being. Pathetic, now, guilt-ridden.

'Well, what of it?'

She sounded level-headed, but reeled, hit hard enough, in her unpreparedness.

'Nothing. She was older. I thought you knew.'

'I didn't.'

'I'm sorry, Hilda.' He took her hand this time, knowing advantage. 'Hilda.'

'Never mind buttering me up.' She managed to laugh, shook the ends of his fingers in mock formality, dropped his hand. 'Save your blandishments for Linda.'

Jeremy laughed with her, and soon afterwards the young pair left, the girl carrying pot-plants for her window-sill, flushed, cheerful, talkative.

'She seems better,' Edward said, pleased with himself.

'Down again tomorrow.'

He asked about his son, but she could not determine what he wanted to know. Big boss-man. He did not throw his weight about, but that was because he saw no advantage.

'If she were free to marry him, Edward, would you try to prevent it?'

'You ask awkward questions, don't you?' Something of his son's charm there, but more assured, less concerned with the result. 'I don't honestly know. I think not. I've got into the habit of seeing him as my only charge. I'd written Anna off. Now I've got you, but I keep forgetting.'

'Flattering.'

'In a way. Yes, it is. How's the angel-antagonist?'

'Eh?'

'One of my prep schoolmasters used to say that, about a curly-headed child who wouldn't learn his Latin verbs. I'd forgotten till just now. No, I meant the Countess, Gaw' bless her.'

'Not a word.'

'Ummh. We must have blotted our copy-book.'

At that moment, she sat down, desponding. She'd failed with Jeremy except in a little hole-and-corner sexual way as she'd failed with Elizabeth. As she lounged she wanted some word of apology, attack even, some acknowledgement of herself. That this should matter troubled her. Elizabeth Marcroft, snobbery aside, wasn't much-of-a-mucher, to use Edward's phrase, a middle-aged, painted petty tyrant . . . The lexis, the mental picture gave the secret away. She would please Elizabeth if she could, creep round her, touch a forelock. But more? Mistress Night-work? The rain had stopped and the wind raked the clouds fine into blackish cotton, patterns of thin smoke, in front of a bright, watery sun. The world promised better.

That night they attended the parish church for the harvest festival.

Usually Edward turned up once a month, at morning service, without his wife who worshipped with secateurs and hoe. The cramped nave, was hung bright under clumps of electric bulbs with flowers, greenery, ribbon, as if the whole population of the village had taken to scissors and indulged in a kind of rough art. The greenhouse chrysanthemums, curled, variegated horrors, flashed proud; laurels were polished, while the end of their pew was handsome with an upthrust bunch of rowan, rust-gold now in autumn, smart as the Sunday suits of the thankful people.

A moment before the choir straggled singing, 'We plough the fields', in procession up the aisle, delayed on this account, the Earl and Countess of Marcroft arrived. They were recognized, greeted with a chatter of prayer-like fervency, shown flauntingly after consultation and rearrangement for the church was nearly full, to a seat behind the rector's wife, provided at the door with books which were replaced in the pew a minute later by grander editions. For a time there was a paradox of flurry, flying sidesmen, nodding hair and hats, and yet stillness, a postponement of the first hymn, as if eternity had been announced and last-minute adjustments were being made before the final trump sounded.

William and Elizabeth knelt briefly.

His suit, country tweed, looked excellent from the rear, but she shone, magnificent, purple, black, fine blue, acid green, simple yet complicated as the vegetables on the sills. Even from this distance she seemed to distil perfume, setting her apart. The villagers, faces placid with excitement, stored the moment, prepared the report for those who had been unlucky enough to prefer television. As they savoured the lord, they forgot the Lord, and that was just, approved on high. The electronic organ wheezed a unison line from its speaker perched high over the pulpit; the choir took it up behind the curtain at the back of the nave, shuffled out, clumped, singing as the congregation hutched greyly and multi-coloured to its feet and the nobility was lost in the upstanding of humanity. Fourteenth-century walls, restored and dark, were observable again and the Crucified Christ above the screen, writhing with wheat and leaves and flowers, showed untouched dust once more along His muscular arms, thick on His thorn-crowned head.

The service gained significance, Hilda thought, from the unexpected visitors. The rector's slow prayers, the responses, gabbled psalms, bawled hymns, the lay-reader's cultured barrack-square stiffness, the anthem 'Thou Visitest the Earth', led, misled, by a short, stout woman in a navy straw-hat hooting alto, the sermon with its reference to pollution and world-wide starvation with white hands laid solemnly on a scrubbed potato and a hunk of coal on the pulpit's edge were honoured by the observation of those two people, one quite still, the other restless, crossing his legs, sniffing, dabbing his moustache. Such feudalism, and Hilda could not be sure it existed outside her mind, seemed pleasing to God, an earnest of His presence. When the last hymn and benediction were done, the congregation waited for their lord-and-ladyship to rise first, lead for the door.

It seemed impossible, rehearsed. Then men reached for their hats and waited. Women knew their place.

William and Elizabeth exchanged a word, no more, with the rector's wife, moved off, unwilling to delay the peasantry, but as they passed the Fieldings Lady Marcroft smiled, brilliantly, like a stage-star, signalling acknowledged friends to follow them out, straight out. They complied.

The rector shook their hands in the porch, the Earl all gruffness, his wife floridly congratulatory on the inventive beauty of the decorations; Fielding said little, Hilda proffered modest thanks for the service. Under the outside lamps, William had taken Edward's arm to invite them back to Marcroft. The women, who had arranged, who would decide, hung behind in well-dressed unemployment. After they had walked the drive, stood outside in the street, the east window, with its half-dozen panes of medieval glass amongst the hundred unstained, alight, dully above them, its foliage, flowers mere shadows, Elizabeth said,

'We're lonely. Will you come?'

Her husband looked affronted as if the confession diminished him, but he smiled when they made no demur, perhaps because he would not be left to his wife's untender mercy.

'We'll use B-roads,' Marcroft said. 'Follow me.' He moved to his Rolls-Royce. Once they had started Fielding, grinning, said to his wife,

'Follow me, and I will make you fishers of men.'

The command hung in her ears, so that she understood, resisting with him, but obeying.

They entered Marcroft by one of many side-doors, along a tiled corridor with dark-green paint on the walls, and then into a sitting room with four armchairs round a lighted gas fire. After an exchange of remarks about the service, the weather, the local fair, the Earl said he must ring the assistant estate manager before it grew too late.

'Take Edward to your office,' Elizabeth said. 'He'd like to see it.'

Marcroft huffed and blew, but seemed pleased enough in his doddering way. When they were out of the room, Elizabeth wheeled on Hilda.

'Willy's ill.'

'I'm sorry.'

'Seriously. Cancer; of the lung.'

'Does he know?'

'I don't know. I think he must, but I'm not sure.'

'Inoperable?'

'No, they are going to take him in, and the surgeon thinks there's a chance of success. But he's run down, and age isn't on his side. We get on each other's nerves. That's why we went to church. I'd seen Edward, and he'd told me you'd go, and I thought we could inveigle you up here.' She spoke clearly, but with dull delivery. 'This is my sitting room. My office's next door.' She jumped up, threw a door open, switched on a light, while a snarl of draught caught at their ankles. 'He's really down, and I can't say any more. I've worked through all the comfort. It's awful. He's in pain, and he's frightened, and I know it, and I can't help him.'

'But you say it will be all right?'

'So it may. He doesn't believe it.'

'And you?'

138

'I don't know. How can I tell?' She looked ready for death. 'Tom's better. He took his re-sits at the end of September and has passed them all. He can do it if he wants. Oh, God. It's all bloody silly. He'll learn management, and accounts and the rest, and he'll end up like his father with a pain in his chest, terrified.'

'Why doesn't he go to bed?'

'He does, but he can't lie. He enjoys driving. And he'll like showing Edward round the office files. "This is big business," he says, but he needs the reassurance from some-body who really does handle commercial contracts. He'll feel better, that and the church and the car-ride. And he'll drink a bit more than he should. God, I wanted you here, Hilda. That scares you.'

'Does it? I don't know.' She was sore.

'I need you here to tell you this, somebody I can run up to, and say, "My husband's got cancer, cancer, cancer." '

When he dies, Hilda thought, Elizabeth will be confined to this room; this will be her dower-house, and Milord Tom will flaunt his shire-end beauty or his mannerless tart in the state rooms because Father William had dared snuff it on his wife. Hilda pushed up to her feet, walked across, sat on the arm of Elizabeth's chair.

'You tell me,' she said, in compassion.

'That's all there is.'

'Are you afraid?'

'I don't know what I am. I want to do something for my husband. He's frightened. He flares into a temper for nothing. He can't concentrate for more than ten minutes at a time. He's never been ill before. What can I say to him?'

'You don't love him?'

Why Hilda asked that, now, she did not know, but she blamed it on her own pain, her own acid of anxiety.

'We've been married twenty-five years,' Elizabeth an-swered. 'Love doesn't come into it.'

Hilda did not argue this.

'The gin will be up,' Elizabeth continued, 'in a few minutes and we shall all feel better. But when you've gone . . . ' She blew a sigh comical in its magnitude.

'What can I do?'

'You can show me you bother with me, and that I shan't be out of your head five minutes after you've left the place. Hold my hand.' Hers was out, over-young, small, pathetic. The other took it, minutely cold. There was not, as Hilda feared, any squeezings or rubbings. A hand for the present was within a hand.

'Now I'm better,' Elizabeth said. Hilda understood, imagined herself more stable. 'You mean a great deal to me, Hilda.'

'I don't know why.'

'I shan't make a fool of myself, if that's what you're afraid of.'

'No.' Now, Hilda had had enough, felt ridiculous herself. Suddenly she felt her hand moved, settled on to Elizabeth's thigh, into the crotch. This was achieved without tugging, gently, with a firm calm; as it were, 'There.' The body under the cloth seemed finely alive, unleashing itself, leaping at her flesh. Though this must have been imagined, was to be discounted, it demonstrated with expressive power the other woman's infatuation, as though every pore of her skin mouthed for help. With a small gasp, an expulsion of exasperated breath, Elizabeth laid the hand back on Hilda's lap, and walked away towards a cupboard, from which she took bottles.

'Gin?' she asked. 'It? Ginger? Tonic water? Those men will be all night.'

Hilda, wary, defensive still, felt that the dry tone announced success in the other endeavour, accepted a small glass, concentrated on bubbles. Elizabeth, sipping already, smiled conspiratorially.

'It was pleasant at Rempstone Church,' she said. 'They do things like the harvest remarkably well.'

'You know the rector?'

'Yes. He had one of our livings. When he was first married. That's one reason why we decided to go there. That, and Willy's driving. And you. Of course.'

The men returned.

'Boozing. Already,' Edward said, uncharacteristically. Willy looked ghastly, sagging inside his suit, his face clayey yellow.

'Good idea,' Marcroft said. Huff; puff. Their shares were poured and Edward called out, 'Your health', jabbing the air with his glass.

'William's due for hospital,' he said, then, in the silence.

'Elizabeth told me. Are you afraid?'

She winced at her inept question, but Lord Marcroft screwed his ugly eyes and considered.

'Don't know. Really. Seems a bit like somebody else. Know what I mean. Happening to somebody else.'

'I should be terrified.'

Edward and Elizabeth joined in a duet in praise of surgery. They seemed to know exactly what to say, as if they had practised together.

'I think you're brave,' Hilda said, naively cunning. 'I'd be petrified.'

Marcroft smiled back, squared his shoulders, sipped gin with a movement of his elbow like a military salute, so that she felt proud of herself.

'Not exactly afraid,' he said. 'Not ready f'r it. Y'know.'

She looked at him.

The good checked suit over beautiful shoes, polished to horsechestnut brown; the wide-striped shirt, gold tie signalled his money and his taste, but above the stiff-standing collar his face seemed in a state of collapse. Wrinkles dug painfully deep, while each outline was blurred, rubbed shapeless. His eyes looked listlessly over heavy bags, and his eyebrows spurted like dead branches from a fire-ravaged earth. His hair, white now, lacked life, drooped, thick and untidy at front and sides, thin over red scalp. She thought again of a baked apple, skin cracked, surface broken. The hand round the gin glass hunched huge, like cement, but ridged with veins, and brown-spotted.

'You'll be fine,' she said. The others had abandoned them.

'I expect so,' he said. 'Very odd, Bates from the estates Office going in with much the same. Stomach, though. He's back at work. Doesn't look well, d'you think, Elizabeth?'

'He started back too soon,' she said.

'You'll have more sense.' Hilda.

Here was a man in the face of death, and afraid. Suddenly she had to put her glass down, lean hard on the arm of her chair as she realized what she had thought. Somewhere, at last now, with his family, his Sunday papers, his jade or lathe, a surgeon took his ease, knowing exactly what chances William had of survival. Title, lands, mansions counted for nothing; the Earl nervously toed his wife's carpet, topped his glass with tonic-water so as not to fill full with gin.

Hilda recalled a photograph she had seen in a news-paper.

Two dead children, little girls from Wisconsin at the turn of the century, dead of diphtheria, laid side by side in their wicker cradles. Flowers brushed their faces, and their hands were gently clenched. No evidence of pain showed; the two smiled as if at any minute they would shift in their sleep, breathe, settle more comfortably, for the black-dotted print revealed no pallor, none of the harsh stillness of death. In that picture the children lay beautiful who would now be aged and ugly, or dead in less comely shape. That moved her, not fiercely, like a charade, a play, a delicacy of words:

142

Pray be silent and not stir
The easy earth that covers her.

And not two yards away, brown boots perfect, sat this uncouth man, himself within touching distance of death. Hilda
shuddered, her body recoiling from the vast iceberg of a
hand, the coldness of shadow.

Edward began to talk, she loved him then, inanities.
Glasses were filled so that soon they felt the warmth of the
room. William described some curious dealings with a
London banker whose ancestors had worked on the estate.
As he talked, in a low voice, sapped by illness, but with the
bark of his class still implicit, he seemed genuinely interested in his own anecdote.

'Was there a lake? man kept saying. With wooded hill on
one side. Was there a lake in Marcroft? And a grove?
Seemed important. Handed down by word of mouth. A lake
or a stew with trees. What the old chap had done there,
God knows. 1850 or thereabouts. And here was this fellow,
Eton tie. Was there a lake?'

He spoke animatedly, pleased with his own energy.

'Well, was there?' Hilda asked. William's face creased
into a smile.

'Could think of two, if not three, places here at Marcroft
fit the bill. Had a photograph of one. In Train's book. Might
have been. Fellow didn't know. Couldn't.'

For two hours they talked desultorily, with both Marcrofts drinking heavily. They showed no sign of incapacity,
as they rallied dying topics. The room was hot, and twice
William went out, and several times stood, tottered to a
table as if he could not bear immobility. Hilda felt desperately sorry for the man, wished she had the nerve to
throw her arms round him, to treat him as a child to be
mothered, but then the flash of light on toecap, the elegant
suit, the scarred face, would replace the agony inside the

man, the Earl, not to be touched in his show case of caste.

Edward demonstrated golf strokes, surprising his wife who knew he neither played nor watched the game on television. He talked about the price of wood, which led Willy into a long complaint about the difficulties of cutting down, marketing timber; he spoke at his best when he deplored, happy in misery. Her husband, Hilda thought, was much like his son; socially diffident, never open, but utterly attractive. He couldn't push a lock of hair from his eyes without bringing the ladies running. His dark eyes were alight; his hands sketched white vaguenesses in the air. Nothing he said was worth attention, yet he saved the evening.

When they got up to leave, Hilda stretched across, took William's head between her hands and kissed the leathery cheek.

'B'God,' he rasped. 'That was nice, if you like.' She could smell the gin.

'Don't I get one?' Elizabeth.

'Now, Edward,' said his lordship. Fielding stooped, touching her cheekbone with his lips, mischievous eyes meeting Hilda's. Elizabeth, putting a good face on, held out a hand to Hilda, mannishly shook, stretched for a kiss.

'Small matter to sort out before bed,' William told them, parade-ground sharp.

'Not tonight.' His wife, exasperated. 'He walks over to the stables.'

'I feel like it. I talk to Delia, my mare. Somehow, they're alive, everything is. I'd sooner stand in that place, saying my silly words, and listening to the movements, and touching their heads . . . Y'know how it . . . ' He stopped, caught out in his sort of poetry.

Lady Marcroft was nodding, solemnly, smally, with all the effect of a great bell deeply chiming, tolling. She led them outside, while her husband leaned on his table, head sunk to chest, eyes closed.

10

'That poor bugger's going to die,' Edward said, driving back. She was not sure he wasn't talking to himself.

'We don't know.'

'He does.'

They sat for a few moments, unwilling to go to bed. Hilda, head dizzy with gin fumes, hummed to herself, staring into the empty fire-grate. The phone shrilled.

'Who the hell's that at eleven-thirty?' Edward made for the door, was back shortly. 'It's Jeremy. For you.'

'What's he want?'

'Christ knows.'

She touched him on his sleeve as they passed, recognizing extremity in his voice. He paid no attention.

A bulb glowed by the phone, throwing a junk-sail of radiance up the wall. She drew out an elegant chair from under the table, composed herself before speaking. Jeremy said straight away that he was sorry, but this was the fifth time he'd rung. She explained, succinctly, where she had been. 'It's Linda. She won't go to the house.'

'When are you due to move?'

'Tuesday.'

'I see. Does she say why?'

'No. She'll hate it. She won't be dependent. Mrs Make-peace hates her. It's a plot of my father's. Irrational rubbish like that.'

'But she's serious?'

'Ye'. Seems so.'

'You've not lost your temper?'

'No.' He had the grace to laugh.

'She means it. I see. Let's forget her, then. What are you going to do?'

'How can I forget her?' The boy interrupted. 'I've got

to consider . . . I'm sorry.'

'What do you want to do, Jeremy? Move house?'

'Yes.'

'That's more important than splitting up from her, if she really means what she says?'

'That's what I don't know.'

'So you want me to tell you?'

'I've argued with her. I've written it down on bits of paper so that she can study it when she's not confronting me. We've had nothing else for days. Will you talk to her?'

'Let's say, Jeremy, I do, and she still won't budge. Will you go?'

'That's not easy.'

'Do you want to move?'

'There's every advantage for both of us.' He set off breathlessly, detailing. Clearly he'd committed all this to his paper, worked out a competent brief and yet the quick voice gabbled, spoke in uncertainty, snuffled anxiety. Hilda allowed him his head, encouraged him to continue though she did not listen. Her eyes played listlessly, almost drunkenly, on a print of a hunting scene where corpulent men in top-hats, red coats, set their horses' manes and tails flying at the call of a horn. The hounds pursued, legs parallel to the earth. She was tired. Mrs Makepeace would have an evening meal ready. No clearing. A garden to sit in. Hilda could not read the copper-plate script on the print, had no notion why so long a titular line was needed. The house was beautiful. Father paid. They'd save money. It was more convenient both for the hospital and the university. She'd nearly nodded away, chin sagging to chest. Nostrils were wide, reins taut, hooves flung under a winter tree. She heard him out.

'Now let's have this straight,' she said when he'd finished. 'Suppose I talk to her, and it makes no difference, what do we do then?'

'I'll deal with that if it happens, when it happens.'

'I can't work miracles, Jeremy.'

'She likes you. She'll listen to you. You're not my family.' He stopped; she could hear him whistling tonelessly. 'It's like this. It seems a shame for us to break up about just a thing . . . We've lived together.' The shame-faced boy she imagined resembled his father, shaken rigid by a confession he meant, hang-dog and suspicious. 'It means something. It ought to mean something.'

She was touched, promised intervention, asked where he was ringing from.

'A phone-box on the other side of the street. It's very windy. Can you hear it?'

'Where's Linda?'

'In bed, but I can see she's got the light on.'

'Waiting for you? She knows where you are?'

'I suppose so.'

She stifled a yawn, but did not speak until she was composed. 'I'll call tomorrow.'

'Thanks, Hilda.'

He rang off, immediately. Phone down. End. Now he'd be crossing the road towards the light as the wind rattled sash-windows.

The trees outside his flat fluttered last leaves away as she parked her car next evening, rang the outside bell, groped up the dusty single staircase. Jeremy opened the door, said nothing, made no welcoming gesture.

'Where's Linda?' she asked, inside.

'Gone.'

They both sat down. He seemed unruffled, quiet as usual, in no difficulty. When he began to talk, he did not speak fluently, but clearly, distant. He'd returned from the phone call, which Linda knew about, and had reported the conversation, Hilda's promise of a visit. This had annoyed the girl, who'd shouted angrily at first, then sulked, rebuffed, at a guess, his physical advances. At breakfast, which she'd prepared without a word, though both were laconic first thing in the morning, he claimed, he'd tried to raise the matter again. She'd burst into tears, left him to finish on his own, hurried out breakfastless to work; again Hilda surmised that this behaviour had been not unusual of late. He'd washed the dishes and gone off for a nine o'clock lecture. As soon as his afternoon labs were over, he rushed home, found a note announcing she'd deserted him.

'You expected something like this?' she asked. 'You dashed back?'

'No. She's usually in about five-twenty, and I wanted the house warm, kettle boiling, toast made. That sort of thing.'

He offered the information modestly, staring all the time at the hissing gas fire. It struck hot in this long room, which was now kept exceptionally neatly, as if he'd been over the faded carpets with a vacuum cleaner, round the furniture with a duster this evening. It seemed more likely since he wore a dark suit and a white shirt showing like a parson's collar over his high-necked sweater.

'And the note?'

It lay folded to hand on a miniature table by his arm-chair. He passed it over. 'It isn't any good, I can see that now. You're better off without me. I've taken my clothes. When you leave for Magdala Avenue you might send the things that belong to me. Or I'll have them fetched if you leave a message for me at work. Linda.'

'You've no idea where she is?'

He shook his head, at too great length.

'There's no way of finding out?'

'I expect she's staying temporarily with one of the girls at the hospital.' He blew a long sigh at this, ridiculous and involuntary, running his hand through his hair.

'When did she come? In the lunch hour?'

'That I don't know.' He was long enough answering,

searching round for words. 'Nobody seems to have seen her.'

'What will you do?'

He put his forefinger into his mouth, sucked the knuckle solemnly.

'I suppose I'll try to get in touch with her at her lab.'

Suddenly he held out his hand for the note which she rustled between her fingers. The gesture seemed right, demanding back this extension of Linda. She remembered a radio talk by Clifford Curzon who owned the last holograph page of Mozart's G Minor Quintet, K 516. Simply, Jeremy-like, the pianist had finished, '*His* hand had rested on it.'

She looked again at the boy, who, with eyebrows almost comically high, re-read the note, re-stared at it. He did not appear bothered; his face expressed mild amusement if anything at his plight. Pickle.

At that moment she realized, as if her head reeled, that she did not know him. Ignorance suffused her. What he thought, what he wanted, what he expected were all unapprehended; she felt perhaps if she touched him he'd blurt out some truism that would bridge their apartness, but he and she sat, staring, not seeing, the note in his hands. Her body was pinned to her chair.

She did not know this boy.

That was understandable. They'd met barely a score of times, and he said little. She thought suddenly, dartingly, one living fibre in a dead brain, of the Earl of Marcroft, the dying man, who loved a Rolls-Royce under his hands. What did he know, want? Then Elizabeth who craved possession of her, who flaunted dominion even when she apologized, was another unknown, a lay figure, a cut-out, an actress in a bad play. Immediately she remembered the Shacklocks, whom she saw every day, and asked herself who they were, how they occupied themselves. Dizzied, her head lurched towards her husband, the man she knew naked, who talked to her every meal, extended himself for her benefit and found he, too, had retreated behind a plate-glass screen where he could act out his work, his crises, his antics without her assistance or knowledge. There was neither knowledge nor telling.

This sense of being frozen away from her world lasted a few frightening seconds, so that the thaw was both a relief and painful. That she could have acted herself into such a singularity of ignorance scared her because her body had occupied itself, driven the directing mind from its house, replaced it by a cold observer who recorded its own strict limitations. Now she realized that she must talk to this boy.

'Did you think she'd do this?'

He shrugged, and that was enough. To understand her question, and make some sort of answer, however impolite, momentarily sufficed. Warmth could grow, glow later; for the present she had breached her own inadequacy.

'If I rang her at work, do you think she'd mind?'

Jeremy smiled; dark-blue eyes under dark hair.

'She could always put the phone down,' he said. 'Or not come to it.'

'Write the number for me.' He did so on a slip torn from an envelope taken with the biro from his pocket. 'Do you want her back? I mean.' Now, her turn to smile. 'I don't want to be rude, but I don't want to bundle her back and find you can do quite well without her.'

'I see.' He spoke the words in his father's office manner putting twenty years on his age, a foot round his flat belly.

'You're moving into Marchmont? No compromise?'

'I'm going. I've given my notice here.'

She expected that, she supposed, made a becoming face for its reception. 'Is there anything I can do for you now?'

'Such as?' He grinned, looking his boyish age.

'You ask me to interfere. I know nothing about you or Linda.'

He grasped the implied accusation, and, taking a step or two about the room, finally adopted a position by the mantelpiece, one arm outstretched to a flat hand.

'You seem to me to, well, have your wits about you. You might notice something obvious we've missed. My dad's sharp enough, but he doesn't care. I'm a part of my mother, if you understand me, and he's pushed that out of his mind. He'll help me; I don't mean he won't. He'll fork money out. But when he sees me tangled with Linda, he thinks, "Anna Latham again", and shies off. When I talk to the people at the university they're pleased, most of 'em, to get away from home. They dislike their fathers who are always under their feet, yapping and snarling. I've never got near mine.'

'Disadvantages to both,' she said.

'You're just being polite, now,' he answered.

'And that's no good to you?'

'You know it isn't.'

He seemed to grow in these last sentences into moral stature that reproached her frivolity, as if he had access to a world of principle, of emotional depth from which she was barred. For the first time, she was herself involved, perhaps because she was condemned.

'I'll ring her, tomorrow or the day after. Though I don't know what I'm going to say. You've got to sort this out for yourselves. You write to her tonight. Post it first thing. Then the day after I'll phone. Do you know what to put?'

'No.'

'Will you do it?'

'If you say so.'

Now he was nobody, blowing air-bubble sentences, a froth.

'Ring me. Tell me what you've said, and then I'll try.'

'Yes, ma'am.'

She remembered as a girl being taken by her mother to see a cousin whose husband had been killed in a car accident that day. The house was full of sympathetic friends, providing cups of tea and consolatory conversation for each other, while Susan, the widow, sat, strode, bright-eyed, brittle, uncrying, efficient, saying she couldn't grasp it yet revelling in the excitement the stardom, numb to everything but surface sociabilities. She'd pressed Hilda, in a slimming phase, to a huge slice of fruit cake, praising her last exam results before dashing off to kiss the newest arrivals. In a week Susan had broken, but then she postured as if at the village dramatic society.

'Will you be all right?' she asked, determined.

'Why shouldn't I be?'

'You've had a shock. I don't want you doing anything silly.' That was out with it. 'To tell you the truth, I don't like leaving you here on your own. Come on back to Rempstone.'

'I'm not my mother.'

'Your father will . . . '

'He won't give a monkey's.' He slapped the outstretched arm down, hand to thigh. 'I shall be right enough here.'

'Make me a cup of coffee, then, before I go.'

The brusque, friendly command embarrassed him, so that he blushed as he shambled towards the kitchenette, bending forward. They drank together while she questioned him about the university; he genuinely enjoyed his work, did not begrudge the time it occupied, but asserted that he would not go on to research.

'I'll have had sufficient.' He smiled, a Victorian clergyman, saucer balanced.

He accompanied her downstairs, came out into the street, stood with one foot on the low wall with its stumps of iron railings.

'You'll ring me tomorrow,' she said, through the car window.

'I will.'

11

Hilda telephoned Linda at the hospital where the girl allowed her two minutes' dull time. No, it was between her and Jeremy and that was all there was to it. She showed neither resentment nor truculence. Hilda begged her to ring at the end of the week, pleading Edward's interest, and the other half-promised but without enthusiasm. A note conveyed the information to Jeremy.

Lord Marcroft went into the Pay-Bed Wing the same morning.

Hilda immediately called Elizabeth, inviting her round, offering services, but there was no answering warmth. The Countess had geared herself to trouble, and she'd endure it.

'I'm perfectly well. And desperately busy.'

'You don't want me to come over, then?'

'No. I have to drive in to the hospital most afternoons.'

'Call in here on your way. It'll be someone to talk to.'

'There are people on my back, round my neck all day. I'm very grateful to you, Hilda, and to Edward, but we'll leave it.'

Lady Marcroft's secretary rang to tell them that the Earl had survived his operation, but was in the intensive care unit and receiving no visitors. Her ladyship would be delighted to see Mrs Fielding.

When Hilda was shown into the office, Elizabeth was haranguing her agent about plans, which covered her long table. She stood, rather mannishly, with a finger out, laying down the law to a body shrunk inside its suit. The man held a notebook and biro, wrote now and then in shorthand, murmured sycophantic agreement in her pauses. Whether Elizabeth put on a show for her benefit Hilda did not know, but her tone hectored. 'I thought we made it clear,

Bates . . .' 'Yes, y'r ladyship.' '. . . that this was not to be extended.' 'No, y'r ladyship.' The visitor was pointed into a chair, apologized to, treated to a sight of more feudal despotism. In the end, at a gesture, Bates straightened and rolled the papers, tied them with tape. The bundle he stuck, awkwardly angled, under his arm.

As he turned, Hilda saw his face for the first time. He was desperately crumpled, like a tin on a vacuum pump, fingered by death. All vitality had been drained so that only his false teeth seemed lively. The eyes, briefly meeting Hilda's, begged from her, though she did not know what. She smiled and he wanly twisted his mouth, shuffled for the door where he fumbled.

'He looks ill,' Hilda said.

Lady Marcroft glanced up, as if still considering her decisions, said, lips thin, briskly,

'Incurable cancer.'

'Does he know?'

Elizabeth shook that one off.

'He wants to work. He might as well, while he can. It occupies him.' Hilda remembered the snapped instructions, corrections, of a few moments back.

'How long has he got?'

'They don't say. Not long. One morning he won't show up to work, and a month or two afterwards he'll go.'

'It's dreadful.' Elizabeth sat, crossed her legs, knitted her fingers. 'How's Willy?'

'He's had the operation. You know that. They say he's doing well.' Her eyes switched shiftily to the door. 'He looked on Bates as a kind of portent. He got through.' She seemed old, harassed, dry, without trace of the smart, imperious female with the plans. 'So shall I.'

Hilda crossed the room, put an arm about her. She knew the practice was dangerous; she also knew her duty.

Elizabeth briefly smiled, then shook the circling arm loose.

They went out together, walking towards the walled kitchen gardens.

'Two of the old glasshouses are going. We've decided to replace them and build two more while we're about it.'

The sky was grey, without breaks, although it did not rain. The raw air chilled. Only one man was working outside and he ignored them, keeping his head down. They pushed into a glasshouse bright with chrysanthemums, huge and spectacular; the air stung with their scent. Elizabeth pointed out faults in the woodwork, began to talk prices and times. Hilda shut her ears, concentrating on a regiment of dark-brown blooms, reddish and shaggy. At a stoppage of talk she asked,

'Will you use the old glass again?'

'No.' A further flurry of horticultural economics, deafened her. Why must Elizabeth bang with this hard voice? The paths between the beds were paved with bricks, holed bricks. Bates, one paper only in hand, entered at the far door, clattered towards them.

He bobbed, making as if to pass.

'If these greenhouses were yours, Bates, would you replace them?' Authority.

'Yes, certainly.'

'Mrs Fielding imagines we're throwing thousands of pounds away.'

'No. We don't want accidents, for one thing. For another, with an enormous estate like this, one must put aside, we always do,' a beck towards Elizabeth, 'a certain sum for replacements, just as we do for current expenses, contingencies, developments.'

'Can't you go a year without renewing anything?' she asked. In face of death, she must whip an argument up.

'Possible, possible.' His voice was strong. 'But usually we have to decide where to spend the money, and what will stand being neglected for a year.' He laughed. 'Next November, now, this will look magnificent.'

'With chrysanthemums?'

'I expect so.' He touched a leaf, with his eaten hand, like a lover, a baby.

'You won't improve on these,' Hilda said. 'They're superb.'

'We pride ourselves. We pride ourselves.'

With muttered courtesies, he moved on, carting his death out into the open air. In a year's time he'd be underground. The door clattered shut at the far end. Suddenly, taken aback, Hilda found tears on her face, her chest stiff with a powerful regret that the polite, sensible man who'd just spoken would die, did not know, did know, while she stood amongst this mass of prize exhibits, this coloured uproar of curled petals. Her throat contracted; she heard sobs, felt herself collapse round them. She did nothing, did not rummage in her bag for a handkerchief, stood, a jelly of grief, an un-self.

She felt no luxury of relief in her weeping. Her body had learnt crude pity and now taught it to her. With her arms in front of herself, shoulders bowed, seeing nothing, nose clogged, she cried, until, with a spurt of energy, tearing, lacerating, she looked up to where Elizabeth Marcroft, leaning on a brick pillar, lawn handkerchief to face, wept quietly with her. Impossible. The blue painted lids hung silver with tears; the harsh mouth trembled. At the sight, Hilda's energies were gathered, without her will, into a great whoop, a scream of distress. This neither shocked nor frightened her, seemed natural, eased her, strengthened. She poked into her handbag, wiped her eyes and saw behind Elizabeth the big stars of blooms, yellow-gold, white, ugly in their pots, impersonal, proud, each a thing in itself, a beauty owing them nothing, comforting not at all, a cold yet rough perfection.

She had calmed herself, found herself without tears. Elizabeth, perhaps three yards away, wept still, but awkwardly, with embarrassed sniffs, dabbing hard now at her face as if to punish its weakness. Hilda squared herself up, thought it ridiculous that two grown women should choose this spot to howl like whipped children, pronounced, to herself, that it was sane, responsible, beautiful even, and said,

'We'll be all right.'

Elizabeth made the effort; one sensed it. She shook fear from her back in one imperious, fierce movement. She could not answer.

'It seemed so sad. With all these flowers, he . . .' Hilda dared not continue, knowing her own uncertainty.

'And I thought of Willy.' The voice rang brassy, plangent. 'He loves this, this . . . ' She broke down again, but briefly. 'He hates it, there.'

They stood for five minutes before they walked along together, by common consent neither speaking nor touching. Both had bared themselves; each dreaded the consequence, but neither would seek help. Two well-dressed women, slightly dishevelled, eyes red-rimmed, progressed along the path, eyeing the flower battalions, while outside the sky threatened in gloom. Indoors they laconically drank a glass of gin.

Hilda drove away, comfortably sure in the warmth of the car that she had acted exactly right, though she felt the soreness still. Edward had come home, grumpily complaining that he could get nothing done, that his employees obstructed him at every turn. He had, however, cheered himself by buying his wife a bunch of chrysanthemums which Mrs Shacklock had divided into three vases. Hilda, surprising herself, looked at them without emotion.

Her husband prepared to travel down to London, where he'd stay for a two-day conference. For the next half-hour she'd make sure that his clothes were ready, though he in fact would pack them. She had no difficulty here, and both enjoyed the exercise, carrying the cases together out to the Rover 3.5, chattering, giving instructions, receiving such.

'Just have a cup of coffee before you go,' she said. 'There's plenty of time.'

She derived pleasure from her man, in his sober suit, broad-shouldered, razored smooth pink, touched with aftershave, his thick eyebrows lifting as he perched neatly on a stool. They sat together in the kitchen, since the Shacklocks had gone visiting, would not be back until late.

'You look a credit to me,' she said.

'And you make a delicious cup of coffee.'

This love-banter seemed warm, so that he pulled her to him, kissed her, nuzzled.

'Not in your best suit,' she said.

'I'll take it off.'

'And miss half those delicious vodkas they'll be handing out.'

He clapped his hands round her buttocks, half-lifted her from the ground.

'I have never preferred alcohol to sex,' he proclaimed. 'Upstairs.'

'I haven't finished my coffee.'

'Nor will you.'

As they lay warmly naked in bed, sated, lapped in comfort, lavish with love's calm, he said, suddenly, touching her thigh:

'Do you want children?'

Mindless, unruffled, drifting in and out of a daze of pleasure, she pressed his hand into her flesh.

'Not really.' She spoke as through a cream bun.

'I'm serious, darling. Would you like a child?'

'No, I don't think so.' Pause. 'You think I should.'

'I don't know.'

'I'm not unnatural,' she said. That sounded silly to herself. 'Only conservative. For the first time in my life I feel easy. Something will come along and upend me. I'm sure it will. But I'm enjoying you, and this house, and the garden. Just as it is. If I start a family, there'll be pressures. I'll do it willingly if that's what you want. But there's nothing but distraction in it for me. Just now.'

'Could be. Yes.'

'I'm not a full woman till I'm a mother?'

'You've thought of that?' His voice, steady enough, implied criticism, and immediately as at noon, her throat filled, choked so that she lay silent. Immediately he showed contrition, hugged her, but the nakedness which encouraged love obstructed pity. He lay strong, as she leaned on to the warmth of his skin, but he had distanced himself from her by turning post-coital joy into an examination. He perhaps, she was capable still of imagination, had used the excellent time to speak seriously, to hear her without effrontery, embarrassment or persiflage reply, and she, like his first wife, had toppled into sullenness, seared his concern with her unbalance.

She recovered quickly, and as she hurried him to his car, returned to the empty kitchen, she felt as if she'd come round from an illness, glad at the first faint stirrings of health. When she'd washed the cups she put her coat on, stepped on to the terrace. It was already dark and the wind had risen, shifting the cloud-pall roaring and clapping. Trees thrashed about as stars hung bright as cold glass. Her feet cracked on the paving-blocks while in the distance car headlights swept, blazing, and passed. She leaned against a buttress feeling the chill of the stones, their roughness on her hand.

In this darkness, with only the light of the doorlamps, and they well behind her, the park, grassland and copses, seemed alive, at movement. There was about this activity nothing unfriendly or threatening; it consisted of blown grass-blades or hedges, the odd scuffle of a nocturnal animal, or bird, a swaying of branches, purposive humming of tyres and engine, kisses of lovers, the scud of clouds before stars and it seemed to impel her towards decision herself. She had no idea what to do; probably she'd an overplus of energy from her idle day and this had no connection with the hustle of the world about her. Yet to stand still, half-sheltered, palming a rough wall, seemed insufficient. Whether her action should be physical, a run in the fields, or social, a visit or phone call, or spiritual, a prayer, or mental, a directed stream of thinking, she'd no idea. She was urged to do, not suffer. She drew herself up, like a guardsman, thrusting shoulders square, marched towards the portico. This for a few seconds seemed an answer. She slapped one of the round pillars harder than she meant, hurting her hand. A car's headlights turned in from the main road, made towards the house. She slipped inside wondering if Edward had come back, or the Shacklocks early, and stood inside the hall, before a mirror waiting for the bell.

The car stopped. She heard its door. Felt, if that were the word, the light vibration of footsteps on the flagstones. Bell.

Outside, scarf loosely round his neck, stood Alan Gascoigne.

He smiled politely, wished her good evening, seemed not put out that she did not immediately invite him in.

'There's something I wanted to ask you,' he said. 'If you'd give me a few minutes.'

She stood back, as he advanced. Once inside he slipped off his short fashionable coat, hat and college scarf and handed them over. She led him into the large drawing room, where she had to draw the curtains at both ends. There was a chill about the place as she showed him to an armchair.

He leaned back, crossed his legs, smiling. His suit, a dark

grey with the faintest red pattern of squares, was well cut, newish. Though he breathed slightly heavily, she'd forgotten that, he seemed much at his ease, smiling, youthful, slim, athletic. Only his hands, which were stringy, with the skin round his nails bitten, gave any indication of the nervous dynamism she knew drove him.

'I hope you don't mind my appearing like this,' he said, 'but I've been this afternoon at a teach-in, so that it wasn't much out of my way to call in here.'

She asked if he'd like a drink.

'No, thank you. I'm driving. And besides I don't want to trespass on your time.'

She felt herself shrivel at the quiet, rather breathy voice; she might well have been the new English mistress of ten years back being interviewed again by the headmaster. An effort on her part shook fear off. He'd not aged; at this distance, with the fine head of neat fair hair, he might have been in his late twenties. The styling was old-fashioned, rather youthful, like that of a pre-war public schoolboy or undergraduate.

'I wanted to speak to you about Elizabeth Marcroft.'

His use of the forename surprised her; she did not answer. He did not continue at once, but stroked the arm of his chair, not in any exploratory style, but thinking out carefully what he had to say.

'You may know,' he began, pausing to show his teeth, 'that in these last months I have had quite a lot to do with her. She is a remarkable woman.'

Hilda shifted slightly.

'We talk together, and, I think I may claim, she has to some extent taken me into her confidence.' He examined his finger nails. 'She occupies a lonely eminence.' He paused to savour his phraseology. 'Once or twice, especially in these last three weeks, she's spoken about you. You hold rather a special place in her life.'

His quiet mannerisms, voice, confidence annoyed her; this devious man adopted exactly such a heart-to-heart tone when he was about to unload extra work on members of his staff. He'd now ask her if she'd assist Mr Burrows in the library, or organize the sixth-form conference he'd invited to his school. She looked away at a Victorian still life, apples and a flagon, in a wide golden frame, ornate as fretwork.

'Her husband is very ill. She has no one to turn to. You are probably the one person capable of helping her, or, perhaps the one person she would allow to do so. You understand what I mean?'

Hilda opened her eyes wide, stared him straight in the face, said nothing. He smiled again, sadly and handsome, closing his eyes, nodding.

'She is lonely. And though she is a woman of remarkable self-possession and resilience, she needs a confidante at this time.'

'Elizabeth asked you to call?' Ironically grave.

'She did not.' He leaned back in a pose of elegant defeat, spoilt by those fierce hands. 'I've no right to do what I have done. She certainly would be angry. But I don't think, perhaps, and I may be wronging you, that you quite understand the position you hold in her esteem.' He paused on that, reconsidering it, before gently massaging his right eyebrow so that it rustled. 'That is not putting it strongly enough, but I do not wish to be accused of exaggeration. She is in need of assistance for which she will not bend to ask. She would refuse help from most quarters, but not, if I am right, from you. I cannot stress strongly enough that I come on my own account, that I . . . this is no embassy from her.'

Though frustrated by the soft voice, its insistence, its air of certainty, Hilda ceased to listen. Why had he appeared? She did not believe him capable of an altruistic action, or rather that any disinterestedness on his part was merely self-interest disguised, pranked up. He would enjoy doing Lady Marcroft a good turn; he would please himself if he manipulated his former wife like a puppet; boast obscurely to his cronies. Again she listened to a critical encomium of William. Perhaps Alan's motive was different, that vulgar curiosity had driven him in here with a cock-and-bull story to see how she lived. Let him look his longest. This room was beautiful, with its pictures, its few pieces of furniture, the great faint-gold curtains at either end. He'd never afford this, if he'd saved, and he was mean, his every penny till he died. '. . . And so you, you see, Hilda, that if you could find it in your heart . . .' The peroration swelled as she waited for the final full stop when he'd raise his eyes to stare blue and candid into hers. He obliged.

She did not answer for a time.

'I'll ask her about it,' she said.

He grimaced, a small pinching of the mouth, but he covered his sourness.

'This is no time for inquiry,' he argued. 'She needs immediate assistance.'

'I said I'll ask.' Mulish-stupid.

'Immediacy, there's an immediacy about this.' She rembered this construction; he flung an out-of-the-way word at you, then used it in a sentence. His energy sapped; he worked now, drove himself to browbeat her.

She nodded, in a glum agreement, then settled to stare him out.

'Thank you,' he said. 'Thank you, Hilda.'

She knew he was done for, was surprised he'd capitulated so easily. This setting was too grand, herself too remote or his excuse too specious for him completely to deploy his reserves. He cast his eye round, at the magnificence, first, of the marble mantelpiece, the one extravagance in this long room; cherubs lifted trumpets, baring small pot-bellies; fruits and bannerets intertwined, in a veined thickness of white, amongst sturdiness of upthrust pillars, under the weighty shadow of the cross-slat. Now his finger tested his chair-arm, as his eye placed, priced the *chaise-longue*, the three tables, the de Wint on an easel, the bust of Byron, the chandeliers, the gold frames, wide, crinkled, of mirrors and pictures. He looked at the naked flesh of the girls in the Alma-Tadema, their hair neat as Victoria's, and as straight, their dresses unnaturally dropped to their waists and the faint silver of water at their feet.

'I mustn't delay you any longer.'

She stood immediately; he followed suit.

'It's been delightful to see you again,' he said. As he came upright, he held out his hand. She shook, withdrew, stepped back. Her limp response was not what he'd anticipated, so that he stood, musing, mending the situation; she'd seen him thus in a staff-meeting when he'd been unexpectedly opposed. He seemed to be collecting the answer and yet by his very reasonableness to rebuke his tormentor. For all she knew, it might merely be a habit he'd acquired, and now carried over from public to private life.

'I don't really understand people like the Marcrofts.' He spoke disarmingly, blandly ingenuous. 'Their responsibilities are very great. In people and plant.'

It took her some seconds to understand the last word, but when she did she grinned.

'Edward says it's like running a fairly large business . . .'

'Does he now?' He'd not foreseen this answer either, or perhaps the mention of her husband's name flustered him. 'I suppose there's some truth in that.'

As he made for the door, he seemed dwarfed by the room, and yet she knew she hated him still. It was difficult to grasp that they had been man and wife, known secrets, shared chores, copulated, concocted plans, taken holidays, lived together. Hate had jammed down between them a barrier of thick plate-glass so that she could see him as one sees a tropical fish in an aquarium, unaware of its needs, its wishes, its limits of either knowledge or existence. He was in her home, a not unattractive man of forty-three, just younger than Edward, and she hearing the soft voice again, seeing the insidious presence, was galvanized into an energy of detestation. She did not approve of herself. She had no choice.

Through one door into the hall, through the next and heavier, and she stood outside with him in the chill, in the wild wind, the starlight. He donned his smart hat, a middle-aged man in a raincoat.

'I've enjoyed our talk,' he said. He'd invariably congratulated members of his staff who'd attacked him, before beginning to pay them out. 'You won't forget what I've said. You are badly needed there.'

She stood under the portico, not answering. She had done her bit.

'Good,' he said, 'good. This has been a profitable exchange.' He looked up. 'It's a beautiful night.' Sighing, sucking air through his teeth. 'I'm lonely sometimes.'

'Yes,' she said.

'Busy, and lonely.' The voice evinced no self-pity, was coldly clear as the sky. He waited; she allowed it, and then he raised his hat, strutted across the terrace towards his car, a new Cortina. Hilda rushed indoors, sat on a radiator by the window listening to his departure, trembling at herself. That man had treated her with cruelty, disdain; he had savaged her for his own pleasure when she had no defence. She felt the bruising soreness yet, the scalding pangs, the tears, the despair, and she heard the soft voice urging her to reason, to eschew infantile practice, to be a grown woman. She had thrown a cup and saucer at him, and, missing, had learnt her feebleness, her vulnerability, his spite. In this secure place for a few minutes she became the terrified girl who'd staggered from her marriage like a blind, wounded mole. Almost at once now she recovered, knew herself assured, a woman of consequence. Alan called to ask favours, and she did not encourage.

She was pleased, however, to find that when Edward returned he expressed his disapproval of the visit with warmth.

'We don't want that stupid sod here,' he said. 'I hope you choked him off.'

'He might have been here for exactly the reasons he gave.'

'Doubt it. He could have rung. Wanted to poke his nose in.'

'That as well.'

'Sometimes, Hilda, you act like a daft whore. You'll be inviting him up next.'

'And you don't want that?'

'I bloody well don't.'

She fussed him out of his short temper which derived as much from his conference and his flog up the motorway as from his disapproval of Alan. Later that evening, while they were watching television, he suddenly said,

'Gascoigne's not rational.'

'Do you think not?'

'I've never seen anything like those letters he wrote.'

'He feels deeply.'

'You think he's sane, then?' Gruffly.

'Yes. And two-faced. Clever. Cruel.'

Edward rasped the bristles on his face, rolling about slightly in his chair.

'Will he marry again?'

'I've not the remotest idea,' she said. True. She tried to consider the matter. His proposal to her did not now look sensible. For a man of his position, opportunities, ability to marry, almost at random, one of the young women on his staff seemed to argue some lack of balance, some emotional inadequacy in him. She said as much to Edward.

166

Again, the chin rubbing, the slumping lower into his chair.

'You're a bit of a bloody fool tonight,' he groused. 'You were, are, a very striking, an outstandingly striking young woman. Make no mistake. It's not surprising in the very least that he picked you out. He'd have been blind otherwise.'

'He wouldn't have made any such error appointing a deputy or a head of department.'

She knew he thought her right, that Alan Gascoigne was crippled emotionally, a baby reaching for the nearest bright bauble.

'I was surprised to see him here, though.'

'Don't encourage it.'

Now Edward sat glumly, jealous, she guessed, making hard work of his evening.

12

Hilda failed to reach Linda Lawrence by telephone, was told the girl had taken a few days' leave. She informed Jeremy by letter, but had no answer from him. When she complained to her husband, he was surprisingly unsympathetic.

'Don't interfere. That's my advice.'

'But he asked me to . . . '

'He's in Magdala Avenue now. He's access to a phone. He could ring you this minute if he wanted. But he doesn't. Leave it there.'

'These young people,' she argued, 'are embarrassed. They think they're occupying your time when they shouldn't.'

'I've no complaints about Jeremy. He's moderately sensible. But he doesn't take two steps to let you know where he is, or what he's up to. He'll tell you; he makes no secret of his goings-on, but only when you've put yourself out to ask.'

'That's what I should do.'

'Not if you take my advice, you won't. We can interfere too often. Let him get on with it, and he'll scream soon enough when he's hurt.'

'I'm worried, Edward.'

'Inquisitive.'

He spoke calmly, without anger, and yet with great force as if these few words of his represented hidden acres of volcanic experience. He conveyed his concern; it was not that he lacked interest, but that he warned her gently away from danger. She wondered how she could have reached such a conclusion; how does one tell whether or not a low-speaking, unfrowning man is deeply gripped with what he is about, or merely uninterested? Colour, perspiration, pulse-beat, movements of eye, head, hand, trunk? She had no relevant evidence to advance.

What she decided about Edward seemed a fiction, constructed from what she knew of his life. He'd married the right woman, an intelligent, lively bride from a suitable background who after a few years had changed, not quickly, into a nervously exhausted invalid unable to cope even with simple domestic duties. He'd forced himself, no, he'd willingly tried, to help; he'd supported, loved, struggled and she'd slipped away from him into hospital wards, periods of convalescent unease, the psychiatrists' couches, back again to hopeless, black despair and the futile swapping of drug for drug. She had staggered towards suicide, the one success of her middle-age. Edward, baffled, had stepped away from hope and compassion, had withdrawn into himself, had hardened his heart.

This was a pretty fancy, but how could he love her? He'd taken her in from Alan's mental assaults, had cherished her. The word just about described it, a quiet, middle-life loving, living, a watered glass of table wine. She looked across as he raised his whisky. Handsome, wonderfully composed, sad, uncertain, savouring the drink but incapable of any height or depth of feeling. That she wanted; somebody to allow her ease, to make no killing demands, to lag her in his money, insulated from trouble.

But he was now only a half-man. Alan, her first, was more vivid, more fierce, more alive.

At that vague statement, she ordered herself to have done. Such was nonsense, however served. This man sat sanely here, ruled three large businesses, made money for her comfort. But he did not want her to interfere with Jeremy, who was, she guessed, an extension of Anna, another imponderable, who might change, under the hands of firm love, for the worse. She'd begun again on her novelettish notions.

'I can't just sit,' she said.

'No?' He appeared to peer at her through his glass.

'I shall ring him up.'

'You do.'

'You were trying to stop me just now. Told me not to poke my nose in.'

'Yes, but I see I'm wasting my time.' Gentle, melancholic.

'Do you know what I was thinking, Edward?'

'No. No idea.' He put down his whisky, sat at sharp attention.

'I thought you'd intervened with Anna . . . ' She stopped, afraid now, brought to breathlessness by her presumption. She wished she could laugh at herself again. Intrepid Hilda.

'Go on.'

'And you'd done your best, and nothing came of it, and you'd opted out of interference.'

He shook his head.

'Nothing like it,' he answered, but he took the decanter and filled his glass to the brim, neatly and neat. 'When we were first married, I'd work twelve, fifteen hours out of the twenty-four, and be away for days on end. It didn't suit Anna, but it wasn't the cause of her, breakdown. She'd had trouble before. They hoped, that is her family, that marriage, a family, might cure her. It didn't. I tried to help her through, but I had no idea.'

'Didn't she improve?'

'Oh, yes. She had quite long periods when she could order meals, shop, see friends, go to church, but she invariably slipped again.'

'What was the basis? I mean didn't she see a psychiatrist?'

'Several. They uncovered matters. They helped sometimes.'

'So,' Hilda pursued, 'nobody really knows what was at bottom?'

'Some chemical imbalance. And they never came up with the right drug, if there was one. They'd perhaps do better now.'

'And you?'

He took a long sip at his whisky, crossed his legs, fingered his creases.

'When I think back now, I see there was nothing I could have done. I've not much to boast about. I left her to the experts. I took other women, and she knew. I may be deceiving myself, but I don't think it made much difference.'

'And Jeremy?'

'His babyhood coincided with one of her long, better periods. Then had a nanny. I put some time in on him. He went away to prep school.'

'And his mother? Did she ... ?'

'I don't know, Hilda. By the time he was ten or eleven she was very much of an invalid. She talked to him, sometimes. He was always nice to her. But she could ignore him for day on day. And sometimes she wasn't fit to be seen.'

'Did it worry him?'

'One doesn't know. I should say not. Took it all in his stride. I thought at one time he was considering doing medicine on this account, but it came to nothing.'

'Didn't he ever talk about his mother?'

'Yes. I made something of a point of it.' Edward ran his thumb-nail edge under his front teeth. 'I felt guilty. To some extent I do still. About Anna. Not about the boy. And so I tried to explain what was wrong with her. He used to listen solemnly enough. No idea what he . . . what effect it had.'

She moved across to him, put her arm round his shoulders. He sat still.

'You've never talked to me about this before,' she said.

'I find it,' he spoke slowly, prising words loose, 'profoundly depressing.'

'But why? You did nothing to reproach yourself with.'

'Even you don't believe that.' His voice scorned her. 'I could have done very much more, though it wouldn't have affected the issue.'

'Then, why do you . . . ?'

'My shortcomings, not hers. I got on with my life and left her to the nurses. It made not much difference, I think, but morally there's not a deal to be said in my favour. I tried at first, but not for long enough. That a beautiful woman should shatter herself as she did seems incomprehensible now, but it happened. I saw it with my own eyes. And I feel like death when I think about it.'

He stared moodily forward, shoulders sagging. She reached for, clasped his hand, which was, surprisingly to her, warm, comfortable. He did not return the pressure, but sat like a stranger. As she looked down, she knew the thick hair, brushed back with a dappling of grey above the ears, the wrinkling at the eyes, the eyebrows, the suit, its smell and his, the whisky, the well-kept hand she held and yet she could not get at him. He'd no resistance; he welcomed her advance, but he had been so much that she could not know about that now while he was sunk in reverie he was deaf and blind as a corpse to her love.

Suddenly he tugged on her arm, smiled bigly, stretched for his glass, drank. He nuzzled her breast.

'I took you on,' he said. 'I was frightened to death.'

That was adequate, a statement of return, resurrection.

'I shall ring him,' she said.

'You do.'

He pulled her on to his lap, and they wrestled in a half-hearted intimacy that led nowhere, but was itself lit with joy. That silliness pleased her often enough later when she remembered it; two scuffling adults who did not want sex but touched each other, touched and played for reality.

She did nothing about Jeremy for some days, hoping he'd contact her. She rang one Friday evening, found him in on Magdala Avenue. She explained she'd tried a second time to talk to Linda without success.

'Yes,' Jeremy said, sounding the s, stupendously polite.

'Did you write to her?'

'Ye'.'

'And didn't she answer?'

'No. A friend of hers telephoned me. Earlier this evening, in fact.' He giggled in embarrassment. 'One Susan Goddard.'

'Hadn't Linda come back?' He said nothing. 'From the leave?'

'She's made it up with her husband, this girl said. While she was with her family.'

'He took her back?'

'Presumably.' A tremor?

'I'm sorry, Jeremy. I really can't say how sorry I am.'
She stood in mindless misery, jaw loose over the mouth-
piece, and then recalled, had pushed into her mind, the
occasion when, as headmaster's wife, she'd rung the home
of one of the staff, expecting to find out from Mrs Phillips
how Hugo, the PE man, had fared in hospital over some
exploratory tests. Phillips himself had answered; he'd been
discharged from the ward that morning because his wife had
died, of a stroke, a brain haemorrhage in the night. Hilda
had rung Alan at once, and he'd ordered her to go round.
Phillips looked ghastly, face drawn, bunches of wiry hair in
the nostrils, coping with one of the neighbours who came
in to sit glumly with him. She had stayed until Hugo's
married daughter had arrived from Derby. She hadn't
known what to say; she doubted if there was any formula
that would have managed. She'd sat, drunk tea, floundered,
until she'd been relieved, and then her heart had leapt as
soon as the man had shown her to the door.

Now with Jeremy, knees weak, she must try.

'I am sorry,' she said again. 'It's awful for you.'

'Unnh?'

'Would you like to drive up here? For company?'

'No, thanks.'

'Shall I come down?'

'There's no need, thanks very much. I'm all right.'

'This is terrible, Jeremy. It really, it's dreadful. You must
feel . . . ' She'd no idea how he'd feel.

'No. I'm perfectly well, thank you.' The little gentleman.

'Did you have, y'know, any inkling that . . . ?'

'She'd left me? She said she wasn't coming back.'

'You've not heard from her?' She must continue to talk.

'No.'

'Only this Susan girl?'

'That's right. She said there were one or two things to
return. She, Susan, would handle that.'

'Linda's back here? At her job?'

'I don't know. No idea how much leave she had. Probably she is.'

'Jeremy, let me come round to see you.'

'Look, Hilda. I'm quite well. Makers is getting me all that I want. And I've a fair amount of work to finish.'

'It's not that. I'm inquisitive.'

He coughed, rather importantly as if giving himself the time to make his mind up, then laughed, voice steady enough.

'You win. As long as it's short. I've an essay to get done tonight.'

When Mrs Makepeace showed her into the study, Jeremy was writing. Yes, he told the housekeeper, they would have a cup of coffee.

'It's five past nine,' Hilda said. 'I'll go at half past.'

'I don't mind a break.' Smiles of peace.

'Tell me about it.'

'There's nothing to tell. Susan Goddard rang up at about six. She'd a message from Linda. She obviously knew all the story.'

'Was Linda with her while she was phoning?'

He glanced up in surprise as if the idea were new.

'Don't know.' Now he seemed disgusted, perhaps at her suggestion, or its implications.

'Were you surprised?' Probing healed, she hoped.

Again the shying. Why complicate simplicity?

'She said she wasn't coming back. She meant it, I thought.' He now made the effort. 'She went home and they persuaded her.' That strained his imagination, she guessed, unless he covered his hurts. They sat in silence. 'What does my father say?' The question caught her napping.

'He's away.'

'I see.'

Again an awkwardness of silence, until he slapped his knees, said crossly,

'Oh, come on, Makers, with that coffee.'

That was the first signal of distress. She'd reply.

'You are upset.'

'I don't know.' Sullen now.

'I think you should talk about it. And if not to me, then to Edward.' He snorted. 'Or one of your friends.' He pulled wry faces. 'No, Jeremy, it's no use bottling it up. You hardly know me, so you should get hold of somebody you can confide in.'

'It would have to be a beautiful woman like you.'

The pleasantry did nothing to convince her, so that she nagged all through the coffee and until she left at ten minutes to ten. Edward had arrived home in her absence, had read her note of explanation, but seemed comfortable in his slippers, inclined to rib her fears.

'The boy is capable of looking after himself.'

'He sat there, all buttoned up, with nobody to turn to. I feel so sorry.'

'He's twenty.'

'That's not very old. He needs looking after.'

'Makers will see to that. For the inner man.' She hated his cliché. 'He'll get over it. You know what I think, don't you? She wouldn't have been my choice for him, and so I can't say I'm sorry she's gone. I didn't interfere; it wouldn't have done any good. But now she's pulled out, it suits me.'

'But the boy?'

'He'll be sore, I expect. But he'll know when he's well off. My father was a hard man. He sent me to the university, right, but after that it was in at the bottom end of the works. And he didn't pay well. Even though I was married. Arthur Twells and I spread the business in all sorts of directions the old man wouldn't have thought of. Make or break. I don't know now whether it was good or bad, but it was efficient.'

She sat straight-backed and beautiful.

'I don't know whether you're certain or not,' she said.

'What's that mean?' Lazy as a cat in sunshine.

'You made quite a long speech. It's unlike you. I thought perhaps you were covering up.'

He shook his head.

'You should hear me at board meetings. I never stop. Still to please you, m'dear, I'll see the boy. Won't be tomorrow, but as soon as I can.'

Again she knew his consideration for her, his love, that in the ordinary commitments of daily life would only show itself in a lazy smile, a refusal to be angry, a promise to do exactly what she wanted after a token bluster of resistance. It was, however, nearly a week before he had time to make his word good. He fixed the appointment meticulously with Jeremy as with a business associate, and on the night, she noted with amusement, bathed and changed his suit. She waited up for him. He returned after an hour and a half, from which she deduced he'd spent perhaps forty minutes with his son.

'How did you get on?'

'Much as I expected.' He accepted his drink. 'First ten minutes nothing but grunts and ye', ye'. A little of that goes a long way with me. "I'm not here to listen to your monkey noises all night," I told him. "Hilda's sent me down to see that you're alive and not breaking your heart." '

'He'd like that.'

'He knows me. And he becomes rational straight away, even eloquent. He said he thought it was a damn' silly thing to part over, just moving house, and even odder that the girl slipped back so quickly to her husband.'

'Could he account for it?'

'We all proved too much for her. That's what he thinks.

"None of you wants me." She often said it, apparently. While we were all spreading good will thick as butter, she felt outside. Nobody loved her. Not even Jerry. He was one of us. The toffee-nosed bastards.'

'Did he say this?'

'You don't think I'm making it up, do you? He said it, and I think it's about right. She didn't feel in.'

'If he knew this,' she persisted, 'then why didn't he try to do something about it?'

'Yes,' he grinned, complacently. 'I even asked that one for you. He didn't think it was very important at the time. She complained about, well, a great deal, and so he didn't listen ever so carefully. Got out of the habit. I can understand it.'

'What about sex?'

'What about it? I didn't ask, and he didn't say. Sex to them is like, oh, a bottle of wine to me. A pleasure I can afford.'

'Having children,' she said, doggedly, determined to pin him down, 'is the most important thing we ever manage. They can't just dismiss it.'

'They can. They do. Contraception. Abortion. The world's changed.' She knew he was pulling her leg.

'Just like cheap plonk.'

'Not cheap. Or not of necessity. They probably practise more, learn the ins-and-outs, to coin a phrase. Any system has both drawbacks and advantages. He'll get over it. In fact he had arranged to take some young woman to a university ball. That doesn't look like a broken heart.'

'Might be. Or worse, he might be about to do something silly.'

'I'll risk it.'

He stressed the pronoun, dismissing her concern, but wary still, unwilling to commit himself too far in opposition.

13

Elizabeth Marcroft left a message that her husband had returned home, and demanded their company.

'How does he seem?' Hilda rang that evening.

'Changed.'

'He's very ill, then?'

'I don't want to talk about it on the telephone.' Face slapped.

'I'm sorry.'

They arranged a visit, but Edward was called to London. He spent more time on his business than he had for the past four or five years, but explained it away, claiming that this was a difficult period, that they were reorganizing and that decisions had to be made at the top. She believed him; Arthur Twells, the financial king, had called in person three times in the last month. Edward's line was ever mildly ironical. Just when he'd thought he could get out of the works, just when he'd really lost all interest, he'd been made to start again. Hilda, frightened, asked if the firm were in any danger. 'No,' he told her, 'we're swapping about to make money, not lose it.'

'But with all these financial crises,' she persisted.

'We've several options open. All the firms are thriving. There's plenty of scope even nowadays to make a bob or two. If we pulled in all our slack, you and I would still eat.'

'But the papers? And you're always . . .'

'I'm always grumbling. The government's feeble, but they won't bring us down. They don't exactly encourage my sort, don't give us any presents, if you know what I mean, but we don't need them. We're not shaping too badly.'

'Edward.'

He began to explain, and again she enjoyed the experience. True, she was quick enough to understand how many imponderables existed, but through his sobriety, his low-key exposition he spoke confidence. He did not boast, except about one or two of Twells's plans, but at the end of half an hour she thought she grasped, could explain to a third person, how, for example, the contracting firm could hold, expand its markets for the next five years, in spite of enemy action by home or foreign governments. She admired her husband most after these sessions, surprised that he did not recognize how much he had impressed her, and that it was only at her importunity that he'd bothered to talk at length. He was not a first-rate teacher, for he made no attempt to catch her interest; the material either was worth a hearing or not, and the hearer decided that. 'I'm not selling anything,' he said. 'There's plenty of that going on, I admit, but it's not my thing. We employ our smooth talkers.'

'I read in *The Times*,' she said, 'how a cabinet minister said his senior colleagues didn't know that a crisis was imminent. They made speeches about success, and expansion.'

'That doesn't surprise me.'

'But this man was clever, Edward. He'd been an Oxford don, and God knows what.'

'Politicians work in public, need to justify every step. In that chap's case, against a hostile press. We've been trained to our jobs. We make the changes, dictate them if you like, and we don't have to go kowtowing to every Tom, Dick and Harry to ask 'em if they approve.'

'You've got rivals.'

'Yes. But it's to their advantage to keep us busy.' He laughed at his paradox, her puzzlement.

Now she had a real husband, she felt. Alan had hawked his schemes around, even spouted on television about this educational advance or that notional advantage, but his arguments were bounded by, founded even on, enthusiasm, on some man's drive. With Edward she felt that money backed his empire, safes and great supporting ingots, so that if one accountant took his talents elsewhere the work would not crumble. Alan spoke fire-in-the-belly with consequent smoke; Edward toed the solid earth because it belonged to him.

She saw him off, then, warned him not to overwork.

Her lunch, on her own, prepared by herself, was a sad little affair, a prelude to a visit to Marcroft. The secretary greeted her with news that Elizabeth might be some time; she'd gone to see drainage works with the agent. The girl, a Mrs Tenby, made coffee, provided a large-armed chair in front of a fire, a pile of magazines, even a friendly Labrador bitch to give the effect of home comfort, but Hilda fretted. Elizabeth could have put her off. It seemed, she did not exaggerate for herself, that she was being tested, found fit or wanting for the ordeal. The vigil mortified her: she fumed as she failed to read; she fidgeted annoyed at the knock of Mrs Tenby's typewriter, her busy jaunts, her sociable enquiries.

She'd been waiting thirty-five minutes when Elizabeth burst in, flinging a broad-brimmed felt hat skimming into a corner.

'I didn't know what to do,' she said. 'Whether to put you off, or go with Bates.'

'Is he better?'

'Who?' Genuine, sharp surprise. Explosive.

'The agent. Mr Bates.' She ought to have meant William.

'Not really. He drags himself around.' The sharp tone suggested that he did so at her expense.

'And William?'

Now she screwed her face into an exasperated grimace. Bile.

'We'll go in and see him,' she said. 'He knows you're coming.'

For the next ten minutes Elizabeth feverishly sorted papers, hissed orders, cross-questioned Mrs Tenby, ungraciously, signed cheques. The whole exercise demonstrated evil temper, unnecessary hurry. Finally, she picked up the hat, folded it this way, that, in fury, slapped it like an ugly bird across her legs and told Hilda they'd go. She used the same imperious tone as to the secretary.

They clacked along passages, badly lighted, solid and whitewashed, all with flag-tiled floors, until they moved upstairs, stone first, then carpeted wooden on to a wide, pleasant landing with clear-glass, leaded windows through which one saw the damp branches of trees close by. Outside busy voices whispered and an attempt was made to start up some machine.

'This isn't his usual place,' Elizabeth snapped, pushing the heavy door open.

The end of the room, a large square place without pictures, had been screened off to make an office or dispensary, and there by the window and its radiator a uniformed nurse sat knitting, able presumably to keep an eye on the patient. She rose at once, laid her work down, skewering a needle through the ball of wool.

'He's asleep.' She made signs indicating silence, as if the visitors prepared to bawl. Elizabeth snorted annoyance, pushed round the screen towards the invalid. Hilda followed.

The room was unfurnished except for a double bed, one chair, one small table, and one slightly larger by the window on which stood a vase of yellow and white chrysanthemums. The effect was bare, shabby even, comfortless, though the air was warm. Carpet, coverlet, table runner, curtains did not match; here were articles for use.

The Earl almost sat asleep, propped up by pillows, his chin on his chest. His hair hung thin over a pale scalp as if he'd been shampooed a dozen times until all life had been shifted with the dirt, leaving these cleanly, sugar-spun strands. His hands with fingers, thumb-ends enlarged, were laid fragilely scrubbed, blood-empty and without health, in front of him.

'Does he have to sleep like that?' Elizabeth asked.

'No. He was sitting up when he dropped off.' The broad Nottinghamshire accent, up, did not conform with the uniform, the smartness.

'How has he been?'

'Oh, very quiet this morning. I told him you were bringing him a visitor. He seemed pleased. He's very weak, of course.' This she directed to Hilda.

'Yes.'

The nurse acknowledged the word, tinkered with the ends of the bed clothes. Marcroft stirred, groaning breathily.

'You've got visitors.' She massaged his arm gently. 'Come along. Wake up now. You've had a nice little sleep.'

The patient opened one eye, painfully, against gravity. Though Hilda had never undergone surgery, she imagined she would jack her lids up so, mouth gaping, as she came round from the anaesthetic after an operation where death was as likely as life. So she'd push open in dread, fearing in dazed sickness a chill world, this or the next. One eye first, shut, peering again, then both, small, squinting, bloodshot.

'It's her ladyship,' the nurse said, with a first reference to rank.

The pig's eyes gimleted about the room and he made some sort of sound of recognition, a phlegmy hack, barked.

The nurse was now at the pillows in a flurry of energy, pulling, pummelling, carefully propping the frail figure. Then she smoothed the lapels of his dressing gown, and flattened his hair with a flick or two of fingers.

'There you are,' she said. 'That's more like it.'

He moaned, and she darted down for a drinking vessel with a spout. He sucked weakly. She dabbed at his lips.

182

'If you'd like ten minutes off,' Lady Marcroft said, 'put the bell through to your room.'

The nurse nodded, quitted the room with thanks. Elizabeth sat side-saddle on the bed, motioning Hilda to the chair.

'Well, now. How do you feel now?' Though his eyes were open, he said nothing. 'Look who's come to visit you. Can you see who it is?'

His eyes dragged themselves in her direction as he inched his head round. He mumbled a monosyllable of assent.

'I said Hilda would come.' Elizabeth rammed the words at him, knives into a corpse. 'Did you have lunch?'

Again the breathy grumble.

'Good. The marrowbone soup was delicious.' Elizabeth talked, not exactly as to an imbecile, but fiercely, keeping him awake. She described the week's menus, the need for building him up, the doctor's orders, the nurse's duties. Under the shrill energy, Hilda guessed a kindness in desperation; here was a woman conjuring her husband back to life. Now she outlined the matters about the estate that needed attention, and once she even canvassed his opinion, about thinning Douglas's Wood. He snored through some answer to this, and it satisfied her so that she set off again, sharply with her information sorted, her schemes cut and dried. He paid little attention, precariously intent on keeping himself martyred upright. She continued, stressing that outside life ran on. In the end she stopped, lifted the hat she held by the brim with both hands, and sat, a puritan at prayer; she had to shrug to liven her body.

'You haven't said a word to Hilda.'

Marcroft turned now, wrinkled his face into a smile: he looked gaunt, so drained that she thought his skin might flake off in dryness.

'Thank you for coming.' That was clear; without power, but human.

'How are you, now?' She took his hand from the coverlet.

'Better.' He seemed surprised that he'd spoken.

'They're looking after you properly?' Her cheerfulness cracked false. He considered the question, and it seemed as if it were being answered by his whole body, as if the reply lifted, flooded upwards at slow pressure. His lips trembled in violence; his eyes glittered with tears, which spilt over as soon as he spoke.

'Everybody is so good.'

For some moments he cried, without sound, as if he'd no idea what was happening to him, before he weakly sought about with his hands. Elizabeth produced a handkerchief from a drawer, wiped his eyes.

'Don't upset yourself,' Hilda said.

He apologized in a voice not unlike that of every day, said he'd no strength, but when he repeated that people were good to him, again his face crumpled and tears were dashed from cheek to chest.

Neither Hilda nor Elizabeth showed embarrassment. William was old, sliced by the surgeons, full of strange blood, dizzy with weakness and drugs; it was not that he was nobody. The concentration camps, the torture chambers were full of men like him, screaming, battered, incontinent, willing to die, all the outward signs of manhood ripped off them, leaving raw, bloodied humanity. Inmates of cells in mental hospitals, the wired bodies in intensive care units were so reduced, but would totter out like Lazarus in time to make something of a show. A show.

To Hilda the whole world seemed at a standstill. Nobody moved or lived; no laws physical or social held. All froze, all congealed. Like the yokel in Theodore Powys's pub, the petrified universe announced: 'Time be stopped. Eternity be begun.' The chasm of silence was inside herself as she recognized, in no time, and soon the voices from the yard,

184

below the shining branches, edged back. William finger-ended the sheet, cautiously coughed. Elizabeth crossed her trousered legs, flapped the hat like a black bat rising.

They stayed perhaps half an hour longer and in that time Marcroft spoke six times. His wife drummed with energy, voice soaring and plummeting, eyes and mouth electric. She ordered, counted, judged, encouraged. Now and then Hilda intervened with a sentence or two, once at length to tell them Edward's views of labour relations and her own gloss on them. Elizabeth was not grateful for the relief: she was like a concert pianist on a breakneck encore, rippling out the seconds. The performance was superb, practised and dazzling, but the only audience was the half-listening Hilda, the half-living William.

They rang for the nurse, who thanked them. Goodbyes were curt. William, hand in Hilda's, whispered to her to come again, and the visitors were back in the corridors. Not until they reached the office, which stood empty, the type-writer covered, did Elizabeth speak.

'Well?' She threw the word.

'Is he going to get better?'

'They say so. They've removed a lung. He'll be an invalid.'

'Won't he be able to drive his cars?' Important, crucial.

'Yes. He will.' She dashed the hat on to a peg. 'He's lucky. The other's unaffected.'

'He seems very weak.'

'You should see the scar. It's a cruel wound.' Unlike herself, Elizabeth outed the adjective.

'Has Mrs Tenby gone?'

'I should think so.' Elizabeth consulted her wrist-watch.

The door was flung open, and a young man burst in, smiling. He shifted his top-coat, whirled it on to a peg, wished them a forceful good afternoon.

'Hello, Mother. Thought you'd still be down. How's Dad?' The heir, Lord Ravenshead.

'What are you doing here?'

'They gave me an hour or two off to visit my father.'

'You're not dodging work again?'

'How could you suggest such a thing?'

He threw a comical, huge smile at Hilda. A tall boy, with his black hair oiled smoothly old-fashioned on top, though long in the neck, he wore a bushy beard which contrasted with the excellent whiteness of his teeth. His mother re-introduced Hilda, who'd met him once before, briefly described his father's condition, asked how long he was staying. He sprang for the kettle, dashed outside to fill it, plugged it in, and sat down.

'We'll have a cup,' he said.

'Tea will be made upstairs.'

'We'll do it down here. Pinch a few of Phyllis's biscuits. Nip up and see the dad, and then back to my studies.'

His mother shook her head ruefully, like any old street-corner mum at the mischief of her child, and lifted down the biscuit tin.

'Your father will be glad to see you.'

'Uh. Cheer up a bit. You as well.'

'I'm cheerful enough.'

He came across, slapped his hands on her hips, made as if to lift her.

'None of your horse-play, now.' But she enjoyed it, as he chaffed her, set out the cups for him, allowed him to pour. He explained there'd been a football match that afternoon, from which he'd truanted to get some work done, and then had dashed out. He'd all his mother's energy, and with a charm she lacked. It was not exactly the common touch, his accent, she noted, was high public-school, but a deter-mination to show interest, to make his concerns subservient to those of his listeners. His attitude to his mother was assured; he had no fear of her, pulled her leg, but gave the impression that he'd taken careful note of everything she said. When she described her visit with the agent to the drainage scheme, he not only asked questions, he asked them from knowledge. He wasn't exactly confident that Bates and his calculations were correct, and the ding-dong catechism was beautifully, forcibly put and answered. Hilda took delight in the drive of these two, and was enthralled when, at the whistling of the kettle, they apologized for boring her with technical matters.

'I've not enjoyed an argument so much for heaven knows how long.'

They handed her a cup, in modesty, and Tom turned a pretty compliment about her kindness. He drank his tea with the same *élan*, dipping his biscuits, commenting on his mother's unusual silence. He then turned his full attention on Hilda, as he poured his second cup of tea; he must have drunk the first boiling.

'How's Jeremy?'

She answered noncommittally.

'There's a fellow to admire,' he said. 'He settles down to that botany or physiology or whatever it is he's doing as if nothing else matters in the world.'

'Is that good?'

She could not help smiling at his verve.

'It's what he's supposed to be on with now, so he's right to concentrate. But surely he'll join his father? And forget his flora and fauna?'

'So he really lacks judgement?' she said, wanting to stretch herself in opposition.

'No. Matter of temperament. I've done moderately badly at exams so far. I may be wrong but I don't attribute this to brainlessness at all.' Elizabeth tutted. 'I've always had other things to do.' He smiled openly, like a film-star naval commander. 'Now, the stuff we learn in the agric department has some connection with the, the estates.' The hesitation attracted. 'I'm doing better. Not that the lecturers are much cop, but they show you one or two ways round problems I shall need to look at myself, one day. I can see the sense of that. Mark you,' again the brilliance of teeth, 'I'd do better to go around with old Bates. He's got the responsibility. He can't just say, "We've this alternative or that." He must make his mind up and get on with it.'

'I don't see Bates quite like that,' his mother said, drily. 'He can decide.'

'Within reason.' They left it there, as if to be argued at length some more convenient time.

'Of course,' Ravenshead said, 'my mother's quite right to put me out. We see other estates. We study other schemes. If I learnt at home, there'd be a big danger I'd just continue in the same old pattern. Very conservative, landowners, y'know.'

'I see.' Hilda wanted him to go on.

'My father read history at Oxford. It bored him. And he wasn't interested very much in the gay life. The grand-parents were tartars, and the old man never recovered from 'em. Reminds me. I'll nip up and see how he's getting over the surgeons.'

He was off and out, leaving a chair askew, a cup empty.

Hilda congratulated his mother, who said,

'He's improving. Never used his head at school, but now he's started.'

'He's very good-looking.'

'The girls seem to think so.'

Elizabeth praised him, but hedging all with cautions. He'd only do what he wanted; he could be obstinate; he didn't see eye to eye at all with his father.

'But he's come home to visit him?'

'I'm surprised, really.'

Until Tom came down, Elizabeth acted without social

grace, flicking through a file, pencilling a note, once looking up a telephone number. Ravenshead entered rather soberly, commented optimistically on his father's progress, and then said to Hilda,

'Last time I saw Jeremy, he told me a curious thing.'

'What was that?'

'That birds have regional accents.'

'Birds?'

'Is this a riddle?' Elizabeth asked.

'A blackbird or thrush from Yorkshire will sing differently from a Gloucestershire one, and yet quite like another from his own county. Odd, isn't it?'

'I'd say it would be next to impossible for a human being to test,' Hilda said.

'I don't think they do it by ear,' he said. 'Electronic machines. Wiggles on a screen.'

'Worse.'

They laughed; Hilda left. Now she walked to the car, accompanied by mother and son, greatly cheered. The human race progressed. A handsome young man supported, usurped, succeeded a decrepit father. She drove faster than usual in her excitement, braked sharply in a village as a black shadow thrust into her headlights, drew into the side of the road, trembling. But as she sat, leaning on the wheel, she felt her warm gust for life through the temporary discomfort. She had learnt; she knew. Yet she shook with fright when a dog had crossed her path and she'd had to brake fiercely.

As soon as the physical twinges at her fast reaction died, she was able to summarize. The present discomfort, real, with a real cause, could not hide her sense of well-being. She sat, shaken, but convinced. She did not immediately move, deliberately called up disclaimers, objections, trying to nudge herself back to pessimistic agnosticism. She did it well enough to succeed. There was little joy left, few traces of her previous happiness. She did not forget, allowing herself the luxury to think she had momentarily deceived herself and received due warning. That was grudging, and safe.

It would be sufficient.

14

Hilda spent some time explaining to Edward how impressed she had been by Tom Ravenshead.

His agreement was, as she expected, qualified.

'If I've got you right,' he said, 'you're comparing him favourably with Jeremy.'

'That's very intelligent,' she answered.

He grinned, pleased.

'He's not without brains, and he's considerable personal magnetism, but I wonder sometimes what sort of a sticker he is.'

'Sticker?'

'Jeremy's clever. He doesn't give up, either. That's why I'm willing to have him in the firm. He's young for his years now. I know you're surprised to hear me say so. That's why I want him at the university. Just to get older.'

'He can do that anywhere.'

'Yes. Yes. But I'm not having him do it with us. He's sharp enough to pick up our drill at any time, and it'll be better if he does so when he's a bit more experienced. It doesn't do for kids to handle men.'

'Oh, oh.'

He laughed again.

'That's what it is. Compromise, compromise. Carrot and stick.'

'And Tom would be no good?'

'He'd be good for six months, if I have him properly taped. But he'd be bored when Jeremy was still unravelling it all. That's what. I'm going out to the Dukeries complex some time. Fancy a trip?'

It was not, however, until after Christmas that they travelled twenty-six miles to the new town the firm was building. They walked round in gumboots, supped tea in warm, well-lighted huts, where Hilda listened to colloquies she failed to understand. In the end a young architect took her off to see a shopping centre while her husband held some sort of conference.

She grew excited then bored as she clumped up and down unrailed stairways among the huge concrete half-darknesses. The young man believed in his boss, his work, almost naively, praising every feature. When she made fun of him suggesting that the place was like every other concrete palace put up in the last twenty years, he marched her, talking volubly, to an office where he unleashed a folder full of plans and with stabbing finger pointed out original touches, unique designs. As she was not convinced, he argued the harder, but this time from the architects' picture, his own work, where the centre shone under an April sky, and small trees, cars, hurrying humans made one glad of the stern straight planes of the design. He almost genuflected before a piece of sculpture which squatted in the forecourt. It seemed like an octopus, flattened, an uncouth jam butty inside its circle of pink stones.

'Is that done?' she asked.

'Yes.' He dragged down a smaller file, displayed photographs of the work which now seemed like a disintegrating sphere. This young man, he'd be thirty, with his pointed face and his eyes appealing to her through comically large glasses, demanded her admiration not for himself but for the grandeur, the imagination of his principal. She could not give it; overwhelmed by the technical resource of the builders, she stood for minutes watching a crane hoist enormous girders, ginger with rust. Surprised by the economy in manpower, a bare dozen and a half spidered it over any one site, she said nothing for the beauty of the place. It impressed; it was huge. She supposed the same could be said of the pyramids. Size is god. She noncommittally soothed her guide, and he packed away his folders, shot long cuffs, exchanged a few bluff words for her benefit with the clerk of the works and the site foreman and led her back, dodging the clayey puddles, to where Edward waited.

Again, the group royally welcomed her, and she noticed that once more they made the curious piece of sculpture the nub of conversation. That was fine art, the one piece, and she, a woman, she deduced, would intuitively interest herself in such matters. But what they spoke of, these men of affairs, was the difficulty of transporting and placing so huge a piece, not its visual or tactile satisfactions. If by chance some cloth-headed underling settled the thing the wrong way round or even, she suspected, upside down, they wouldn't have noticed, or cared. Neither, in honesty, would she.

Edward, though affable with a mug of tea in his hand, seemed in a hurry to leave. Nobody pressed him to change his mind.

'What do you think?' he asked, as they drove from rutted mud to concrete road.

'Bloody awful,' she said.

'Why?'

'Would you live there?'

'Yes, I would.'

He added no more; she believed him. As long as he was warmly comfortable, had room for his armchair, desk and cocktail cabinet he wouldn't complain. They said nothing

until after fifteen miles he turned off the main road, muttering, 'I've always promised myself a look down here.'

'Where's this lead?'

'Clipstone. My great-grandfather's cottage.'

They drove along a country road, unwidened, with
ribbon building on both sides, detached suburban from
thirty-eight, a tin ramshackle from the twenties, but mostly
semis and link houses of the last ten years. Behind, at one
place, a colliery headstock towered over its tips of rubble.
They passed through what might have been a section of a
corporation housing estate in a large town, and now ran
past open fields, flat, straw-pale, reedy. As they reached,
left behind a factory, a newish, glassy affair on both sides
of the road, Edward slowed.

'Hereabouts,' he said.

They drew up under the tall arch of a viaduct, in slate-
blue bricks, which crossed the valley. Below the road they
could see the grey meandering of a small river. Twice it
looped through the bridges. Edward helped his wife over
the fence.

'Are we allowed here?' she asked.

'I own the land.'

The ground struck damp under their boots and once they
jumped a shallow stream, brown and oil-stained. The viaduct crossed the low land magnificently, spanning two roads
and a railway as well as the river before running out either
side into an embankment, furred with the same pale grass
as the flat. In the low winter light the bridge stood both
solidly and delicate, high-arched, straight as a die, with the
spring of metal in its dark structure. Edward pointed to a
clump of buildings over to the right.

'Used to be a lake.'

'Lake?'

'Pond, then. Skated there as a boy. Bulldozer squares
it up in no time.' To the left perhaps a mile away were raw

houses, with chimney smoke straight in the still afternoon. Ahead a large sun burst bloodily from rags of cloud, blackening the arches, spraying wet grass tips with gilt.

They were making towards a stone cottage, not twenty yards from the viaduct.

'Is that it?' she asked, uncomfortably. Now footsteps splashed.

'Yes.'

'It'd be flooded half the winter.'

'Actually it's built on a little rise, an outcrop. Would be damp, though.'

They crossed a stream, by a step, squeezed between two pillars of brick which had crumbled to pencil shape.

'The garden gate?' she demanded.

'End of a bridge, I'd guess.'

There was no sign of a path to the door-hole and inside patches of weed sprouted on the edges of the floors. The house gaped; even roof beams had gone, but the walls were solid, well-cut squared blocks, differing in size, of the local yellow limestone. Even where the mortar had fallen out, the rock seemed settled, immovable.

'Two up, two down,' he said. 'Seven children survived.'

'When did they live here?'

'My great-grandfather was born in 1850, so he'd be here in the seventies.'

'Is that when the cottage was built?'

'Oh, no. Earlier than that. Might be eighteenth century.'

'Why did they build it in a place like this?'

'No idea. Perhaps the land went cheap, or the occupant was employed on the water-meadows. Then, as soon as the Industrial Revolution started, they knocked up all sorts of little concerns along the river.'

'As mills?'

'Not water mills. Too sluggish. Bleaching, dyeing, hosiery. That's how my great-grandfather made his first money. In

194

partnership on the other side of the village.' He pointed southwards. 'Then he began the building firm.'

'When did he die?'

'Early nineteen hundreds. 03, I think.'

'And he'd made his fortune?'

'Hardly that. But he'd left two growing concerns for my grandfather to work on.'

He plucked at the feathery weed growing by the wall, rubbed the leaf between his fingers.

'Smell,' he said.

A bitter, herbal scent like rue.

Some of the plaster had fallen from the wall, and that remaining was brown-stained without trace of wall-paper or paint. The little wood surviving from the window-frames had crumpled into blackness. The floor, though uneven, was solid with, here and there, red tiles left intact but discoloured.

'It's so small,' she said. 'For nine people.'

'They'd be out, I reckon, by the time they'd reached that number. But this is the house William Fielding brought his bride to.'

She liked the word 'bride'; it hinted at history, at a different people, absorbed and industrious, growing rich on bread and water, on prayer. Inside the walls all was shadowed though beyond the gaping windows the red sun brightened wet land. Behind, the viaduct towered, a master-piece of beautifully intricate brickwork above the hump of the house below.

'When was that built?' she asked.

'Late nineties, early nineteen hundreds, I guess.'

'Your grandfather had gone?'

'Oh, yes.' Oh, yes? 'He was up in Ravenscroft Villa, then.'

'What was your great-grandmother like?'

'Go-getter. Pushed him. Constantly shifting him into better houses. Read the Bible; worked round the clock. I must have seen her, though I can't remember her at all.'

Edward spoke away from her, staring up into the black holes of the beams, hands deep in pockets. He seemed shrivelled inside his top-coat as if this visit had reduced him, warned him that this ruin measured the worth of the Fieldings. She shivered.

'When did the last people live here?'

'In the twenties.'

Fifty years derelict, then.

'It ought to be pulled down,' she said.

He shrugged from his reverie, gently slapped his palm on the wall.

'Well built. Won't collapse, this. In a picturesque spot, it'd be worth doing up. But it'll go when I sell the land.'

'Is that likely?'

'Oh, yes. Quite a valuable site.'

The Fieldings had prospered, but not lived long. Edward, Jeremy, two aunts, three cousins made up the tally now. Energetic, competitive, they'd died off in their prime, with leisure unsampled, sweating all the way to the grave. She looked at her husband, noticing his pallor, the pinched delicate nostrils, the fragility of face that his breadth of shoulder denied. He was forty-five now. How long would she have him? A cold depression undermined her life. In distraction.

'I wonder what they said when they first came?' She made herself speak, to clear away superstitious fear.

'I wonder what we said when we were first married?'

That rang harshly, as if he'd no notion of her dread. He was tapping gingerly at a tumbled stone with the toe of his shoe.

'We lived together, first.' She repaid unkindness.

'When you first came to Rempstone, then?' He should have kept his mouth shut.

'I don't remember.' Miserably.

They returned to their silence; she mooched into the far

room. Smaller still; no cleaner; the fireplace ripped wide open, oven gone. On the floor a few charred sticks where children had recently warmed themselves. They must have brought the twigs in with them; no tree grew here-abouts.

Outside, faintly an ambulance hooted its double warning.

She stood still, a casualty, waiting. Nothing happened. No graffiti cheered the bare wall, not an initial. She moved to the window, listened for the sounds of the river. There was none. No wind shifted the pale grass. The sky, slightly misted, stretched a blanched blue; the only clouds lay over to the west, flat on the horizon. They could expect a frost. She imagined this place under occupation on such a day, the fire bright between boiler and blackleaded oven, the deal table, the one worn rug, the bunch of bodies, the aroma of potatoes, of watery stew. His people.

Try as she could she made no connection between her husband and these his imagined ancestors. He stood too large; they crouched as dwarfs, as they needed to in this hole. A dog, black and thin, raced solemnly over the flat land, loping away for no reason, silently beating out his course.

'Are you ready, Hilda?'

The polite, standard accent where his forebears had bawled broad. She looked again at the damp fields, the great blue-black spans of the viaduct, at the four walls, and walked back obediently.

'Yes.'

His right glove was off, held in the left, and he sucked his, bit on his, thumbnail. The babyish pose spoke his puzzlement.

'Cheer up,' she said. 'For heaven's sake.'

'We're not dead yet.'

She gulped at his sentence, his death-sentence. Without hurry he took an arm to lead her out. They recrossed the stream; he felt for her hand, beginning to hurry, jerking her along.

'I'm not going to run,' she said.

'You'll do as you are told.'

He eased off so that they approached the fence by their car soberly.

'Over you go.'

She turned, once across to lean on the wooden cross-bar, looked back at the cottage which stood black against the low brightness of the sky behind it. The sun had gone; mist seemed to seep upwards from the sodden soil. He bent by her, face on hand, comfortably eyeing the darkness.

'This fence is wet,' he warned. 'Stain your coat.'

She smiled, ran a small hand along his upper arm.

'Not much of a place,' he said.

'Have you never been here before?'

'No. I've passed it on the road times enough. My grand-father had a factory further back. That's where we came to skate.'

'It's been derelict too long.'

He scratched his neck, holding his head back, so that he looked fierce, predatory as an eagle.

Inside the car, she sat warmly as her husband pressed for home, through the industrial town, on to the ring-road, the motorway, then quietly into Rempstone along a dark-ened lane. She left silently, upstairs to a bath. Lying in comfort she could not melt the ice of the cottage from her veins. She despised herself, did not feel superior, but flinched from that God-forsaken square of walls, the damp, the sluggish stream, the pale grass. She had no right to flaunt herself there, nor had she done so. She had stood by her husband, and dreaded neither the consequences, nor the past. It was as if the chill dampness of the place had blemished her. It should cheer, sustain that the energetic great-grandfather had burst out of a slum; she imagined the man giving orders, standing his ground, taking risks to benefit the sharp wife who, prayed, goaded, outlived him to enjoy the affluence he'd founded. No. People passed constricted, crippled lives under great bridges, palpitating railways, and died in pain, not escaping as the goods wagons clashed and lumbered past above. Warmly comfortable, she walked downstairs discomfited still.

Edward poured her a cup of tea.

'You're late. Bath too pleasant?' He still wore, she noticed, trousers with a mud-streak on one knee.

She began to explain how she felt.

'I understand it,' he said. 'I understand it.'

'Did you . . . ?'

'No.' He interrupted. 'An interesting quarter of an hour. I'm bothering about what those boys told me up at the site.'

'Something bad?'

'No, not really. Very minor, in fact. But I hadn't thought of the possibility. Narks me.'

'So all the time we were down by the cottage, you . . . '

'Yes. Telling myself what a bloody fool I was.'

'You didn't say anything.'

'I don't want to advertise it, do I, now?'

They sipped; windows were curtained against the frozen stars.

'And you've got over it?' she asked.

'Yes, yes. It's nothing.'

'I'm pleased . . . for you.'

He looked up, surprised, curled his lip and went back to contemplation of his slippers. Idly, without result, he brushed with his fingers at the mud-stain, then more carefully scraped with a nail.

'Tell you what,' he said suddenly. 'We'll visit Jeremy this evening.'

'Ring him first.'

'Right.' He glanced at his watch. 'Too early yet.' He waved the teapot. 'You recovered?'

'I can't account for myself. It's silly. There are plenty of people I know with illness and tragedy on their backs, and I ...'

'Understandable.'

'You've said that before. I don't understand it.'

'Temper, temper.'

'Ichabod,' she said.

'Oh, yes?'

She did not trouble herself to explain.

Two people had said words, but had skirted reality. Both had been found wanting, though trivially, marginally. Neither liked it.

15

Elizabeth Marcroft called, brogue-shod, slapping leather gloves.

'I'd like you to come up and see him,' she said, when Hilda inquired after her husband.

'I thought he was better?'

'He is.' Elizabeth stretched her legs straight. 'He's fallen in love.'

The voice croaked, killing humour.

'The nurse. The day-nurse. Do you remember her? Stocky girl? It's quite an idyll.'

'I see.'

'His eyes follow her everywhere. They sit holding hands.'

'He's up, then?'

'In his room, yes.'

'I imagine,' Hilda ventured, 'that it's not surprising. He must be weak, and that makes one susceptible. If I read some rubbishy novel when I'm recovering from a cold, I weep by the bucketful. Is she nice to him?'

'Yes. And efficient.'

Again Hilda sat back, in need of explanation.

'You find it ridiculous?'

'No,' Elizabeth snapped.

'Why do you want me to see him, then?'

'I don't think he wants to get out of that room. It's his world. He and his Susan. He's no responsibility. Neither has she, for that matter, now he's so much better.'

'How does . . . does the girl . . . ? Does she know?'

'She's as bad as he is.'

They both thought that one out.

'How old is William?' Hilda asked.

'Sixty-two next.'

'And the girl?'

'Twenties. Twenty-five.'

'Married?'

'Yes. Her husband works in one of the factories in Ripley. They've no family.'

Now Elizabeth sat still as a stone, hands crossed on the gloves on her lap. She seemed to be trying to recall some quotation, some tune to whistle, not displeased, convinced that the errant phrase would soon be tracked down.

'Is it serious?' Hilda asked.

'What's that mean?'

'Has any misconduct taken place?'

'If you mean "Have they had sex?", then I'd say, "No." He's pretty seriously incapacitated. But if you mean, "Has he pushed his hand up her skirt?" then I'd say he has. She, of course, until recently has done everything for him.'

'Do you mind?'

'I can't tell. That's why I want you to come up and see

him. I want some outsider to have a look at him, and tell me what's happening. He's very happy, I'm sure of that.'

'And doesn't feel guilty?'

'No idea.'

'You want it stopped. Is that it? Is it?'

'I can't even answer that. I think I rather approve now, so long as it's kept within bounds. I don't want him to do anything foolish.'

'That's likely, is it?'

Elizabeth shrugged, smiled, stood up and poked at her hair in a looking-glass. Hilda promised to call on the next day.

'I oughtn't to ask you this, but please don't say anything to Edward, will you?'

'No.'

'You would have told him?'

'Yes.'

When Hilda arrived at Marcroft Hall she found the Countess ready for her. A few military orders to the secretary and they moved into the corridors, to wait on the landing by a window overlooking bare trees. The grass below stretched bright green, spring-like round the paths swept clear of leaves.

'I don't know why I have to worry you.' Elizabeth had taken Hilda's arm. 'As soon as I came back yesterday, I knew I'd done wrong. You can't do anything.'

'We don't go in, then?'

Elizabeth took her hand, caressed it.

'Now you're here I suppose you might as well.'

'Now, look . . . '

'No. We'll see. We might just manage something.' She disengaged herself, walked to the door, rapped, waited without expression, for decorum, perhaps, to be re-established inside.

William sat, in his dressing gown, at a window. The room

smelt hot, not medically, nor stuffy, merely as though the radiators danced with heat, and flowers wilted on their stalks. The nurse, with her back to the patient on the other side of the room, busied herself with a bottle.

'Tablet time,' she called.

The Earl eased himself round. Hilda had expected some remarkable change in him and so was taken aback by the puffy ugliness, the small eyes. He greeted them gruffly, drew himself upright in his chair, held a hand out. The nurse waited, with tablet and glass.

'Here we are, then,' she said.

The capsule lay on a plate, two-coloured on one whiteness. He took it, shoved it in, gulped, coughed, muttered thanks. She stood still, hand ready for the tumbler.

'Thank you, Susan.'

'Shall I . . . ?' she asked Lady Marcroft.

'No. We shan't be a few minutes, Mrs Pennington. Unless you . . . '

The nurse sat on the chair furthest from the patient, scrabbling in a large paper bag for her knitting. He seemed intent on the world outside. On inquiry he briefly described the improvement of his condition, asked after her health and Edward's, snuffled, sighed, rearranged his hair with the left hand.

Hilda drew a chair towards him.

First, rushing at it, she questioned him again on his health, persisted, bullied him into a full account of the operation, the present treatment, the visit of the physiotherapist, exercises. Truthfully, he was not averse to answering at length, so that she felt no compunction when she pressed him about his feelings as he was wheeled into the theatre, as he came round. Here he was less comfortable; the other he'd been through before, heard it in the jargon of surgeons, but nobody had asked him to reveal himself. Inside a few moments, Hilda had convinced herself that he did not know the answers, had never tried even to remember, let alone seal into words. His red-rimmed eyes darted from the lizard-skin; he fingernailed his moustache, hauled at his dressing gown.

By this time, in their first stretch of silence, Hilda had become aware that Lady Marcroft, in full whispering spate, ushered Nurse Pennington from the room. William directed glowering attention entirely to that exercise.

As the door snapped shut, he set his face, glared out of the window. Hilda asked him what the trees were along the drive. If he heard, he did not answer.

Without warning, he jerked round, shifting his chair an inch or two.

'What's the idea?' The question was unclear, phlegmy major-general. Hilda signalled incomprehension. 'Taking her out, like that.'

'I don't know.'

'She's talked to you, hasn't she?' He combined military gruffness with petulance.

'Yes. Of course.'

He expected evasion, was taken aback.

'What's she say?'

'She's pleased that you're recovering so well.'

Now, he lowered his head, thrusting it forward from his shoulders. His eyes lacked life, hatefully dull.

'You've been told to ask about Susan, haven't you.' The voice, no louder, carried authority. Hilda prepared resistance.

'You tell me,' she said.

'She thinks there's something between us, doesn't she? Between Susan and me?'

'Is there?'

'She's said as much to you, hasn't she?'

'Yes.'

'What do you think?' His eyes clustered with tears,

204

lustrous. He begged, she thought, for her approval, or a
word of encouragement.

'It's true, then,' she said, betraying him, herself.

'Tell me what you think.' Voice rose; a trill of hysteria
quickened, but he sat squat in his chair, lumpy hands
crossed on his stomach.

'What I say won't be much use,' Hilda began. 'There's
a big difference in age. Even bigger in social status. Special
circumstances have thrown you together. She's an attractive young woman in a healthy sort of way. But as soon as
you're up and about, as soon as you start making social
contacts you'll know how, how impossible it all is.'

'That's your opinion.'

'You've been ill. When you're well you'll see matters in a
different light.'

'Is that all?'

The last was in a hoarse whisper. She saw the hair at the
back of his head, thick, coarse, untidy.

'I can tell you,' she said, speaking like a schoolmistress,
'what commonsense dictates. Elizabeth hasn't asked me to.
She wanted me to look at you. Perhaps she expected you to
talk.'

'She was right then.' He drew back from his window,
clutched his thigh in a big left hand. 'I've enjoyed having a
young woman's arms round me.' A flash of devil crooked his
face. 'Do you blame me?'

'What about her husband?'

'Forgotten. While she's in here. Never mentioned.'

'Outside?'

'Outside?' He echoed the word.

'At home. She still lives with him, doesn't she? Acts as
his wife.'

'I presume so.' Aggressive, as if he knew life.

'I see.' She folded her hands in her lap, and occupied
herself in smiling towards the window. He rattled his false

teeth, pushed a cushion about under him. Ill-temper demonstrated his weakness. If he could have flung himself at her,
he would. 'He deserves some consideration.' Silence.

'Come on, then. Come on. Out with it.' He might have
been addressing a gardener. Or a dog. She continued to
ignore him pleasantly. 'I'm a fool, aren't I?'

Slowly, as if with reluctance, she refocussed her attention
on him.

'What about the young woman, Susan?' she asked.

He pulled at his chin.

'When you're well enough to move about,' she continued,
'she'll be given a leaving present, and that will be expected
to be that. How will she feel.'

He nodded, not concerned.

'You've enjoyed this,' she went on. 'It's a bonus. You
recover from a serious operation, and find an attractive
young woman attracted to you, touching you. It's good. It
feels good.'

'Why shouldn't I please myself, for once?'

'Your position.'

His big hands hung together. She felt no aptitude for
her role.

'You lived with your husband before you were married.'

His tone neither accused nor hinted childish tit-for-tat,
seemed explanatory.

'I was desperately unhappy with my first husband.'

'Yes.'

The single word touched her; sad, understanding
sadness.

'Is that how you are?' she asked, laying a hand on his.

'When you get to my age, you can expect nothing else.
Elizabeth's a lively woman. You know how it is. She can
organize, run the estates and houses. Apart from that, and
there's not much else, she goes her own way. I don't suppose
I was ever very attractive to her, physically. She's indepen-

dent, and headstrong.' He removed his hand grudgingly from under hers. 'No. Privately she is. In her public capacity, she's admirable.'

Now, chin spread on his chest, he seemed worn out.

'You and Edward get on well?' he said, in the end.

'I'm happy now.'

'You're lucky. You've not been married long?'

She thought about that.

'I was nearly off my head in my first marriage. And I didn't have the strength or wit to escape. I ran to Edward. It was almost by chance. I'm amazed now. It was as if it were pre-ordained it seemed so unlikely.' They sat unspeaking again, watching trees in winter light. 'Then, his wife, well, was alive. He intended to divorce her. I felt guilty, and I suppose he did. I don't know, though. He'd had such a battering. I tell you, I didn't realize that for long enough. And I had. So we were cautious. Didn't give too much away.' She stopped, gulped, looked about for something to handle, to touch. 'We're still like that. Groping.'

Now he nodded.

'As soon as I start saying these things,' she began, 'I see they're silly. It's not like that in the slightest. It's more complicated. I'd say I was settled, and content.'

'You could fall violently for some other person?' Each word coughed out separately.

'I think I'm in love with Edward. I'm sure of it.'

'Aagh. Does it solve my problem?'

'What are you going to do?'

'God knows. I'd like to keep her here.'

'She wouldn't?'

'I don't honestly know. There isn't any discussion with us. We don't use reason. We touch each other, and say we love, and enjoy that.' He was near tears again.

'And she's . . . ?'

He brushed his face with a large handkerchief he had

pulled from the pocket of his dressing gown. After a moment he collected himself, apologized.

'You'll have to forgive me. I can't keep it back. Everything seems too much, and it bursts out.'

'Never mind.'

He mopped his face again, as his lips quivered.

'I love her, Hilda. Honestly I love her, as I never did Elizabeth.'

'Is this the first time?'

'Yes. For years. I thought it didn't matter. I'm like a young man. Not physically. I'm weak. It's the, the love I feel.'

'You've told Elizabeth?' Hilda pitied him.

'I've tried. Susan doesn't demand anything. I've tried to tell Elizabeth, but she won't listen. And I burst into tears. It seems,' he spoke in monotone, as if he dreaded excess, 'ridiculous. I cry as soon as I think of anything serious. It's no wonder Elizabeth won't listen.'

'Do you want to divorce her?'

Now he looked wildly about, as if she'd stilettoed him, threatening more.

'She wouldn't hear of that.'

'You wouldn't force it on her?'

'How could I?' The skin hung yellow from his cheekbones.

'Then you can't be fair to Susan, can you?'

'I know.' He admitted it, like a schoolboy culprit. 'It doesn't seem to matter, though, while we're here. We're together. We don't think any further.' He'd shrunk so that his dressing gown held itself newly together. 'Oh, I know all about it.'

'How long will you be cooped up?'

'A week. It depends. Longer perhaps.'

'Enjoy yourself, then.'

'You don't mean that, Hilda, do you?'

'Yes.'

His face puckered round the trembling of his lips. Elizabeth was rattling the door-knob, warning that the inverview was ending. He dabbed at his eyes as she flounced across.

'You shouldn't upset yourself.' Voice steely, cruel. He did not answer, miserably low in his chair. Susan Pennington held herself subserviently in the background. 'I shall have to go over to Cheevor tomorrow. Did Bates mention it?'

'Mr Bates hasn't been up today,' the nurse said.

When they were ready to leave, Hilda bent, quickly kissed William on the forehead, shook Susan's hand.

'Thank you for all your trouble.'

Mrs Pennington smiled. Her teeth were even, white, her skin excellent. One forgot her stockiness, thick legs, the broad rump, as one saw her youth, the pretty hair, pleased eyes.

Outside, Elizabeth led the way, a yard in front and intent on keeping there. When she reached the office, she passed through to the sitting room, not pausing as she ordered the busy typist to brew tea.

Leaving Hilda to close the door, Elizabeth slapped herself into a chair, knees close, teeth biting into her lower lip.

'That silly female upstairs thinks I don't know what's going on,' she said.

'Did you ask?'

'No. Evasions. Medical titbits. She really is stupid.'

Hilda, suddenly tired, sat in silence.

'Did you speak to him?' Peremptory, this time.

'Yes.'

'Did you get anything out of the man?'

'He says he's in love.' She summarized the interview. 'He won't try for a divorce.'

'What do you think?'

'I felt sorry for him, and happy for him. I'd say he was pleasing himself for the first time for . . .'

'He's selfish. Has always been so.' The eyes narrowed in anger. 'He doesn't work now. He leaves it all to me. I'm not saying it was always like this.' Hilda closed her mind as the bile spurted. Soon the voice sharpened to such an extent that she felt she was the accused, but it did not rouse her. She made soothing noises, handled the air ineffectively.

'Elizabeth. Does Tom know about his father?'

'Nobody knows except you and me. I warned him I'd tell you.'

'He didn't say so.'

'He talked to you. I said he had to. To put it into plain words for a third party to see what it sounded like.'

'Every time he mentioned the girl,' Hilda said, 'he wept. He's in an unbalanced condition, emotionally.'

Another tirade from Elizabeth, a fierce direction of energetic, spitting words at her companion's head. There was no excuse for him. Weakness of body did nothing to cover this caper. If he acted like a bloody fool.

'I think it will come to nothing.' Hilda interrupted, grudgingly.

'What's that mean?'

'He'll recover. The girl will be paid off, and go home. That will be the end of it.'

'And what's happening now doesn't matter?'

Hilda again moved her hands pacifically waiting for the outburst. It did not come.

'Does it affect you? Are you angry? Or jealous?'

'I am.'

'I see. At least, I don't. I'm sorry. You think nothing of him physically. You ask nothing.' She stopped the other's mouth. 'Listen. It may seem ridiculous. Or shame you. But as long as neither of them is hurt, then this, this idyll means something. You're buying it cheap. Your husband has had his last fling groping the young girl who empties his bed-pans. If she comes out of it unscathed, and her husband, then it's fair enough. I don't know that they will. But if they do, then I've no time for words like "ridiculous", or "morality".' Again she prevented Elizabeth's interruption, revelled in her power. 'I know morality's there because people do get hurt, can't just forget, won't leave off, but this seems such a piddling, dead-ended affair that every-body'll be glad to drop it for good in a month. So leave them. Let them alone. They know what you think, don't you worry. They're frightened of you all right. But let them get on with it.'

Elizabeth sat silent.

Suddenly Hilda knew victory. It reminded her of her days in the classroom, when she'd suddenly realized she was in control, that they listened.

'You immoral little bitch.'

Elizabeth stood by her, close, hands on her arm. The vulgarity of the phrase, with its trite appeal stiffened Hilda, angered her coldly. The secretary brought in tea, was invited to join them in ladylike conversation, and when Hilda withdrew twenty minutes later no attempt was made to detain her, though Elizabeth asked Mrs Tenby to show the guest out.

Hilda examined her disappointment half the way home.

16

Buds reddened; a clump of iris reticulata bloomed in the borders; blossom on the mahonia stood faintly sweet.

Edward twice visited Jeremy, reporting both times that the boy was well, working hard, walking girls out. Mrs

Makepeace praised his meticulous tidiness, found him utterly considerate. He'd brought young ladies home, one at least had shared his bed, but all discreetly, without noise; not a car door slammed after midnight. He'd had a party or two, when the stereo had thumped, but there were no beer-marks on the wall, even if fine china plates were black with cigarette ash. The boy, according to the housekeeper, was a paragon, sitting at his desk with his files, writing, studying. Jeremy made no such claims for himself, was genuinely pleased to see his father; he did not gush, but at least he smiled as he failed to enlighten.

Lord Marcroft who was now up and about again occasionally took to his Rolls-Royce. He made no public appearances, but did not stay at home. When Hilda rang Elizabeth, neither mentioned Susan Pennington; both promised to call, failed to do so.

It was still too cold to work for long in the garden, but Hilda fetched out her mackintosh and walked the lanes, head scarfed against the wind. Edward was busy, preoccupied, very cautious, sometimes called from the dinner table to the telephone. After meals he'd describe what the firms were about, claimed in fact that it honed up his mind to explain these matters to her, but he seemed not altogether cheerful. Hilda suspected that she just began to know him, that she read this new seriousness into him because she realized for the first time what snags he reckoned with. That sobered her; she stepped humbly. 'You seem to work longer hours,' she said, 'than when I first came here.'

'I was considering retirement then.'

'And you're not now?'

Again he explained what he was about, why it needed supervision, and during the exposition he became cheerful, animated. But when she came across him on his own, his mouth drooped, he frowned, muttered, curled the edge of the *Financial Times* round his finger. Expecting the bankruptcy court, or the police, she said so.

'Nothing so drastic.' He was as incommunicatively obstinate as Jeremy.

'I'm worried.'

'So am I, to tell the truth.'

For the first time she saw how good the last few months of marriage had been, how when she ceased to be mistress she had become wife in unexpected fullness. She had not appreciated this until there was a possibility of its ending, and now she tiptoed round her treasures in dread. Once, when she was a new first-former, a girl in the upper sixth had spoken to her, walked a few times along the road with her to school. She remembered Janet well, womanly in her uniform, with a bust, curling fair hair. She'd felt proud, telling the older girl breathlessly how she fed the goldfish in the garden pond, how she had trained them to swim up, mouths open, when she scattered the ants' eggs. Janet had listened like an adult, making grown-up noises of encouragement, and had announced that her young brother kept a fish in a bowl on the sideboard. Those two or three conversations were clear yet; the girl with the prefectorial badge, who ordered boisterous fifth-form hockey-players about, had noticed her with her freshly ribboned hat, unscuffed shoes, bright satchel. One evening, during the Christmas holidays, fiddling with a jigsaw, she suddenly realized that her parents were discussing Janet's death; she had been killed in a motor accident in France. They asked as she looked up if she knew the girl; they had met her parents at the bridge club. Hilda had been shaken, cold about the spine, but it had not lasted. When they got back to school the headmistress had pulled long faces, said what promise had been lost, so that one child had burst into a squeal of tears. Hilda kept a straight face.

That had seemed to be that. Slightly scarred, Hilda forgot.

But in these last weeks she had recalled those conversations, remembering how she and Janet had stepped through heaps of sand, amongst piles of bricks, as they had taken a short cut on ground where a house was being built. The talks, the autumn sunshine, the stiffness of pride seemed not poignant, but clear; they did not relate to imminent death, were pleasurable as though Janet had recently attained distinction and one brightened one's dull life by recollections, perhaps exaggerations, of the contact.

Hilda had no idea why she remembered these snatches. Perhaps they warned of disaster. The past is always good, even wretchedness, in that one knows one survived, lived to tell the tale or keep one's mouth shut. Her marriage had been good, solid, substantial, reassuring but was now, possibly, to be splintered by some newspaper heading. 'Local business man arrested. "I am penniless," claims magnate. Tragic accident in Chamonix. Fielding bankruptcy (from page 1).'

'I'm worried,' she said. She knew she must drop identical pennies in this machine.

'So you tell me.'

He grinned, eyebrows bristling. The good mood encouraged her to probe.

'You're working all the time now.'

'That's true.' His whimsy didn't suit.

'Is everything all right? When I read the newspapers . . . '

'Tell you what. We'll have a thousand each to invest. Little competition with real money. You can ring Annerly for advice.'

'I'm not fooling,' she said. All at once she spilt it. Sentences about bankruptcy, prison, penury, return to the classroom. Even as she spoke she felt shame, but the compulsion, like a reflex, forced her to spew on. He should tell her. It was worse for her because she'd no idea what was happening. Her imagination stabbed; could he not see that?

He listened, apparently without surprise. She now spoke with force, but without heat, condemning from principle, not from emotional involvement. He took her hands.

'I see,' he said. 'The truth is, I've got my second wind.'

'What's that mean?'

'When I first took up with you, I wasn't going to do anything to lose you. Moreover, I was sick with guilt about Anna and Jeremy. It all coincided with a period when my fellow-directors were doing well. What you'd call their creative period. They didn't need me. I didn't have to raise a finger.' He looked down, grimly solemn. 'Anna died; we married. One or two snags, or opportunities, if you like to call them such, appeared. For four or five years we've been embroidering the same tune. Very profitably. Now a new theme's called for.'

'And you . . . ?'

'I provided it.' He smiled, teeth white. His huge fingers were locked together, like those, she thought, of a television politician both concerned and at ease. 'Not surprisingly, if you look at it. I'd had a rest. I was pleased with myself. The sap was rising.' He determined not to keep it serious. 'For the first time in ten years, I was something like settled. And I give you the credit for that. That's how it is with me. When I'm easy in my mind I can get on and do my thing, which is making money. It's not so with everybody. Some work at their peak when they're worried stiff, can slave to forget it. Not me.'

He held a hand up.

'I've made a packet these last weeks, believe you me. And I had further confirmation of it this morning. That's why I'm talking like this. Because you're responsible in your way. But I'm pleased. Damned near overjoyed. Usually I'm like Jerry, tell you nothing about what matters. I'm so chuffed with myself today I want to stop people on the road and shout, "I've got a beautiful wife." '

'When you mean, "I've made my pile"?'

'Same thing if you could see it.' She felt the joy in this, for she understood. Her face glowed, seeming to relax, to melt. 'There's a drawback.'

'There always is.' Thank God for clichés.

'It means more and more work. If my partners had done this, I'd have said, "Let's have a jaunt for a week or two." Now, it's me. And I say, "You'll see even less of me for a bit." And it's because you're such a marvellous woman. What d'you say to that?'

She kissed him, but both seemed incapable for the moment of any large physical demonstration until she had absorbed his praise and he had grasped that this was done.

'We should have a drink,' she said.

'What?'

'Whisky and water. That's what you like best. And I'll get it.' She did so. 'It's silly to drink champers when we like this better.'

'You?'

'Yes. I have a nip or two when you leave me on my own.'

'Anna did. At one stage.'

'She breathed. And walked. And went to sleep. She was a human being.' Hilda spoke with a vulgarity that caught him like a punch, jolted melancholy out of him. 'I'm pleased with you. And with myself. So look like it, will you?'

'Yes, ma'am.'

'We shall be down in the mouth tomorrow. One of my plantlings will snuff it. Your fortune won't appear quite as huge as it might have been if you hadn't overlooked something or you neglected it. But not tonight.'

They drank.

'This is what marriage is about,' he said, flourishing his glass.

'Sometimes.' They lifted spirits.

'We're up in the air,' she said. 'I can't help but think of

216

your great-grandfather in that damp cottage. What did he think of marriage?' She laughed. 'The fire burning. And his new wife spitting on the iron.'

'Why?'

'If the spittle flew off it was hot enough. Or if it evaporated.'

They laughed, and she took his arm, forcing him to perambulate the long room, stopping here and there at a picture, the bust of Byron, at the curtains where they stared out across the night-shining fields to the black hedges, the wild quiver of twigs on distant trees. He seemed to understand her action, as if it were a procession, a beating of bounds, a resettling of solid property. She could not speak for powerful joy; two people arm-in-arm having achieved a little who would make love, would sleep sweeter for this success. When they reached the door, he opened it, led her to the hall, to the draughts of the front door and the portico where they shivered in the lamplight, darted back in thumping the great doors shut.

'That's good,' he said.

She was breathless, with a splatter of rain on her face.

'I wonder how many nights like this we shall have?' Hilda asked.

'You're tempting providence, my girl.'

'And your great-grandfather never did that.'

Next morning they were sober-sided as Edward occupied himself with his newspaper, but as he left, he touched her breast recalling their climax. Almost as good, he telephoned to say he'd be home at six sharp for dinner, and she confessed her pleasure.

When he arrived he looked serious.

'Have you glanced at *The Times* today?' he asked.

'Yes.'

'You've seen it, then?'

'Seen what?'

'Gascoigne.'

Fear rammed her weak.

'Has he died?' Why did she ask that?

'No. Announced his forthcoming marriage.' He passed her an already folded paper. The engagement of Alan S. Gascoigne, O.B.E., M.A., son of Mr and the late Mrs S. Gascoigne to Edwina Mary, only daughter of Mr and Mrs Frederick Leigh, Whitemoor Hall Farm, Pately Bridge, Yorks. 'Who's she?'

'No idea.' Not Hilda Marguerite, only daughter of Lt Col and Mrs C. R. Kennedy.

'Elizabeth Marcroft hadn't said anything?'

'Nothing.'

She could not deny an element of jealousy. He should have confessed her superiority by remaining celibate. He'd be forty-four now, wanting to start a family. And his father, the old platelayer, thin as his son, wiping his breakfast platter clean with bread, was still alive. She'd disliked him, with his nasal tenor, and cropped hair thick as his son's. He was a snake. Two, thin, handsome, slimy creatures, one uneducated, one cultured, both rats, gnawing with malice. They were sharp enough to recognize very early that Alan had made a mistake choosing her, but they'd put up with it so long as she kowtowed, worshipped at their grubby bethels. She'd hated that house on the border of Lancashire and Yorkshire, that stone box, that belonged to Sid, the only platelayer to buy his own place. By what dishonesty had he managed that? She was no longer angry now, but as Edward watched her, she blushed.

'No wedding present there, I think,' he said, drily.

She could not look at him.

'Sensible, really. I don't know, though. He didn't act like a sane man. I'm talking about those letters. That wasn't the behaviour of a grown-up.'

She could not speak about it.

'Edwina Leigh?' he said. 'Doesn't mean anything.'

He did not press her, but circled her shoulder with his arm.

'I'm going up to see the Marcrofts tomorrow,' he announced. 'We're doing a job on the estate.'

'Why are you . . . ' She was glad to be able to ask a humdrum question.

'We should send one of the junior architects. He'll go with me. I owe 'em a visit. To see William, really, though it'll be Elizabeth who'll be laying the law down.'

'Poor Willy.'

He returned from that visit highly delighted.

'Oh, M'lady Liz took over. She dismissed young Baines to talk business with the estate under-manager, led me in for two minutes to see William . . . '

'What was he doing?'

'Sitting in a chair with a newspaper, dozing. I was allowed to ask how he was, and listen for a bit to his complaints, when she rushed me out, shoved me into an armchair and delivered me a lecture.'

'About what?'

'You guess.'

She sat primly, thinking.

'Her husband's shortcomings.'

'Well, yes, that was part of it. But it was mainly my wife's superlative qualities. How about that now?'

They chaffed each other through six sentences.

'She told me about William and his nurse. Said she'd had a tottering time. Bates, the estate manager, was off. He's seriously ill again now. She had to do everything and there was milord slavering over this dolly. She was acid.'

Hilda did not answer.

'But you, she claims, kept her going. You talked to her. Sensibly. So that she could begin to think straight. And

219

you talked to him with such effect that he was never quite so stupid again.'

They laughed, not exactly comfortably.

'She was full of it,' he said. 'You know the way she lays it on the line. Banging it right through your ear drums. You'd sorted her out. You'd made it possible for her to go on.'

'That's nothing like the truth.'

'That's what she believes. She was surprised I knew nothing about it. "I'd asked her not to say anything," she said, "but I thought she might tell you." That led her off again. That you were beautiful, and intelligent, and your word was utterly to be trusted.'

'How did you answer all this?'

'I agreed with her, of course.'

'And what did you think?'

'Um,' he said, laughing. 'That's different, now, isn't it?' He straightened his face immediately. 'I was surprised.' He held a hand as if to prevent her from striking him. 'It seemed truthful enough. I thought she might ask us to do something, but she didn't. She thinks, m'dear, whatever your views, that you are outstanding. Upstanding and out-standing.' He shook his head as if clearing his brains. 'And I agree.' He settled comfortably, board-room fashion. 'She's sharp. Don't you find her so?'

'Well, yes. Knows her mind.'

'That's what I'd say. And yet she claims you kept her steady through this business.'

'It's not true, Edward. I hardly saw her.'

'You were a kind of ikon. No, it's right enough. You don't realize the effect you have. It's true. On me. On pretty well everybody. Liz claims that when she was in trouble she could turn to you and you'd talk sense. And more. She'd look at you, and be certain that things weren't as bad as they seemed, that somebody, some few people, saw reason, acted on it.'

'I wish to God you were right.'

'I am.'

'I thought at one time she was attracted to me. That's probably the answer.'

'Sexually?' he asked.

'I suppose so.'

'You mean she made advances? Didn't know she was that way inclined.'

'Not really. I mentioned it at the time.'

He screwed his eyes, dug chin into collar.

'I see I'm not going to get anything out of you on that score. That's what I mean. You rouse my curiosity, and then clam up. No wonder people are impressed by you.'

'She wrote a letter or two, said how much she depended on me. They seemed over-stated. And I thought one explanation was sexual attraction. One. I wasn't sure. One among many. I may be wrong.'

'You stir our letter-writers up, don't you?'

'You . . . ?'

'Gascoigne. I've read nothing like them. They weren't the work of a sane man. And it's on your account. He wasn't steady because he knew what he'd lost. I've picked a winner, my girl.'

Delighted, she allowed the conversation to peter out; her husband had made his point, was certain it was grasped, had left it. He mentioned that Elizabeth had also reported that Tom, her son, had been quite stunned by Hilda, couldn't stop talking about her. Edward affected pangs of jealousy. She could not make her mind up whether these encomia were of her husband's designing, but sat exultant, even as she warned herself not to be a credulous fool.

'And while we're talking about the younger generation,' Edward said, 'I think I'll arrange for you to try the celebrated influence on Jeremy.'

'What's he done?'

'Nothing out of place, so far as I know. But I did say we'd call.'

Fielding himself rang the boy, who taciturn as ever, invited them over at their leisure. Yes, all was well. Mrs Makepeace grandmothered him. He'd won a prize for an essay on marine biology. No, that wasn't really what he was studying. Something he'd done with another fellow last summer. Nothing to write home about. No, he wasn't particularly pleased. Why should he be?

They received an invitation, to call in on the Marcrofts on Saturday night. Edward, at this shortest of notice, found it impossible, but Hilda was pressed to come on her own.

'Reason,' her husband said. 'Upstanding and outstanding.'

Neither felt comfortable.

17

At Marcroft Hall, Hilda sat down to dinner.

The three were in a room she had never seen before, and which, though sparsely furnished, had something of Victorian comfort about it. The table, chairs and sideboard were darkly ornate over a crimson carpet, and the walls were papered with a wide brown pattern, wreaths of wild flowers and corn, on dull gold. Over the fireplace, tall itself in oak, hung an eighteenth-century oil painting of a Marcroft ancestor in a frame of fantastically convoluted extravagance. Hilda looked for a likeness between the fourth baron and William, but found none. This did not surprise her; the face seemed sketchy, rapidly daubed, unobserved as if the artist had lavished his skill on the lace of the coat. The features were a nothing in the upper middle of a huge canvas which became interesting at the edges and was surrounded by the craggy gold caverns and horned, leafy bridges of the frame, the real achievement.

The meal was simple, as if from a steak-bar, with substantial helpings. William ate slowly, in effort, while his wife chaffed him.

'Good of you to come, Hilda. We bore each other when we're on our own. We need distracting.'

'Don't know about that.' Suck at his Beaujolais.

'Don't you ever read a book at table?' Hilda asked.

'William never reads. Not even the paper.'

'Well, now. That's not true. Read that thing about Japanese war-crimes. What was it called?'

Marcroft made little effort to entertain his guest, concentrated on the forking and masticating of food, speaking only to defend himself against his wife's gibes, and that without enthusiasm. Hilda seeing no sense in domestic quarrels, talked about her own husband, forced Elizabeth to describe what Edward's firm were building on the estate. This led to a fierce account of how her ladyship had proved to some whipper-snapper of an architect that he neither knew his job, nor could listen to plain instructions. This lasted until the pudding, ice-cream and prunes, and again William made no intervention, but spooning up the fruit, he'd chuckled, said forthrightly, 'Black-coated workers. Very necessary to me since the operation. Too much sitting about. Constipation.' He blubbered his lips, smiling still.

All agreed they enjoyed prunes, said appearance gave them a bad reputation. Hilda explained they were the only comestible allowed to be sold in Jacobean brothels. That wiped the smile from Marcroft's face, sent him lugubriously back to squinting down at his dish, searching for impurities.

At the end of the meal, he asked them, almost absent-mindedly, to excuse him, and stumped off, a glass of port in his hand.

'Where will he go?' Hilda asked.

'Television. If he can be bothered to switch it on. Otherwise he'll just sit in a chair.'

'Drinking?'

'No. Hardly at all. In a chair. Moving sometimes. Groaning. Though he probably doesn't realize it.' Elizabeth looked much at ease, like a solicitor with a raw client. 'I wanted to see you. I wanted to talk to you.'

'About Lord Marcroft?'

The formality of the phrase seemed to throw Elizabeth momentarily so that she drummed five-finger exercises on her chair-arm, conjuring conversation back.

'Partly. But we've seen so little of each other. You're the only person hereabouts I can sit and talk to. And you won't come. At least, you haven't.'

'You're busy.'

'Not to see you. I'll tell you something. Your former husband is going to remarry.'

'I saw it in *The Times*.'

'Oh.' Grunt of displeasure. 'He told me all about it. Are you interested?'

'Yes.'

'Are you sure?' Elizabeth took up a commanding position, which Hilda ignored. 'He's been very helpful to me, as perhaps you know. He's a quick mind, incisive. Ask for a scheme and he'll come up with it. I can use people like that. There are too few. Plenty who'll address envelopes for the party; not many who can decide what to put inside them.' She seemed pleased with this. 'But I didn't know Alan Gascoigne intimately. We were always formal. Though he spoke so beautifully, and dressed well, I don't think . . . Wasn't his father a working man?'

'A platelayer.'

'What's that?'

Hilda, mildly triumphant, explained. Elizabeth did not listen.

'We were never close. Then one evening, in the office, we'd been arguing about the Tenfield by-election, he stopped and said, shy as one of his own schoolboys, that he was going to get married. He opened his eyes very wide.' Hilda could imagine it; Alan had hustings tricks galore. 'He said I knew you and he confessed how devastated he had been when you walked out. He seemed genuinely surprised that you'd done so.' She waited for a comment.

'He's convinced himself, has he?'

'Apparently it threw him into depression. He could barely keep up public appearances. It ruined his world, he said. But then he found out you were living with Edward Fielding. It was as if every moral standard in the universe disappeared. He was stunned.'

Hilda closed her mind to the poison. This woman sought advantage. She would get none.

'For some years he was ice, he said. Or a corpse. He did his work, was efficient, but it meant nothing. It helped keep him level. And the reason was that, and he said this solemnly, bell, book and candle, in making you his wife, he had chosen properly. He had chosen the unique woman.'

As Lady Marcroft talked on, of Alan's distress, distrust, inability to accept her flight, with a detail that seemed nearer fiction than truth, Hilda withdrew, listened carelessly, let her mind burgeon on a chance phrase. She knew this story, had read it in those dozens of frenzied letters, had felt its truth there as it had battered her, but now treated it, in the mouth of a third person, as a twopenny topic to waste an evening on, an hour's telly drama. When Elizabeth described Gascoigne's meeting with Edwina Leigh at a Conservative rally, the short courtship, the proposal by telephone, Hilda took an interest. Miss Leigh was thirty-six, a landowner's daughter, moneyed and smart, but not beautiful. 'She has black eyebrows,' Elizabeth said, 'that meet in the middle, and she does nothing about it.' Gascoigne would marry into the middle class again. But this woman was not young; they'd have to spring the family at once.

'She's old.' Hilda said. 'Why hasn't she married before?'

'Crossed love?'

'Do you know that? Did he say so?'

'No. It's not my business.'

At last, when Elizabeth grew certain that her friend was not vulnerable through Gascoigne, she switched to compliments.

'You put my husband right,' she said. 'He's a fool, but he knows his position, duty. And yet I could not get through to him. You did. You spoke commonsense, with uncommon force. He listened, and he compared your appearance, your speech, your attraction, with that vulgar little woman's and he knew. He knew.'

'I wouldn't say that.'

'You've only to look at a person.'

'I wouldn't bet on that, either.'

'Edward loves you.' Elizabeth spoke with force, hauteur, certainty.

'I think he does. But I don't know for how long.'

Elizabeth bent forward, back hunched ugly.

'Would it surprise you if I told you I love you?'

Hilda blew breath out, uncertain how to answer, before she made her mind up.

'I don't understand.'

'Let me explain, then. I have for you a powerful affection. I want to look after you, to be with you, to take a major part in your life. There's the physical thing, too, I admit. But it's not most important. I tell you there is nothing I would sooner do than set up house with you, share . . . ' Stilted phrases limped out.

'You'd give all this,' Hilda waved a hand, 'up for me?'

'I think I would.' Enough.

226

They sat in a warm, well-lighted room, not speaking. In the end, Elizabeth rose, filled Hilda's glass, and standing by her own chair, decanter still in hand, asked,

'All that meant nothing to you?'

'Basically,' Hilda began to speak doggedly, in fear, not knowing exact directions, 'love is for me a physical thing. It's more, I know, much more, but unless there's a bed-rock,' she smiled at her ambiguous cliché, 'of sexual attraction, love of the sort you talk about, isn't on. For me. I could love an old person, a parent, in a different way. Or perhaps a child. But anything else to me is sexually based.'

'You're not shocked at my, my deviation?'

'Surprised. No, not that. I wouldn't know what to do.' She laughed, wildly. 'When it was a man, and I didn't have any real knowledge, I felt some sort of urge, some strange-ness in my body.'

'Oh.' Eyes wide.

'May I ask you,' Hilda began, 'about yourself? No. It's not fair, and none of my business.'

'You want to know,' Elizabeth answered flatly enough, turning her back to return the decanter, 'if I've always been like this.' She sat down, heavily for so small a woman. 'Like you, I was innocent. I didn't know anything. I was at a girls' school, and there were exchanges of a sort. Then I met boys, and William proposed in my first season. He was rich, titled. That seemed enough. I had little out of him. I tried adultery, once, with a young, beautiful man. It was nothing. I was over thirty before I learnt, or was seduced.' There was self-loathing in the last, though whether at her ignorance or perversion Hilda could not guess. 'Is that what you want? I don't mind talking to you about it.'

Pity unbent in the listener; here one spoke desperation.

'William does not know,' Elizabeth said.

'And you don't think to tell him?'

With a puff of air from the lips Elizabeth dismissed the foolishness.

'I'm sorry,' Hilda said.

'Not your fault.' Gruff.

'You'll forget it. If one doesn't cultivate love . . . '

'I shall cultivate you, my girl. Make no mistake.' Then in a softer tone. 'This embarrasses you, doesn't it?'

'Certainly I don't know what to say. I admire you, especially the work you do here. I enjoy your company. In a, a frightened sort of way. But my idea of sex is that with Edward. I want children.'

'Why have you not had them?'

'Convention.' Hilda flashed the word in her face, with panache. Then slyly crumbled her next flat utterance, not clearly. 'I'm very ordinary.'

'That you aren't.'

'You don't see me as I am.'

'I don't want to bore you. Everybody sees you as . . . '

'That'll do, Elizabeth.'

'It won't do. Don't hide things from yourself. I cannot bear to sit here, yet I daren't touch you, even your hand for fear of the consequence.'

'That's you, Elizabeth, not me.'

In mock anger, slapping her hands on her thighs, Lady Marcroft sat straight-backed.

'I could hit you.'

Suddenly Hilda felt, as it were, at home. She was not in control, but was hampered by neither fear nor desire.

'I'd like to do something for you,' she announced.

Elizabeth jumped to her feet.

'No,' Hilda said. 'Not that. Not now. I honestly think I know what you feel. If you asked me to eat one of those wax candles, I wouldn't want to. The idea doesn't nauseate me. In fact, they look rather appetizing. If I started to chew, well, I don't know.' This sounded back-broken, was meant

228

to be so. 'In a way, I feel honoured. By you. Honestly. But let it stop there.'

'No.' Near shout.

'Yes.' She stood, half turning. Elizabeth crossed the yard or two of space, dug nails into Hilda's arm, breast-pressed her, kissed the face that was jerked away. They stood, the pain in the bicep frighteningly ugly, as if the whole skin were scarred, but this time Elizabeth did not wrestle, released the other.

'Good, God,' she said. Her handkerchief she gnawed, dragging it out tight. An inch or two of lace border hung raggedly loose.

'I'd better go,' Hilda muttered. The other paid no attention, seemed, though still, to be writhing as if inside the skin, the bone structure, serpentine entrails reached and screamed for comfort.

'Love me,' Elizabeth asked.

Useless to answer that. Hilda moved to the door, grasped the handle, shook it as if by the rattle to signal her intention. Elizabeth, calm now, faced her.

'William will want to say good night.'

'Where is he?'

'We'll go.'

Hilda hurriedly opened the door, but Lady Marcroft did not touch her as she passed. The guest, like an Indian wife, followed down a carpeted passage, through a huge room and into a television lounge where the Earl sat in an arm-chair, smoking an amber-stemmed pipe.

'Hilda is going,' Elizabeth barked.

He rose, stumbling, uncomfortably, as if deafened.

'Going. Oh. Ah. It's not late, yet, is it? Not late? What time is it, then?'

The television set, colour garishly mistuned, showed cowboys brawling. Elizabeth lowered the volume.

'I've enjoyed my visit.'

'Yes. Oh. Yes. Do you have to leave so early?' He puffed as if at violent exercise.

'She's had enough of us.'

He laughed heartily raucous, wrinkles blackly deep round his eyes.

'Can't believe that,' he answered. 'We're glad to see you. Any time you care to come. Trouble with Elizabeth is she's lonely, but won't do anything about it. I'm no company since the operation. Can't find energy. Not to talk, even. I sit staring at this.' He closed his eyes; his forhead rutted like a disused sandstone cutting. 'All I'm fit for. And if you asked me what I'd been watching I wouldn't know. Bloo'y stupid, really.' There seemed about him an intelligence, a dead-reckoning of his weakness. 'Change for her, to sit at home, and chatter about knitting or belly-ache.' He showed no sense of incongruity.

'I'm glad. I like to come.'

'Elizabeth's good company. She's young yet. Vigorous.' His eyes were red rimmed, heavy with water.

'I enjoyed our meal together, and the talk.'

'You did. Oh. Good. Good. Yes. That's good.'

She held her hand out, found it ignored, but did not move.

He concentrated, shook, inside his own mansion, shook hands with a guest. On impulse, she kissed his cheek, which was rough.

'Oh. Ah,' he said. 'Goodbye, m'dear. Enjoyed it.'

Elizabeth restored the sound to the picture of a man galloping through orange dust. William sat down, though still gesturing, reaching to them through the air. The women left, tramped corridors, found themselves at length outside in the chill.

'Goodbye, and thank you.' Hilda.

'Will you come again?'

'Certainly.'

That seemed unexpected, quietened them in the rustling dark.

'Kiss me,' Elizabeth said.

'What?' She'd been engaged elsewhere, rapt, chill-caught.

'Kiss me.' Sharp retort. Knuckle-hard. 'You kissed my husband.'

'So I did.' She bent, touched the cheekbone, cool, perfumed. Lady Marcroft made no other move, held up her face, received the lips, melted and stood straight.

As soon as she sat in her car Hilda found she was trembling violently, would have screamed out if she had been alone. She fumbled to insert the ignition key, physically flattered. Elizabeth said nothing, stately, feet together, stiffly formal.

As the car jerked forward, the engine stalled. Elizabeth did not move. Now, the second time the car made smoothly out for the great drive, headlights proud. Skirr of tyres; gravel shifted; women apart.

18

After a day Hilda recovered.

She said nothing to Edward, and this out of fear of ridicule. That was not exact; she had no idea how he'd take Elizabeth's proposal. Perhaps in a quiet of anger or with three or four obscenities. One did not know with him.

He said they were to visit Jeremy at Marchmont on Saturday night.

'He's invited us,' he announced.

'Anything special?'

'Linda Lawrence is back.'

'What? Since when?'

'I've known for a week,' he said. 'From Mrs Makepeace.'

'He didn't say anything?'

'No. Nor did I. But he asks us round. Bravado, perhaps. Or perhaps she's gone off home for the weekend.'

'You sound cross.' She tried charm. 'Are you?'

'Moderately.' Himself again. 'Secretive little sod.'

'Perhaps,' she said now, determined to rough him up, 'you'll remember that you've said nothing to me about it.'

'No. I haven't. It's my worry.'

'Is that true?'

'God knows.' His face was red, in annoyance, puffy. 'I don't know whether I can do anything about it. I'm pretty sure I can't.'

'And you don't like that?'

'No, I don't. It's happening too bloody often these days altogether.' Slow, the sentence; untidy.

'But you could have told me.'

'I could.'

He nodded, heavily handsome, bemused. She was reminded of Willy Marcroft in his chair, with the television screen apeing life for him. Edward would recover; by tomorrow he'd bounce to work, chase his son, scorch the world with his mark. But this evening, tired, ashamed that he'd been too feeble to confess weakness to his wife, he sat in a dull distress. She kissed him, and he fondled her absently. She guessed old age began for him when she had no words of comfort.

'We're not dead yet,' he said.

'By God, it feels like it sometimes.'

'Not you, surely?'

He put his glasses on so that he looked milder, more puzzled. Soon he'd pull them off, drop them or ram them in a pocket, but for the moment she tasted the future, found it unpalatable.

'See the doctor,' she warned.

'See him yourself.' Both laughed, not immoderately.

She dressed carefully on Saturday night, in a long gown; she'd spent the afternoon at the hairdresser's. When Edward saw her, he whistled, grinned, whisking his tie over.

'Going somewhere?' he asked.

'Isn't it suitable?' Mock innocence.

'Superb. Why tonight, though?

'I thought this would be what you wanted.'

'So it is. I didn't know until now.'

He took the Bentley, and wore a white scarf, a Homburg, so that they stood in the porch without a word waiting for Mrs Makepeace's admiration as she answered the bell. Jeremy already fidgeted in the lounge, where every polished surface gleamed. Though the room was hung full of light, the heavy purple of mahogany seemed darkly to occupy most of the space, and that densely. The gold frames of the pictures shone diffidently, and silver on the sideboard was half-ready to drop into cavernous dark underneath. Jeremy who occupied one of the four chairs round the fire stood politely. He looked taller, thinner, more delicate with his hair waving thickly to his shoulders; his suit, dark grey, threw his conservative white shirt into bright prominence. He had pushed his hands, behind him, like a royal, under his coat tail.

'This is a beautiful room,' Hilda said. She believed it; beige carpet in dark surrounds. Two chandeliers. At the far end hung curtains in heavy blue velvet. Pictures of Victorian mountains by day, and a lake, tall trees, a boat in moonlight gloomed under varnish like great formal, gilt-edged holes in the magnolia walls. And dominating, spread the sideboard, the table, the chairs on which polish shone glassily, inch-thick, cared for from the day they left the craftsman's shop, love lavished, so that Hilda imagined the crowd of busy servants who had achieved this gloss through the drudgery of a hundred years.

'I hadn't noticed,' Jeremy said. She believed him, thought

he'd now begin to frown, to worry in his spare time discovering the attractions of the place. That pleased her. He'd never know. He was asking her what she'd drink. Dubonnet glowed a sober red. Jeremy not having water for his father's whisky, went out.

'Does it bother you to come back?' she asked.

'No.'

'It really is marvellously looked after. I don't . . . '

'They never come in here.'

'Didn't you?'

'We did, at one time. When we entertained. We weren't very well off, then.'

'Hardly a poor man's house.' With mischief. 'Has this room changed much?'

'New carpet. That Highland thing was over the fireplace. No mirror. Furniture swapped about. The smell's the same.'

Jeremy returned with a cut-glass jug.

'Rots your boots,' he said. It sounded out of character as though he'd prepared that during his errand.

'Where's Linda?' his father asked, pouring.

'Linda? She'll be in. She's been a bit off colour today.'

All three paid attention to their glasses.

'She'll be in later, I hope,' he said in the end. His voice had thinned. Again they silently sipped, shifted in their chairs, made no attempt to feel at home. Jeremy crossed his legs, clamping his ankles together.

'When did she come back?' Edward, brusquely, with hostility.

'Ten days or so.'

'I see. Expected?'

'Yes and no.'

'What the devil does that mean?'

Jeremy showed no distress, smiled absently.

'We'd written to one another. There'd been telephone calls.'

'You'd not met face to face, then?'

'Yes, we had.'

Conversation progressed like a game; one must not deviate from truth, merely needle an interrogator. Edward gave up, grimly, widening nostrils. When Hilda, mounting a relief operation, asked some questions about Tom Ravenshead, Jeremy answered at length. Yes, he was clever, and idle, and charming. No, he didn't chase the girls unduly, but he'd given up Caroline, what-was-her-name?, Hartley-Davenport, when everybody, she included, had thought it serious.

'You don't like him, then?' Hilda pressed.

'So, so.'

'I thought he was a friend of yours?'

'We met quite a bit in the holidays, when we were younger.'

'And didn't hit it off?'

'He liked his own way.' Jeremy spoke slowly. 'He usually got it. I wasn't keen on that. No.'

'And he hasn't changed?'

'Shouldn't think so.' He grinned.

Edward listened, glowered still. Hilda distrusted the set of his shoulder. The door opened; they'd heard not a sound outside; the two men scrambled to their feet. Linda was guided into the chair between them.

Her face was white, floured with powder, while she slouched awkwardly under an ill-matching skirt and blouse. She had been crying; her mouth was drawn trap-thin. Jeremy, without inquiry, poured her a sherry as his father, exerting himself, smiled, nudging his chair companionably towards her.

'Your good health,' Edward said, when the girl had taken her glass. Hilda admired the warmth he insinuated into his voice. Linda did not even lift the wine, but stared ahead, mouth and chin trembling.

The visitors glumly ignored this exhibition.

Jeremy leaned towards the girl until his father asked about a rowan in the garden which needed cutting down. They exchanged a few words, but neither was interested. Both avoided glancing at the set, dead-white face.

'Are you still at the hospital?' Hilda asked.

'Yes.' Barely audible.

'I had to call in there the other day. They're organizing a charity dance. They, and the Northern, and the Women's Free.'

Linda did not answer, sip, move; to Hilda it seemed that if the girl opened her lips to speak, the mask would crack and her grief exude.

'I saw a charming man in the administrative block. A Mr Milne. Do you know him?'

Nothing to that.

'He was very helpful.'

'Do you know him, Lin?' Jeremy spoke very softly, but the girl looked up at once so that it was clear she'd not been listening. She made no apology, sat glass in hand. Edward now intervened with questions about the function, its provenance, what they aimed to make, how they'd divide the spoils. He spoke with warmth, lazily, setting the company to rights.

Hilda answered and they developed a little argument as to the probable cost on the market of the voluntary help. Lively, the exchange interested Hilda, so that she forgot the girl and her taut face.

'We're money-grubbers,' she said to Jeremy.

'I like to hear you two ding-dong.'

'You don't often give yourself the chance,' Edward intervened. 'Make him drive you up, Linda.'

'We're busy,' Jeremy answered.

'All the more reason to use your leisure profitably.' Hilda, mock-moral.

'We'll come up one evening, shall we, then, Lin?'

'When?' Whined monosyllable.

'That's entirely up to you,' Hilda encouraged. 'Evening, or weekend. Edward's away quite a bit these days, but he can always free himself. Will you come?'

Linda demonstrated a faint interest.

'Rempstone's lovely in the spring. This is the best time of year. Spring. Early summer.'

Garden-, country-talk for two minutes in which Linda took no part.

'Will you bring Jeremy up?'

She was bunched again, ugly as broken concrete.

'We'd enjoy your company. Edward and I don't entertain enough. The house is beautiful.'

'Make him turn out,' Fielding said.

Linda seemed intent on ignoring them, staring at nothing, wine slopping untasted. Jeremy and his father exchanged questions about grants, university administration, the possibility of employment. Neither posed questions at length; both spoke in a kind of shorthand which demonstrated to Hilda their shared affection, interest. She wondered if, in fact, this was a run through of routine phrases or whether the language would have to complicate itself if the matter became serious, broke into new territory. Still, the laconic exchange cheered her.

'That extended essay? Last summer?'

'Ye'. It was all right.'

'That mean?'

'They gave me an A.'

'Well done. You might have said.'

'Not asked.'

Linda sniffed. The men now argued about a marine biology station at Whitby, but Hilda did not listen carefully enough to determine the point at issue. She organized her features in surprise, interest, exposing the tips of her teeth.

All three performed for the girl who sagged like a thick-skinned balloon on the point of deflation.

'Didn't we holiday there once?' Jeremy.

'We did.'

'Can't remember a thing.'

'Cold.'

This led to a discussion of the best resorts. Jeremy, suddenly loquacious, fancied a pub in the Cotswolds, the site for a detective novel. His elders both chose the sun, but argued placidly, for Mediterranean, Caribbean, even the Black Sea which Edward described winningly, making two laugh.

'Where do you choose, Linda?' Edward who broke the round.

She moved. Grudgingly.

'Skegness? Sochi?'

Glass lifted, she wetted her lips as they waited. She set the drink down, felt for a handkerchief to dab her mouth. All sat encouraged. Sanity.

'Well, then, Linda,' Edward said, voice warm, 'where's it to be?'

She opened; nothing emerged.

'Come on, Lin.' Jeremy spoke easily, unforced.

Now she shook her head, energy battered out of her, quarry within hot inches of a hound's maw.

'Perhaps she doesn't want a holiday.' Hilda, pitiful, rescued.

Edward puffed a sigh out. That had a finality.

'She could say so,' Jeremy snapped. 'She's not dumb.'

Excitement sparked in Hilda. These two had quarrelled. Now no social conventions would restrain them. They'd bite. Linda looked at the floor, dully, her face like putty-coloured charcuterie, petty in silence. Her legs caught by the electric light were beautiful, calves strong, knees, thighs handsome. Jeremy had clutched his lapels in his left hand.

In the pause Hilda decided there would be no fight, that Linda would give in, or defend herself with a dumb mouth.

She remembered Alan goading her.

'Why didn't you say something, for heaven's sake?' Gascoigne in annoyance.

'You knew I had arranged it.'

'I did not. I'd have consulted my diary, and told you it was impossible.' He flicked the small book open, held before her face though she could neither look nor see. She knew that the engagement which prevented this visit would be meticulously recorded there, together with a date of entry. 'We cannot go.'

'I can.'

'You will accompany me. I hope you're not going to be stubborn about this, Hilda. You just need to ring your friend and cancel the trip. Temporarily.'

'She's put herself out, got us tickets for *Don Giovanni*.'

'I'm sorry. You should have been more careful. This,' he tapped a white finger on the still open pages, 'has been arranged for months.'

'An exhibition of pottery and painting at the Training College? They'll not miss us.'

'They won't. We shall be there.'

'That's what you prefer, isn't it? Students' daubs to Mozart. And I'll tell you why. Because the Lord Mayor, and the Deputy Lieutenant and the Director of Education will all be parading.'

'I will take you to Covent Garden.'

'When?'

'Find a suitable date, when we are free, without duties, and we'll go. But you must ring up this Elise and explain . . . '

'No.'

'I'm afraid you must. I insist.'

'I'm bloody going, whatever you say.'

'You can shout, Hilda, and scream, and kick the furniture.

I understand your disappointment. But you have made an error. You failed to consult me.'

She had suspected that Alan filled engagements in every weekend, most evenings in order to make opportunities to dash her. She knew quite well that if the Director changed his mind, decided to play truant from the college, show up elsewhere and invited her husband to join him, this important engagement, this strict obligation, would be dropped easily as one discards a chocolate-wrapper.

In the end she'd give way because her body screwed itself into such agony that she could only buy relief by rushing from the room, flinging herself on her bed and howling knead the mattress. The tantrum would die; the shame of her surrender would rankle, but she could only bear so much of his taunting. Then she revolted in blood and nerves, and collapse alone could redeem her. On the few times she'd defied him, he'd raised the subject day after day quietly, nasally. Once she'd hurled herself at him, but he was a strong man, a fine tennis-player, and had no difficulty in pulling her away, into a chair of his choice. And that he'd done, as he sneered, without overt excess of energy, slimy as a snail.

She'd come to realize, months later, when she'd left him, that he had needed these blood-lettings to reassure himself. He'd seemed unmarked, but fear of his wife led him to humiliate her, with cruel efficiency, planning his assaults. She should have walked out before, abandoned him to his sadism, but marriage had seemed binding, a sacrament, not so much of religion as of education in that she had been chosen, from all the others, to wed, to match with this gifted master. Now she could think of him as a scared infant, ripping with his fingernails at the faces of rivals in the school yard. Not then.

Jeremy was no Alan Gascoigne.

'Sup up, Lin,' he said pacifically.

'A good sherry, is it?' his father muttered.

'Thought you didn't like it.'

'I don't.'

The three laughed.

'Passes the time.' Edward. 'Wetting your whistle.'

'I bought some red plonk the other night, and it made us drunk,' Jeremy said. 'So, isn't it, Lin?'

Nothing there.

'Did it . . . taste well?' Hilda now.

'Like ink.'

'Why did you buy it?'

'We decided, on Wednesday. No. Start again. Mrs Makepeace decided that once a week we should have dinner in the evening. Wednesday. She said roast beef. And I bought this great flagon of jungle juice.'

'Was Makers tight?'

'No. She won't eat with us. Or drink. She cooks the meal. We report to the kitchen. She'll have laid the table, mind you. Lace and candlesticks. Still, we cart the platefuls in, and independence is maintained all round. But I'm telling you, we couldn't have carried the empties out.'

'Tch, tch.'

Hilda enjoyed boyish innocence; his face glistened, closely shaved.

'My head reeled. I couldn't even sit straight.'

'And Linda?' Hilda asked. 'Were you the same?'

The girl began to cry, rather sedately, hiding her face. Hilda rose, like a schoolma'am, put an arm on her shoulder and said,

'Come on now. It's not so bad as all that. It can't be.'

A unintelligible answer oozed from the sobs.

'What do you say, darling? What is it?'

'It wasn't my fault.'

'What wasn't? Nobody's blaming you.'

'You were all laughing. I fell down. I couldn't help it. Jerry made me drink, and I fell over.'

'We've not heard anything about it,' Hilda answered.

'You were laughing. I cut my hand.' She opened her hand to reveal sticking-plaster near the base of her thumb. 'It wasn't . . . ' She relapsed into tears.

'She dropped a plate and cut herself,' Jeremy said, dismissing them.

'You've no call to tell them.'

'I don't suppose I have.'

'You were singing, and you couldn't talk properly.'

'I don't deny it.'

'Don't laugh at me. I'm not having it.'

Jeremy turned away, deliberately in disgust, showing her his back. The action was childish, yet fiercely provocative as a coarse oath. Linda yowled, stood, and moved from the room. This she did in silence, leaving the door ajar so that they heard the squeal of tears as soon as she reached the hall.

'What's wrong?' Edward asked his son. The managing director spoke.

'Oh, God knows. She's all over the place.'

'That won't do, Jeremy. It's no business of mine, I imagine, but if you put this sort of performance on in my presence I'm bound to ask questions.'

'We've had a row.'

'I can see that. About what?'

'Nothing much. She said she was tired, didn't want to come in here.'

'And you made her?'

'Yes. I asked her. Was that wrong?'

'I'm not blaming anybody. I'd just like to know what's up. I suppose you'll please yourself what you tell us, but . . .'

'I don't know what's wrong with her.'

'Is that true?'

Jeremy sighed, shrugged almost whimsically, as if he despaired of his father's intelligence.

242

'She's been depressed since she came back. She's not sure she's done right.'

'Has she been going to work?'

'Yes, she has. She's seen her doctor, though.'

'What's he say?'

'Usual. Sympathy and tablets.'

Edward's face looked hard, grey and without life. She knew in a glance what his appearance would be when he was an old man.

'Go and see what you can do, Hilda,' he said, mildly enough. His voice hadn't changed.

'Where will she be?'

Jeremy shrugged, muttered. Hilda made for the door. As soon as she opened it she heard Linda who was standing by the dining room, hands flat and actressy on the jamb.

'What is it, darling?'

A flash turn of the head before the girl swooped to the knob, let herself into the room. Hilda followed, switched on the light. Linda had crouched down on the carpet in front of the hearth, head on the seat on an armchair, skirt draped wide, her legs tucked in.

'It will do you good to tell somebody.'

A mindless sobbing, without violence, crawled from the hidden face.

'You tell me what's gone wrong, now.'

'He doesn't want me back.' The promptness of this answer startled. One expected glum incomprehension.

'Has he said so?'

The sobbing squealed into a crescendo.

'Has Jeremy said so, Linda?'

'No. He doesn't need.' That came slowly.

'What do you mean by that?'

For half an hour they struggled, Hilda receiving a reply perhaps once in three questions. She spoke quietly, though her own temper was ragged, encouraging and smooth, but felt, resented, failure. The evidence against Jeremy stood small; acid failure seethed inside Linda. She had returned, had looked for and found 'snubs from Mrs Makepeace, then from her man, so that she crept back each night expecting, searching for humiliation.

Hilda talked half-nonsense about the difficulty of human relationships, the complexity of marriage, the mismanagements even the most balanced personalities stumbled on. In the end Linda was dry-eyed sitting in the chair listening if not with interest, then without obvious inattention, while the other became more and more immersed in the techniques of spinning out sentences, sentences which in themselves had no sense, but had magical value, thaumaturgical effect, so long as they only continued.

'I can't stress how hard it will be. Sometimes everything you do, never mind what he does, will seem to set you up against him, when it's the exact opposite of what you want. You say something, and as soon as the word's out of your mouth you know you've offended. But you must work on the principle, however fantastic it appears, that this is the place for you and for him, together. Even if you can't believe it. Even if you're certain you're wrong. This is our place, our decision.'

Crooning stilled childish wails. Hilda wondered if the opposite delivered with the same tonal syrup would be equally efficacious.

Before too long the girl began to talk. She was unsure of what she'd done, because she suspected that Jeremy took her back out of pity or politeness. Her husband would allow her to live with him.

'Do you want to go to him again?'

'I don't know.' Again, stoniness.

'You'll have to decide, somehow. You've been away from him now, and gone back.'

'I'm frightened.'

244

'Is Robert?' Hilda asked without hope, 'kind to you? He doesn't knock you about?'

'No. That's not like him.' Linda lowered lids, tightened lips. 'I think it stimulates him to think I've been with somebody else.' Eyes brimmed, but she held steady.

'He wants you, at least. For whatever reason.'

'I think he does.' A watery warmth coloured her voice.

'That's something. And what about Jeremy?'

'He'd be glad to see the back of me. And his father.'

Under her depression, the girl had commonsense, intelligence, but her condition prevented their use. She had the means to cure herself if only she could apply them; at present she could not. As they talked on, Hilda both admired and disliked the other, who lacked the personality to function for herself, who borrowed colour from her surroundings.

'Your husband doesn't like me, does he?'

'I don't think it's a matter of dislike. He doesn't see this, this liaison as very suitable for his son.'

'He'd be glad if I got out?'

'That's fair. Yes, he would.'

The eyes gushed, but briefly, almost by default.

'I should go, you think?'

'That's not for me to tell you. You'll have to make up your own mind.'

They talked on, not friendly now, flatly, inattentively until Jeremy pushed the door open.

'We're having coffee,' he said. 'What about you?'

'Yes, please.' Hilda.

'Lin?' A nod. Coffee? Amphetamines? The Word of God? Nod on. Linda drank with Hilda in the dining room, prepared to go up to bed, but asked that her apologies be given to Edward. She shyly muttered thanks.

'Jeremy's no good. He's nice in many ways, but he's no

245

idea what I'm saying. For an educated person he doesn't know what to do with words.'

'That's interesting.'

'Well, sometimes you feel better just for talking, letting it out. I don't think he knows that.'

'His father's . . . Perhaps it's because of their . . . of Anna.'

Linda came from her seat to place herself straight in front of Hilda, face only inches away, dumbly, powder-streaked, firm-jawed.

'Tell me whether to leave him.'

'It's not . . . '

'You say. Should I?'

Hilda put her shoulders back; she could stand up, now.

'Yes, then. You should. Go home to your husband.'

'I see. Thank you.' The girl offered the stale politenesses slowly. 'Rob doesn't know I've come, not this time . . . '

'Perhaps I'm saying this,' Hilda answered, gabbling, 'because it's what Edward wants. You should remember that.'

That was shrugged off. Somehow, they shook hands, wetly, dumbly.

'Well?' Jeremy asked Hilda returning.

'Her husband's trying to get a job here so they can live together.'

'I know.'

'You should let her go.'

'I'm not stopping her.'

'What do you want?' she asked.

'It's not what I want. She's the one to be considered. She doesn't fancy trailing back to him. He's a bore. All he thinks about is work. She tried to. It didn't come to anything.'

'She thinks you don't want her, either.'

He thrust his arms out, straight, palms down, like a puppet, but did not deny the accusation.

'I don't wish to interfere,' Edward started.

'But.' Jeremy banged the word out incongruously loud, furious with himself.

'Send her off. It's the best thing.'

'For you?' Jeremy, lively now, on the *qui vive*.

'For everybody.'

'So I go up to bed, do I, and tell her to clear out?'

'You'll manage.' Edward. 'She's different now. She's tried him twice, you twice. Once you've made your mind up, it's amazing what you can accept. Believe you me.'

'My mother couldn't.' Angrily, flung off. Edward crossed his legs, adjusted his trouser crease.

'We have to work on the assumption that people behave somewhere near rationality, that their bodies, at least, and their experience will allow them to. Otherwise it's a case for psychiatrists and treatment, if not incarceration in a mental hospital.' Edward spoke carefully, choosing his words, rounding them formally. She was reminded of Alan Gascoigne, in school assembly, who often used this mode of address ironically, quietly indicating his scorn for the behaviour he castigated in complex, Latinized sentences. Edward seemed to aim for objective care, scrupulosity towards fact, *lexis* and listener.

Jeremy grimaced a collapse.

'Sorry,' he said.

'No. I'm pleased you came out with it.' Hilda looked Edward over in surprise. 'I want this thing to be properly discussed. But if Linda's like your mother, you can give up. I struggled for her long enough. I also feel guilty. Make no mistake about that. Guilty as hell. But there was no saving her as far as I was concerned. Nothing I did or failed to do seriously altered what was going to happen. Now I know what you're thinking, that I've deluded myself into believing this, that I'm covering up. That may be so. But most of the consultants concerned had made it clear to me that your mother was on a one-way track to destruction. What I did was slightly to alter the speed, the run. Again, you may think they were soft-soaping me, that they saw no use or profit in accusing me outright of driving her to an overdose.'

Jeremy gulped, taken aback by the steady force of his father's statement. Hilda, afraid, pressed herself deep into her chair, astonished by the deadly order of her husband's mind.

'I'm being honest with you. You perhaps think, not consciously, that by hanging on to Linda you are paying off part of your debt, or mine, to Anna. I shan't convince you otherwise. Or, at least, not with arguments. But try to treat the case on its merits, if that's the word.'

Jeremy dumbly stroked his legs.

Edward heaved himself up in his chair, as if to deliver some knock-out punch.

'You should send her back to her husband. She wants that as much as she wants to stay here.'

'You don't like her.' Jeremy intervened tentatively, like a boy.

'I don't. I see nothing in her. Not that I've given her much of a chance. She's ordinary, as far as I can make out, dull as ditchwater. She let you into her bed.'

Jeremy's glance registered protest.

'I'm speaking plainly now. You won't shout up for yourself, so I do it for you, however crudely. She'll be a drag on you. And for no good reason. You tell me, yourself, her husband will have her back. If he wouldn't, or took her in to beat her, that might alter matters. You've interfered in her life, admitted, or she allowed you to do so, and that makes you in part responsible. I don't deny that. You owe the girl something. What, and how you repay it, God knows. But what I do not want you to do is to clutter your life now, hobble yourself. When you've given her up, you'll sometimes feel regret or remorse. So you will. But don't spoil your life either out of idiocy or, worse, out of apathy.' He was back now, hands crossed on stomach, smiling at his own animation. 'That's enough preaching for one night.'

But he waited for an answer, Hilda noticed, and when nothing came asked his wife if she were ready to go.

As they stood, Jeremy said shyly, 'Thanks,' and his hand reached out, towards his father, though he stood three yards from touching.

'Don't forget what I've told you.'

'I won't.'

The boy smiled pleasantly, but coldly, mere face-shifting. Hilda noticed a framed, postcard-sized snapshot of Jeremy and Linda together. They seemed to be walking along by a stone wall under a canopy of wintry trees and they were holding hands. An air of unaffected happiness pervaded the photograph so that one could imagine them swinging the linked arms, or humming, or suddenly leaping up to touch a twig. From this distance she could not see the expression on their faces, but for the moment she thought the picture justified the pair, redeemed their bored depression, their quarrels, uncertainties, inadequacies. She dismissed that fancy at once, throat full.

Jeremy looked at her, noticed her.

'The Lamentations of Jeremiah,' he said.

'Don't forget.' Edward checking foolery.

On the way home, her husband did not speak, but drove rather slowly, careful of the dark. Both had buckled the safety harness, unusually, as if they felt susceptible to accident. Edward peered forward, every movement unflurried. She waited for him on the terrace as he garaged the car, but he did not speak, even signalled with his eyebrows his surprise at finding her still outside.

They settled to the comfort of their own chairs, silently.

'What's that?' he asked, after a time nodding at an envelope on the mantelpiece. Hilda fetched it. Mrs Fielding. In Mrs Shacklock's rough writing.

'Lady Marcroft's secretary rang. The Earl has been taken seriously ill again, in hospital. Not expected to recover.'

She passed that over; Edward seemed to have difficulty in forcing himself to read it. He took glasses from his inner pocket, though he could manage without, read, blew.

'I suppose it isn't surprising.'

Hilda burst into tears, as if she'd abandoned restraint, as if her body had disintegrated, destroying her will.

Edward did nothing but stroke the note, his inactivity fearful as her grief. Suddenly she knew it was no longer necessary to cry, but wiping her face felt a debility that emptied her personality.

'We're a pair,' she said.

He looked up gratefully.

'I'll make coffee,' he said. 'Or do you want whisky?'

'Coffee.'

Soon, easily, she hoped, in a hospital bed William would die, and elsewhere Tom Ravenshead would at that second become Earl of Marcroft, Viscount Ravenshead, Baron Basford in the County of Nottingham. A bishop would commit the remains, but Elizabeth would survive on the margin, to be dismissed to the dower-house, to a corner of the estate the moment her son brought his unsuitable bride home. She would fight to remain queen, would win skirmish after battle after raid, but throw away the war and its spoils because she would believe herself ousted by the nature of things. She'd discuss the estate, even manage it, but no matter how mild the new countess, how mealy-mouthed or diffident, the older woman would know she usurped, and hate herself.

What comfort then?

Hilda tried to think seriously of the other's Lesbian approaches. They had typically the directness of Elizabeth's character, but none of the stamina. The young countess had not ridden roughshod once over estate managers, house-keepers, lawyers and snatched instant victory from these entrenched defenders; the campaign, military metaphors seemed invariably in order, had been long-drawn. Elizabeth Marcroft had acted in hope, but desperately, daunted by her own energies or afraid to take a partner she considered capable of equalling or rivalling her. She'd lost her real love. Nothing cured that. Now perhaps she'd take a respectable companion, or search seedily for one-night mates, or surprisingly discover her sexual urges evaporated with the demise of the impotent Willy.

All Hilda could grasp, and the thought seemed tangible, sculptural, was that the lively, dominant woman would soon be diminished. Immediately her intelligence told her that was not so; Elizabeth was not much over forty, would find dozens of outlets, could even master her son and his family if she set about it, but reason meant little this evening. To be mistress of Marcroft was Elizabeth's *métier*; nothing else would do. Willy, even, might not die. But one huge thought, palpable now, visible as a stone shape, discarded, discharged all sense. A reduced figure, a dowager, shrank away from a closing door.

She struggled to rid her mind of the image, listening for Edward's return.

Not a sound from him where he'd be sitting in the kitchens waiting for a kettle to boil or a saucepan. Tonight he'd shown his quality by speaking his mind with restraint. But even while he'd been lecturing Jeremy he'd looked old, disgruntled, and, if one could so describe a face, shabby. She'd not noticed his age until recently; he'd been very much of a contemporary but now he hesitated. He'd never been averse to taking decisions, she'd supposed, speaking his mind in such a manner that suggested he'd be obeyed, and presumably in his business world people got hurt and held him responsible. She'd heard him described as a hard man, had found the words inapplicable, but could easily see that he was perhaps something of an actor. Which was the role, which the real man? Anna, now, the dead Anna.

Why did she feel no guilt for Anna?

At first, flinging herself away from Alan on Edward's pity, she had no ease from her own mangling wounds, and thus no concern for other casualties. When she began to recover, she'd already accepted Edward's version of his wife, a hopeless case, old tat one could not get rid of, but which was kept out of sight. Improper. Unfair. He'd used no such words. She asked about Anna, times enough then.

'Does she know I live here?'

'I shouldn't think so.'

'But she would mind, if she knew?'

'I can't answer that. In her condition she doesn't exist in our sort of world. If she knew, and grasped, that we lived together, she might not object to that, but conceive a violent hatred of the colour of your skirt or the shape of your shoes.'

'It would be dislike?'

'What's that question mean, Hilda?'

'It would be hate, dislike she felt, wouldn't it? Not pleasure.'

'I'm afraid so. But not on account of anything you or I have said or done. I know it's hard for you to believe that. It's the truth.'

She found no satisfaction in his answers, said so, was duly rebuked.

'I don't appear to much advantage in this conversation,' he said. He spoke calmly, without rancour, like a teacher setting aside the objections of a clever pupil. 'But I have had nearly twenty years of her condition and I know what I find and what I don't. I shall marry you. If Anna appeared this moment clothed and in her right mind I should ask her for a divorce. One sums matters up, and makes a decision;

I have done so. On paper it sounds heartless, but in practice it is the only way.'

He'd smiled again, and taken her hand. Help thou my unbelief. Distraction distracting.

Is it nothing to you, all ye that pass by?

'You haven't an inkling of the effect you have on me.' The quietness of his voice always suggested irony to her. 'Physical beauty. Presence. You think I'm overstating it. That is not so. The first time I saw you I was overwhelmed. Now you think that's a daft word, don't you? The con-man's way of saying "mildly interested".'

'Well, you didn't show.' Flattered, eager.

'I don't show it, now. I'm not demonstrative. But practice at work has taught me, now and then, to put my cards on the table. To say exactly where I stand. You see?'

' "There's more enterprise in walking naked." '

'What's that?'

'Yeats.' He ignored the answer.

'I don't think, either, that my view is subjective. So I tell you. So you understand your own effect on people. You can walk into a room, dowdily dressed, unkempt, no make-up, not that you do, and sit down, not say a word, and yet the temperature rises, the atmosphere of the room is heightened. That, my lass, is you.'

'You say so.'

'I do. But I am not on my own.'

She had half believed him but was vain enough to engineer repetitions of this conversation. He did not change his mind, only his words.

As she considered this, now, with her husband out of the room on a chore she was aware of a lightening of mood.

Again she felt ambivalence. The world splintered for others, but because she was not harshly involved she recognized hope. Jeremy would toe the line and dismiss Linda;

the system would try to get rid of Elizabeth, who might beat it, at a sore price; her Edward would become less confident, less able to make his mark, more liable to hurt, thus less distant. So she could be pleased. Why, then, we'll smile. They'd begin a new family, level almost with the one Jeremy would raise. Deaths and revolutions would turn the world upside down, and their domestic life with the convulsion. But she, catalyst to a few, would manage minor distractions and be glad. That sufficed. She remembered Auden's dead Chinese soldier whose name would not be known 'when this campaign is tidied into books'. Auden had blessed the corpse, if he existed, with greater than a name already. Time, ironist in chief, might improve on that. Anna and Linda had retired hurt, one for good, if that was the expression. William Marcroft's hangdog hankering after his nurse seemed a gracious gift. Elizabeth's fierce clutchings for love were proper, human, humane, divine.

These were not truths, merely the results of her upsurge of energy, even if one understood, of chemical or physiological alterations. So be it. She could continue, in love to Edward who'd revived her once, to Jeremy, the Marcrofts, Mrs Makepeace, a crone who'd bedded in adulterous joy with her young man, perhaps even towards Alan Gascoigne, self-important and cruel, as he paid heed to his new wife.

Edward returned, with tray, biscuits.

'We're slimming,' she said.

'I've just brought these for you to look at, so that you can congratulate yourself on your self-denial.'

'Thank you very much.'

They drank. He'd been through to the boiler house to look at Mrs Shacklock's new kittens, but as he described them, she knew Shacklock would quietly dispose of all but one in a bucket of water. All Annas, Lindas, Alans. One surviving Hilda. And who would give twopence for its chances?

Edward sat stock still, a vigorous man, powerfully built, directed, motivated. At ease, alert, he waited for her to speak. She'd detain him a little longer because she knew no better, or plainly, acted perfectly.

Afraid, cheered, she watched. He took a biscuit, waved it at her, grimaced, bit.

'You're quiet,' he said, mouth deliberately full.

'Lucky you. Thinking about holidays.'

'We're going to Canada; you know that. June.'

'Business.'

'And pleasure.'

'As usual,' she said.